LORI WICK

Whatever Tomorrow Brings

THE CALIFORNIANS

HARVEST HOUSE PUBLISHERS

EUGENE, OREGON

Unless otherwise indicated, all Scripture quotations are taken from the King James Version of the Bible

Cover photos © Kateryna Govorushchenko, Chris Inch, and sprout22 / iStockphoto

Cover by Terry Dugan Design, Minneapolis, Minnesota

WHATEVER TOMORROW BRINGS
Copyright © 1992 by Lori Wick
Published by Harvest House Publishers
Eugene, Oregon 97402
www.harvesthousepublishers.com

ISBN-13: 978-0-7369-1945-6
ISBN-10: 0-7369-1945-7

Library of Congress Cataloging-in-Publication Data
Wick, Lori.
   Whatever tomorrow brings / Lori Wick.
      p. cm.—(The Californians: bk.3)
Sequel to: Sean Donovan

ISBN: 0-89081-969-6

I. Title.

PS 3573.I237W48   1992
813'.54—dc20

                                                                92-38109
                                                                    CIP

Printed in the United States of America

08 09 10 11 12 13 14 15 / BC / 12 11 10 9 8 7 6 5 4 3 2

*This book is dedicated to
my parents, Harland and Pearl Hayes,
whose life together began in the
Hawaiian Islands. Thanks Dad and Mom
for the years of love and support,
in times of laughter and in times of tears.
I think the world of you both.*

About the Author

LORI WICK is one of the most versatile Christian fiction writers in the market today. Her works include pioneer fiction, a series set in Victorian England, and contemporary novels. Lori's books (more than 4 million copies in print) continue to delight readers and top the Christian bestselling fiction list. Lori and her husband, Bob, live in Wisconsin with "the three coolest kids in the world."

Other Books by Lori Wick

A Place Called Home Series
A Place Called Home
A Song for Silas
The Long Road Home
A Gathering of Memories

The Californians
Whatever Tomorrow Brings
As Time Goes By
Sean Donovan
Donovan's Daughter

Kensington Chronicles
The Hawk and the Jewel
Wings of the Morning
Who Brings Forth the Wind
The Knight and the Dove

Rocky Mountain Memories
Where the Wild Rose Blooms
Whispers of Moonlight
To Know Her by Name
Promise Me Tomorrow

The Yellow Rose Trilogy
Every Little Thing About You
A Texas Sky
City Girl

English Garden Series
The Proposal
The Rescue
The Visitor
The Pursuit

The Tucker Mills Trilogy
Moonlight on the Millpond
Just Above a Whisper
Leave a Candle Burning

Other Fiction
Sophie's Heart
Pretense
The Princess
Bamboo & Lace
Every Storm
White Chocolate Moments

The Taylor and Donovan Families—1871

The Taylor Family—

William Taylor
Wife—Mabel (May)
Children—Marshall Riggs (Rigg)
Jeffrey Taylor
Gilbert Taylor
Nathan Taylor

The Donovan Family—

Patrick Sean Donovan II (Patrick)
Wife—Theresa
Children—Kaitlin Donovan
Patrick Sean Donovan III (Sean)
Marcail Donovan

Maureen Donovan Lawton Kent—sister to
Patrick Sean Donovan II
Percy Lawton—Son to Maureen Kent

one

Hawaii—January 1871

Kaitlin Donovan smiled as the mid-morning sun hit her full in the face. She'd slipped from her shoes and stockings while hiking among the trees and now, as she moved toward that hot globe in the sky, her toes sank into the pure smooth sand of the beach. She walked until she was just short of the Pacific Ocean waves that lapped in easy rhythm at the shore.

The seemingly endless horizon stretched before her and the wonder of it, a wonder that never waned, made the breath catch in her chest. Kaitlin was content to stand and stare for a long minute before she walked a lazy path down the shore line.

Coming to the beach always brought her thoughts to God in a very special way. Today was no different. The vast expanse of water made her think of His overflowing love and the sand beneath her feet reminded her of a verse in Psalms that said God's thoughts of her were as numerous as those tiny grains.

Some 50 yards up the beach Kaitlin stopped her tour of the shore line and looked once again out to sea. The rest of the world felt so far away and, in actuality, it was. But it was more than just the miles, of this she was positive, even though her remembrance of a home before this one was vague.

Her parents sometimes spoke of their life before the mission but until recently none of what they said had been of much interest to Kaitlin. She couldn't imagine living anywhere else and she believed herself to be content, but there was a restlessness rising within her that she'd never experienced before. It was both confusing and exciting, as if something special was about to happen. But she couldn't think of what that something might be so there was never any relief from those restless feelings when they occurred. She prayed and tried to place her restless heart into God's loving hands; and peace came, as she knew it would.

Much too soon the sun rose until nearly straight overhead and Kaitlin knew it was time to be home for lunch. She'd just laced her shoes when she caught sight of a couple walking along the shore. Kaitlin recognized them immediately as two of the village young people who attended her father's services. Normally she would have called out and waved but seeing their hands linked together made her hesitate.

What would it be like to have someone hold your hand? It wasn't the first time such a question had occurred to Kaitlin and, as always, she looked down at her own hands. But again, as in times past, she found no answer as she examined her long fingers.

When Kaitlin's attention was once again drawn to the shore, she saw that the couple had stopped to face each other. Sure that she was about to be an unwilling witness to an embrace, Kaitlin turned quickly into the trees and walked toward home. As she went she prayed about the restlessness that again reared its head after seeing that couple.

The sun's position told her she was late for lunch and she knew she'd have to apologize. But she also knew she would not be scolded—not today that is. Today was much too special. This was her twentieth birthday!

two

"I don't think it's fair." The little girl spoke to her mother from a stool in the corner of the kitchen.

"It's very fair, Marcail, and you know it. I warned you this morning at breakfast that if you were too far away to hear me calling, then you're far enough away to be punished."

"But I came as soon as Sean told me to."

"I shouldn't have had to send your brother at all. If you had stayed where you were supposed to, you would have heard me calling."

"I'll bet Katie's been to the beach. Will she be punished for making lunch late?"

The attempt to divert Theresa Donovan's attention to Kaitlin didn't work and she sent her eight-year-old daughter a look that told her she had heard enough. Marcail lowered her eyes and sat quietly for her punishment, wondering as she did if someone would remember to call her for lunch.

"I'm sorry I'm late, Mother." Kaitlin spoke as she entered the kitchen and bent to kiss her mother's cheek.

"That's all right dear, but be sure to thank Sean, he set the table for you."

"What did Marc do?" Kaitlin wanted to know, as she looked at her sister in the corner.

"She can tell you if she wants."

Kaitlin's brows rose in question and her look was kind. Marcail cocked her head to one side and admitted in a small voice, "I was down at Loni's."

Kaitlin nodded. Loni was Marcail's best friend but her hut was on the beach and Marcail was not allowed to go there alone. Loni's mother was dead and her father was rarely home during the day. The lack of adult supervision had forced Theresa to decide that if Marcail and Loni wanted to play, it would be at the Donovan home.

Theresa had watched the exchange between her daughters and smiled as she went back to work. Theresa's sweet spirit had given her very special relationships with her children. It wasn't any wonder that Marcail responded well to Katie, who was so much like Theresa.

Not that they were alike physically. In fact Katie's resemblance to her father was almost frightening. She was tall and full-figured with deep brown eyes that looked right to your soul with compassion and kindness. Her face, with its well-shaped nose and high cheekbones, would probably be considered beautiful were it not for her strong square jaw. It lent a look of stubbornness that her nature rarely exhibited.

Marcail's tiny frame on the other hand, was the physical image of her mother. But there the resemblance ended. Marcail's personality was very much like her father's. Theresa didn't have half the energy her husband possessed and never once would she have questioned someone in authority over her. Marcail had no such inhibitions and that, along with her questioning mind, was enough to wear Theresa to the bone.

Sean was already at the table when the food was carried in. At fourteen his appetite was voracious. He was already showing signs of having his father's large build. An inch taller than Kaitlin, people who didn't know them often mistook them for twins.

Theresa sat at the head of the table since she wasn't expecting her husband until evening, and looked at her children as they began to eat. As always she felt a little amazed at how, with their black hair and tanned complexions, they resembled the Hawaiian people to whom they ministered on the island.

"Mother, aren't you feeling well?" The question came from Kaitlin who had observed her mother's untouched plate.

"I'm fine dear. I'm just growing sentimental in my old age."

"You're not too old, Mother," Sean stated in his logical way.

"Thank you, Son." His mother's tone was dry.

"Will father be late tonight?" Marcail chimed in.

"The usual time, I think," Theresa answered, with a little sigh that made her children stare at her.

"Mother," Kaitlin's brow furrowed slightly, "have you lost weight?" Theresa became instantly alert.

"Am I looking poorly, Kate?" she evaded the question neatly.

"Oh, no, Mother, you always look lovely." Kaitlin smiled sincerely, even as she noticed her mother's face was flushed. Kaitlin was rewarded with her mother's beautiful smile.

three

The afternoon moved by quickly as friends came to visit and some baking was done. Kaitlin found herself wishing her father would come home a little early but it was not to be. By the time the supper hour neared, Kate was pacing like a caged animal.

"Katie, you're walking a hole in that floor mat."

"I know, Mother, but I thought Father would be here by now."

"He'll be here, Katie, he'll be here," Theresa said as she worked on her school lessons for next week. She and Kaitlin taught together in the mission school which was attended by both village and missionary children.

Kaitlin flopped onto a stuffed pallet on the floor and tried not to think about her birthday supper and the gifts that would be presented in the Donovan tradition. But it was no use. Her eyes went again and again to the table already set for the meal, especially the lack of gifts next to her place.

After a thorough scrutiny of the table, her eyes swung to Sean. He usually teased her senseless about knowing what her gift was. This year he hadn't said a word.

Marcail was the next person to come under Kaitlin's regard, but she was looking at a book and not at her anxious older sister. Had Katie cared to look at her mother she would have found herself being studied quite intently.

She's a young 20, Theresa thought to herself. *Not physically of course, but emotionally. Her world has been protected. Even when there was trouble in the mission, the children were never involved. She's never known hate or rejection.*

But she has the Lord, and there's nothing more I would ask for her. Oh, Father in heaven, Theresa's thoughts turned to prayer, *please keep her close to you. I trust You to give only what she can take. Please help her believe that too. Her world will be changing so quickly over the next weeks, please help her to keep her hand in Yours.*

"It's Father!" Marcail bounced up a moment later, the first to hear his feet on the path. Patrick Sean Donovan II was greeted with the usual enthusiasm his family afforded him.

"Every man should come home to this kind of love." It was his customary statement but hearing it often never erased the smiles from the faces of his wife and children.

"Are you hungry, Father?" Kaitlin asked anxiously.

"Not really. I think I'll have my evening swim before we eat." Kate, so excited over her birthday, missed the twinkle in his eye. Her face fell with disappointment, but she didn't complain. Grumbling, and rightly so, was not allowed.

"Father is teasing you, Kate," her mother spoke softly to her daughter and then louder to her mate, "For shame, Father. If you could have seen this girl pace around in anticipation all afternoon you would not torment her."

"Anticipation of what?" Father asked with his eyes wide. Katie smiled, seeing that he was not done with her.

"I'm not sure myself," Katie teased back. "Since I see no packages at my place."

"Well, we'll have to see what we can do about that. Happy Birthday, Kaitlin." This time his smile held no teasing and the embrace he gave her warmed her to the depths of her soul. He released her to wash quickly for supper and in a few minutes they were seated around the table.

In the Donovan birthday fashion, gifts were opened before supper. Sean and Marcail were as excited as Kaitlin when father smiled at all of them and began to speak.

"We don't have anything for you to open, Kaitlin."

"What Father means, is that there was no way to wrap your gift. But we hope you'll be pleased," Theresa quickly added with a smile.

"Now, in the past," Father went on, "the gift would have been strictly your own and the choice to share it would have been yours. But this year we are asking you to share your gift with all of us." He stopped a moment, meeting the confused glances of his son and younger daughter before looking back at an equally confused birthday girl.

"I've booked passage on the *Pacific Flyer*. We all leave for San Francisco in a month!"

It took a full minute for this statement to sink in and then questions poured in a torrent from the three young Donovans.

"You mean California?"

"Will we see Aunt Maureen?"

"How big is the ship?"

"How long will we be gone?"

"How long does it take to get there?"

"Can I have a new dress?"

"What of the mission and school?"

"Can I invite Loni?"

Father's hands were in the air in an effort to gain some quiet. His voice was full of laughter as he spoke.

"Hold on, everyone, hold on. I'll explain everything to you as we eat."

Father thanked God for the food and the twenty years with Kaitlin. As dishes were passed he explained the plans for his family.

"As you know, Katie, you were only five years old when we came to the islands and we haven't been back to

California since. Your mother and I both feel that it's time.

"I've written to Aunt Maureen and she's expecting us. I haven't chosen an actual date to return here to the islands, but I imagine we'll be at your Aunt's for six to eight weeks.

"Now, back to your questions. We'll see if we can't come up with new dresses for each of you girls and maybe a shirt for Sean." Father took a moment to inspect his son's hair and clothing. "On second thought, maybe you should just get something from my clothes. Theresa, when did he get so big?"

Sean smiled at the compliment from his father and then Kate asked, "What of the mission and the school?"

"Things are in good shape right now, Katie, and even if they weren't, it's time for us to have a break. Your brother and sister have never been off this island. I also think the other missionaries are overly dependent on us sometimes. We won't be gone for too long, and it will be good for them to see they can do very well in our absence.

"There are at least three men who can fill in for services. Things at the school are a little trickier because both you and your mother will be gone, but I've talked it over with everyone and I'm sure they'll work it out.

"You children were never aware of it, but this is not the first time we've made plans to leave Hawaii." Father saw that his words were a shock. "But in the past God has always closed the door on our plans, and your mother and I have accepted that. This time I feel very certain that, even if something unexpected arises, God's leading is for us to sail to the states."

"Can Loni go with us?"

Father's eyes became very tender as he looked at his youngest daughter, so like his beloved Theresa in appearance. He slid his chair back and held his arms out to her. Marcail settled in his lap and then looked up at him. He kissed her brow.

"You wouldn't want us to leave you here when we sail, would you Marcail?"

"No."

"Well, it's the same for Loni. We wouldn't want to take her away from her family. Think how lonely she would be for them." The little girl looked thoughtful and then asked if they could take Loni's whole family. Father smiled but answered with a definite no.

"Marcail, you need to finish your supper dear," her mother reminded her. "Tomorrow are Sunday services and I want you in bed on time. Kaitlin, Sean, please try to eat. I know you're excited but we're not leaving for a month and . . ." Theresa stopped talking when she saw that her children were hundreds of miles away. Husband and wife exchanged a smile.

"And you thought she might be disappointed about not having something to open," Patrick whispered to Theresa, who gave him an exaggerated sigh and then chuckled.

"You were right, Patrick, as always, you were right."

four

Theresa Donovan called Kaitlin's name three times before she responded, and the children at the school found this highly amusing. Kate smiled good-naturedly at their laughter as she made her way to the rear, but inside she was scolding herself. The day before her father had asked her about something he'd said in his sermon. Not an unusual occurrence, but Kaitlin had been very embarrassed over having to admit that she hadn't been paying attention.

I've got to pull my mind out of the clouds, she told herself, as a child came toward her with a question. Even as she worked patiently with the little girl, she despaired of ever getting over her dreamy state. A trip to California and seeing Aunt Maureen! Who would have thought her twentieth birthday would be so wonderful?

"Miss Katie, is this right?" Kaitlin was surprised to see that the little girl she'd been helping had returned to her seat and Joseph, one of Kaitlin's favorites, was waiting for his work to be inspected.

"This is very good, Joseph, but you missed question 14." Kate looked into the little boy's eyes as she spoke and they told her his incomplete work had been deliberate.

"Joseph," she reproved gently, and watched his eyes fill with tears.

"Are you really going away, Miss Katie? Are you really leaving the island?"

"Yes, I am, but . . ." Kate stopped just short of telling Joseph she would be back. Something inside her wouldn't let the words come. She searched for other words of comfort even as the thought persisted that she wouldn't be returning to Hawaii ever again.

"I'll miss you, Joseph, very much, but you're my little brother in Christ and I know that He'll care for you. And we can remember each other in our prayers." She reached out a gentle hand then, and brushed at the tear sliding down his cheek. Then her hand went to sweep back the thick, black hair on his forehead.

Marcail appeared in the next instant and Kate had no choice but to send Joseph back to his seat. She watched him for a moment and was relieved when their eyes met and he smiled.

"He has a crush on you."

"Do you think so?" the older sister whispered to the younger.

"Yes, I do. His sister told me that he talks about you every day after school, all the way home."

"Well, it's too bad he's not a little older—" Kaitlin let the remark hang.

"Scott Harper is older and I saw him holding your hand yesterday."

"It wasn't what you think, Marc," Kate said, as she remembered the scene with the son of one of the other missionaries.

"You're really going, Kaitlin?"

"Yes, Scott, we leave in a month," Kate answered the tall, painfully thin young man who had been in love with her for years.

"When will you be back?" The question had been asked, almost desperately, and Scott had touched Kate for the first time, grasping one of her hands in both of his own.

Kate had no desire to encourage him but neither did she want to hurt him. "My father says we'll be in California for about two months." Kate gently disengaged her hand as she spoke.

Scott's eyes, big and dark like her own, were looking at her in a way that always made her feel regretful. Here was a man her own age, who was in love with her, and she didn't feel anything. Oh, she cared for him and he didn't repulse her but she wasn't in love with him. With both their families involved in missionary work on the islands, it would have been very comfortable and practical if she had been in love with him.

But when she'd said as much to her mother, Theresa had told her in plain terms that love was neither practical nor comfortable.

"Did I upset you because I said something about Scott?" Marcail's soft question broke into Kate's memory.

"No, Marcail, I'm fine and we both better be about our business."

The rest of the day slipped by, and Kaitlin was thankful that she was too busy to think about California—or the pathetic look in Scott Harper's eyes when she'd left him. In fact she didn't give another thought to him until late that night, when he knocked on the door.

"Well, Scott, come in," Father spoke kindly, as he answered the light tap. "What brings you out at this hour?"

"I know it's late, Mr. Donovan, but I have something important to ask you."

Marcail had been sent to bed but the rest of the Donovan family watched as Father led the nervous young man to a chair. Kate's heart grew heavy and she began to pray when she noticed that Scott did not look in her direction or acknowledge her in any way.

"What can I do for you, Scott?"

"I've come to ask you for Kaitlin's hand in marriage."

Patrick Donovan, a wise and loving parent, was careful not to look at his oldest daughter. When he spoke, his eyes looked directly into Scott's and his voice was gentle.

"Did Kaitlin know of your plans to come here this evening?"

"No sir, she didn't. And the truth is, I know Kaitlin doesn't love me. But sir, I know I've got enough love for both of us and I think in time she would learn to love me."

Sweat glistened on the young man's face and Patrick was deeply moved at the sincere look in his eyes.

Scott rushed on before he could speak. "I'm not trying to keep Kaitlin from making the trip to California. In fact, I was hoping you could marry us right away so I could go with you. I'm afraid if she leaves without me I'll never see her again." Scott's voice had dropped to a whisper, as he continued to look at the man he hoped would be his father-in-law, his heart in his eyes.

"My parents' marriage was arranged Scott," Father began quietly after a moment. "My mother was from a different part of Ireland and my father had never laid eyes on her until a week before the wedding. There was no love at first sight like the books tell about, but it was a good marriage, and I believe they did grow to love each other.

"It was different in my own life. The first time I saw Theresa my heart nearly jumped out of my chest, much the way I suspect your's did when you set eyes on Kaitlin four years ago.

"But Scott, lad, four years is enough time for Kaitlin to know her heart. I'll not force her into a lifelong union when I know she's not in love."

The young man's shoulders slumped but his face wasn't angry or disrespectful. For the first time, he let his eyes go to Kate's. He was thankful that he saw no pity, only the kindness he had come to expect from her. There would be no embarrassment when they were together again, because Kaitlin would treat his proposal as a compliment, not an insult, even though she was not the least bit interested in him as a husband.

"Well, it's late," Scott's voice was hoarse, "I'll be on my way and let you retire. Good night."

"Good night, Scott."

The door closed and no one spoke. Kate's composure, held so neatly in place while in the presence of Scott, slowly crumbled until her face was buried in her hands and the sound of crying filled the room.

Her brother, who was sitting nearest to her, said quietly, "Maybe I should have warned you, Katie. I knew he was coming tonight, but I just didn't know how to tell you. Even though I think he would have been good for you, well, it's not your fault you don't love him."

"When did he talk to you, Sean?" Mother asked as she put her arms around her crying daughter.

"This afternoon. I'm sorry if I—"

"It's all right, Sean," Kate's voice was ragged. "You were sort of caught in the middle. But what really bothers me is that I think Scott's right—that we'll never see each other again—that we'll never come back to Hawaii."

Father came close at that point and waited until he had Sean and Kate's attention. "I want you to listen to what I'm going to say, not just listen but believe it with all your hearts. Our lives will be changing in the weeks to come and even though we are making plans to return I can't predict the future. But whatever tomorrow brings, God will be with us. Whether we're in California or Hawaii or some place we've never even thought of, God will go before us and keep us in His precious care."

Father hugged his family, then, and had a brief word of prayer. Reassuring Kaitlin about her feelings toward Scott, he told her, as her mother had, that love would come in its time. He then sent his children off to get their much-needed rest.

five

The *Pacific Flyer* was a beautiful ship that stood proudly in the water. And to the family of five she would bear eastward, indeed she was the most glorious ship on the sea.

The farewells on the beach had been tearful, but all were aboard now and cast-off was moments away. With the enthusiasm of first-time travelers, Sean and Marcail tried to take everything in at once. Kaitlin was no less excited but the openly flirtatious looks some of the crew were sending her way made her stay close to her parents by the railing. The wind snatched at some of the words, but Kaitlin was able to hear part of her parents' conversation.

"I'm worried about the promise you made to Pastor Graves."

"Why would you worry about that?"

"Because you never break your promises."

"And you think I'll have to break this one. You think we won't return."

The rest of the words were swept away on the breeze, leaving Kaitlin to wonder what was worrying her mother. Whatever the source of her concern, it was causing her mother to lose weight and sleep. She'd never seen her mother so thin and weary. Of course, getting ready for the trip was enough to tax anyone. Why, yesterday she'd been teaching the island children and today she was on a ship headed for the California coast!

"Katie, come and see this," Marcail called to her sister, affording no more time to speculate about her mother.

The next days of the trip proved enlightening as the Donovan females showed themselves to be natural seafarers. Kate and Marcail were rarely below deck and their faces reflected their contentment as the wind drove the trim vessel across the waves. The deck was often slick with sea spray, which added to the excitement of being aboard ship.

Kate's apprehensions did not ease concerning the overly interested sailors but there were a dozen other passengers aboard and she never really felt threatened.

The girls loved to watch and listen as the sails cracked in the wind and to feel the spray that hit their faces when the wind caught a high wave.

"Put your bonnet on, Marcail." Mother said as she approached her "Vikings."

"How are Father and Sean?" Kaitlin wanted to know. Her father and brother had not taken to the sea swells as the women in the family had. They lost most of their meals as the ship moved into deeper waters.

"Both sleeping," Theresa answered with a tired sigh. "I got a bit of broth into them and I'm praying they'll keep it down. I certainly wish they had your sea legs, Kate."

"I have sea legs, too."

"Yes, you do, Marcail and I'm glad. If you lost any weight you'd blow away."

"Mother, why do all the men on ship look at Katie?"

Theresa's head snapped up in surprise and after a startled look at Kate, her eyes scanned the deck. Father had tried to warn her, but he'd been feeling so sick she could barely understand him. "Keep an eye on Kate. She'll draw attention." His words became suddenly clear, and, with her spouse so sick, she felt anxious over not having been more aware. They had all been sheltered for so long.

"Has someone approached you, Kaitlin?"

"No, but the sailors, well, they stare." Kate shrugged rather helplessly and Theresa looked almost stern to cover her dismay.

"Kaitlin, I'm not accusing you of anything, but you need to be careful. You are a very attractive young lady and I'm afraid you cannot be friendly while on this trip. I realize it's not normal for you to ignore people, but a smile on this ship can be taken the wrong way."

The fact that Kate towered over her mother did nothing to diminish how young she looked at that moment. Being leered at was something she'd never before experienced and she didn't like it at all. Her hand went self-consciously to the severely high neckline on her dress and she glanced down at her chest. For the first time in her life, the sight of her full breasts caused her to hunch her shoulders.

Theresa's heart turned over in her chest and she reached to touch her daughter's arm. "Kate, honey, I don't want to make you ashamed of your lovely face and figure, but ship life is unlike anything you've ever experienced. Maybe you should wear your cloak, even if it's warm."

"All right, Mother." Kate's voice was a mixture of sadness and confusion. Theresa felt like something precious and innocent had just been destroyed. The thought persisted even as Theresa watched Kaitlin go below decks to care for the others. But then she remembered the rough life around the docks of San Francisco and mentally compared them to the relative calm of the ship. *Please Lord*, she prayed silently, *please help Patrick to be on his feet before we land.*

"Are things well, Mrs. Donovan?"

Theresa turned to find the Captain addressing her. He was a tall, well-built man and might be considered handsome by some, with his wind-roughened cheeks and full head of steel-gray hair. His eyes were kind and Theresa responded to the kindness she saw there.

"The girls and I are faring better than my husband and son I'm afraid, but we'll be fine. Thank you for asking."

The Captain tipped his hat, smiled at Marcail, and moved on toward another family at the railing. Tempted to call him back and complain about the conduct of his men, Theresa was sure, on second thought, she'd be wasting her breath.

"How much longer, Mother, before we see Aunt Maureen?"

"I'm not exactly sure, dear. Much depends on the winds."

As it turned out, the winds were steady to the east and a week later the docks of Theresa's previous musings were before her eyes.

Father leaned heavily on the balustrade beside her. As they neared land, he began to adjust to the rolling of the ship and believed himself to be on the way to recovery though he had dropped over 20 pounds. Not so, Sean. He was very shaky, staying on his feet by willpower alone, or so it seemed.

The docks swarmed and buzzed with activity as the ship berthed. Passengers aboard the *Pacific Flyer* felt the excitement over the imminent disembarking and even Sean perked up a bit.

As the Donovans made their way down the gang plank, Sean leaned heavily on Kate. Marcail's hand was clenched in the material at the back of her sister's cloak in a hold that was not to be broken. They moved slowly and close together as Father scanned the docks for someone familiar. He was not disappointed when, before he could spot her, his sister Maureen called and rushed toward them.

"Patrick, oh Patrick," was all she could say for at least five minutes as she embraced her younger brother. Like- wise, Sean held his sister close in his arms for long minutes. At 46, she was five years Patrick's senior. Her hair was a beautiful shade of gray, and her clothing was well-made and fit her plump figure perfectly. When her brother released her, Maureen wiped at her streaming face and moved to hug Theresa.

"Oh, Theresa. I've missed you so. How was the voyage? Oh this can't be Katie! Oh, my! And Sean, so tall for fourteen!" Her words tumbled over each other as she embraced everyone again and again until she realized she had missed one child.

"Marcail? Where is Marcail?" Maureen caught Kaitlin's smile over the question and smiled back in understanding.

"Marcail, come out now," Mother spoke gently. "Aunt Maureen is waiting to meet you."

The little girl obeyed with obvious reluctance, and Maureen watched as a miniature Theresa stepped from behind Kaitlin.

"Oh my," Maureen breathed, "she's a picture of Theresa." The tears that had ceased began again, and it was some minutes before Maureen could contain herself and tell everyone that her carriage was waiting to take them home.

six

The sights of the docks were too much for the exhausted Donovan family to take in, so everyone's eyes were trained upon Maureen Kent's back as she broke a path through the fray.

They stepped around massive coils of rope and barrels stacked high. The air was cold and the sky threatened rain. Overhead, flocks of sea gulls made their presence known with the flap of wings and high-pitched cries.

They hadn't walked far and before anyone expected it, Maureen stopped beside a large coach, pulled by two perfectly matched bays. Fascinated, the children stared at the horses and rig, then at the coachman who alighted from his high seat to assist them with their bags. They believed in those few moments that their aunt was quite wealthy. It would be some time before they understood that Maureen's home, carriage and belongings, although ample, were not San Francisco's finest.

"Is everyone settled?" Maureen smiled in genuine delight at her family as the coach lurched into motion.

"We're fine," her brother assured her and smiled. Maureen smiled back and turned to speak with Theresa.

"Were you terribly seasick, Dear?"

"No, the girls and I weren't sick at all."

Theresa was mentally prepared for the startled look that came over her sister-in-law's face. She reached out

27

and took Maureen's hand. "We'll talk tonight, when the children are in bed."

Maureen had to be satisfied with that, but she was shaken. Kaitlin, who had just looked over at her mother and aunt, glanced curiously between them. Theresa, having known that Maureen would see the physical changes in her, was able to smile at her daughter. Maureen was so shaken over what Theresa might tell her later, she could do no more than stare at her oldest niece and then her brother.

"See down this street? Mother and I had an apartment there when we were first married," Father said.

"Can we go see it?"

"Not today, Marcail. Let's get to Aunt Maureen's and settle in. We're going to be here for a while. I promise you, we'll see everything. Oh, Maureen, I forgot to ask you if Mitch is in town." It took Maureen a moment to answer the question about her husband, but she was glad for the diversion.

"No, he's been gone about three months. He did say that this would be a short trip and maybe he'd be back to meet you before you have to return."

"Father, did you know we would be going three months ago?" Kaitlin asked in surprise.

"Yep. Kept a good secret, didn't I?" He winked at his daughter. "Maureen, where is Percy? Still in Europe?"

"Yes. I doubt you'll see him, unless of course, he runs out of money." These words were said with a tired sigh.

"Is this where you live, Aunt Maureen?" Sean asked in awe as the carriage pulled up before a large, two-story home. Maureen did not miss the looks of wonder the house was receiving.

"This is the place. You children may not be aware that my first husband, your Uncle Stan, was in real estate. He left me very comfortable." This was said so matter-of-fact, that Katie blinked. She didn't know her Aunt

Maureen beyond letters over the years and had no idea what a survivor she was.

Her full legal name was Maureen Olivia Donovan Lawton Kent. She was a land owner in her own right and very much in love with her second husband, Mitchell. Mitch's job with a shipping line never had him in port for more than a few months at a time.

The two of them had no children together, but Maureen did have a son from her first marriage, Percy Lawton. He was much like his hard-working father when it came to spending money, but fell short in his lack of ambition for making the money he so wanted to squander.

Percy was Maureen's one weakness. Oh, she was aware of his spendthrift ways and his devil-may-care attitude toward life, but the truth was, she loved him to distraction. She honestly believed he would outgrow his immature ways and settle down some day with a lovely woman who would give her a handful of grandchildren to spoil. That Percy was 28 years old and showed no sign of ever changing his ways was where Maureen was utterly blind.

Life was always quieter when Percy was away, and, whenever both Mitch and Percy were home at the same time, well, it became nearly unbearable. Maureen was, at that moment, saying a prayer of thanks for the very fact that both her men were gone and she could devote all her time to her brother and his family.

"Sean, dear, you're looking so pale," she spoke to her nephew as he stepped carefully from the carriage. "We'll get you right into bed."

Sean wanted to argue. There was so much he wanted to see and explore. He'd never seen a house like this and here was an entire street lined with them. But they would all have to wait until he felt better. He prayed it would be soon.

Marcail had reached for her mother's hand after alighting from the carriage and held on tight. She wasn't sure she liked California. It was so big and noisy. The houses were huge and she hadn't seen very many children. Their trip was just starting and she already missed Loni so much she wanted to cry. Staring up at the house as they climbed the front steps, she wondered if it was going to eat them alive.

Kaitlin smiled warmly at the young groom who had come forward to hold the horses. He was nice looking with blond hair and blue eyes and his smile was respectful and sweet. Kate turned to pick up a small traveling case and before she could take a step he took it from her hand. She thanked him and felt herself blushing, an unusual occurrence. Kate smiled as she walked into the house behind her mother and sister. So far, she liked San Francisco very much.

The front entry to Maureen's home was enough to stop a person in his tracks and that's exactly what it did to Kaitlin. Across from the front door, a large archway covered the stairs going up. Kaitlin watched her mother and sister disappear up those stairs but couldn't bring herself to follow them.

The banister, stairs, and the walls of the foyer were a light, stained oak. A grandfather clock stood against one wall. The rug beneath her shoes was multicolored and plush. Kate finished her inspection with the high ceiling and its beautiful brass chandelier. She stared until her father bumped her with the bags he was carrying in.

"It's a little bigger than you're used to, isn't it, Kate?"

"Oh, Father, it's well, it's . . . big!"

Patrick laughed at his daughter, enjoying her look of wonder over the beautiful home. Maureen bustled back down the stairs in the next moment.

"I wanted to help Sean, but he seemed embarrassed by my being in his bedroom with him. Maybe you should go up, Patrick."

"Thanks for your help, Mo." He bent and kissed her cheek.

She positively glowed at the use of her family nickname. "Percy's room. You know the one."

Katie was still frozen in place near the front door when she turned to find her aunt watching her.

"Your home is lovely," Kaitlin spoke the words almost shyly.

Maureen smiled and her eyes misted. "I'm glad you like it." She stopped when her throat clogged with tears. Kaitlin looked at her in gentle inquiry. "I'm just so glad you're here, I—" the words were stopped again as a tear slid down the older woman's cheek.

Kate went to her aunt and put her arms around her. They were alike in height and she loved the feel of her aunt's sturdy arms tight around her.

"Would you look at me? Standing here getting us both wet with you probably hungry and dead on your feet. I'll show you your room and see about dinner."

❑ ❑ ❑

Dinner was quiet with just Maureen, Patrick, Theresa and Kaitlin. Sean was having a tray in his room and Marcail had fallen into an exhausted slumber that would not be disturbed.

Patrick spent most of the meal answering his sister's questions. Maureen wanted full details on their trip over and it was quite late before she remembered how fatigued they must be.

Maureen would have understood if her brother and sister-in-law had headed right to bed, but, after they kissed their daughter goodnight, they moved with Maureen into the parlor.

A fire blazed in the hearth and Theresa warmed her hands before taking a nearby chair. Patrick watched his wife. When Maureen could stand the silence no longer, she spoke.

"You haven't come for a visit, have you? I mean, it's not a vacation trip for you and the kids is it?"

Theresa shifted in her chair to face her sister-in-law. She was thin and pale and appeared much older than her 39 years.

"The children don't know of this, Maureen, but we've come back to San Francisco because there's something wrong with me and we don't know what it is."

seven

"We've needed a break for a long time, Maureen, you're aware of that. But every time we planned to come back to the states the plans were interrupted. With Theresa feeling the way she does, we knew it was time to come back. We need to see a doctor while we're here."

"Theresa," Maureen said gently, even as hope burgeoned within her that this was not as serious as it seemed, "did you think of your age? I mean, the changes a woman goes through? I hear it's a little different for everyone."

"I've heard the same thing, Maureen, but I've never heard of anyone developing sharp chest pains and a dry cough."

"You have a cough?" The words were almost whispered as the older woman's hopes faded quickly.

"A dry cough and every afternoon and on into the night I run a fever. It keeps me awake. I don't think the children suspect anything, although I feel more burdened every day to tell Kate and Sean."

They talked for another hour and Maureen went off to bed with a heavy heart. Her hopes had been dashed so quickly in the face of Theresa's cough and fevers. For the first time in many years, Maureen Kent was terrified.

❑ ❑ ❑

Kaitlin woke up the next morning when Marcail climbed into bed with her.

"I'm freezing, Katie," the little girl's teeth chattered and Kate pulled her close. They lay in the quiet house and listened to the rain hitting the windowsill.

The previous afternoon they had come into a cloudy San Francisco and thought it chilly. They realized now that yesterday had been warm compared to this cold-to-your-bones feeling brought on by the rain.

"Katie?"

"Hmm?"

"Do you miss Hawaii?"

"Not yet, but I'm sure I will."

"I miss Loni."

"She probably misses you, too. You can write her, you know."

They fell silent and dozed off. They woke again when Sean lightly tapped on their door and came in. Seeing that Marcail's bed was vacant, he slid slowly beneath the covers, shivering all the while.

"It's freezing here," he said in a tired voice. "I thought California was sunny."

"Not in February," Kaitlin said. "How do you feel?"

"A little better. I'm weak, but that's probably because I'm starving,"

"You're always starving." Marcail stated.

"That's true," Sean answered in his logical way. "This is a big room," he added.

"What's yours like?" his little sister wanted to know.

"It's big too, everything is black and gold." Sean looked around the green and white room that belonged to the girls with some envy. His own room was dark and gloomy. The room belonged to his cousin Percy, and he would never have complained. Actually, he was very thankful. The bed was the most comfortable one he'd ever slept in. A small shudder went through him as he remembered the nightmarish days aboard ship in that tiny bunk. The return voyage popped into his head and he stubbornly pushed it away.

❏ ❏ ❏

Everyone took things slowly at first and by the third day all were well rested.

Maureen had come to some decisions on the first night and had already begun to act upon them. She was going to take care of this family. She was going to see Sean on his feet doing things with other boys his age, and she was going to get a playmate for Marcail. Kaitlin, with her looks, well, it would be no trouble finding a few young men to escort her around town. That would give her plenty of time to take care of Theresa.

Why, her brother and sister-in-law were a team, she couldn't let anything separate them! In fact with no cleaning and cooking to do, Maureen could already see that Theresa was feeling better. Maureen had sent for the doctor and he arrived shortly after breakfast. As she paced in the upstairs hallway outside of her brother's room all these thoughts ran through her mind. Both he and Theresa were in there with the doctor. Maureen wondered how long she would be able to stand the suspense.

❏ ❏ ❏

"Did you notice anything, Sean? I mean, did you think mother was sick? I know she's had a cough, but I just thought it was that cold hanging on." Kaitlin looked stricken and Sean felt helpless as he shook his head.

That morning while Marcail was playing in the kitchen, Patrick and Theresa had sat their oldest children down and told them that a doctor was coming to see Theresa because she hadn't been well.

Kate and Sean had said little as their father spoke and now questions came to mind almost faster than they could handle. How sick was she? When did it start? Who is this doctor? Is this why we came to California?

The questions filled their minds again and again, even as they knew they would have to wait for their answers. And as they both tried to pray, Doctor Weston was asking his own set of questions.

□ □ □

"How old are you, Mrs. Donovan?"

"Thirty-nine."

"Have you normally enjoyed good health?"

Theresa looked up at Patrick who stood by her chair. It wasn't that it was a difficult question to answer, it was just something they'd never thought much about.

"We're hesitating, Dr. Weston, I think, because we have enjoyed such good health. Theresa was sick with the pregnancies but, I think as a whole, the five of us have all been very healthy and obviously taking it for granted."

"How many times have you been pregnant?"

"Three."

"But you were always up and about soon after?"

"Sean's was the most difficult, but even then I bounced right back."

Doctor Weston was very thorough. He asked about Theresa's family history, her grandparent's deaths, her parents' deaths and the deaths of any siblings. At times he only nodded and made notes; other times he wanted specifics.

Theresa explained to him that she'd caught a slight cold last fall and had not been able to shake it off. She told him of her reccurring fever and how hot she was at night. When she told of her dry cough, his face went from concerned to grave. Patrick's heart began to pound in his chest as he prayed.

"Do you ever cough up anything?"

"Not until we were on the ship traveling here. I coughed up some blood." The words were whispered.

"Theresa!" Patrick's voice was pained.

"You were so sick, Patrick," tears came to Theresa's eyes as she spoke. "It was just a little blood and you had enough to worry about. I didn't want to do anything to spoil our trip."

Patrick's arms were around his wife and Dr. Weston walked over to the window to give them some privacy.

Paul Weston had known Maureen Kent for years. When she'd asked him to come and see her sister-in-law, he'd cut into his busy schedule and came without delay.

Fifteen years ago he'd have told Mrs. Donovan she had consumption. But they had a name for her ailment now, not that it did any good. Theresa Donovan had tuberculosis, and if she was coughing up blood there was probably little he could do for her. He turned away from the window to tell the Donovans his prognosis, wishing all the time that he'd been out of town when Maureen's note arrived.

eight

"You would think I was already dead by the way you're all acting." Theresa Donovan's family looked at her in utter shock when she spoke these words from the doorway of the library.

"I've had to wait for a time when we were all gathered without Marcail to speak with you. I know I've shocked you but I'm still here and I don't want to see my family in mourning."

Theresa stopped to give them all a few moments to digest what she had said. Doctor Weston's news was over a week old and after lunch everyone had moved to the library, a room as elegant as the rest of the house, to stare at the fire as they'd done every day since the man left.

"We just want you to be comfortable, Theresa, and not overdo." Father cleared his throat when Theresa gave him a stern look.

"I'm not yet an invalid, Patrick, and I think I can gauge when I need to rest. Now, I've faced facts and the first fact is that I won't be returning to Hawaii with you. Secondly, Marcail is going to be nine years old in two weeks and not one plan has been made for her birthday. And finally, all of San Francisco is waiting to be explored and if you won't go sight-seeing with me, well, I'll go by myself!"

"But mother! We thought you were feeling sick and we—" Sean's voice was so young and confused that the anger drained completely out of his mother.

"Please, all of you listen to me." Theresa's eyes moved to each one, Patrick, Sean, Kaitlin and Maureen, holding their gaze for just a moment before going on softly. "I have times when I feel quite good and all of you know that. Just sitting around and waiting for my fever to go up in the afternoon accomplishes nothing. Starting tomorrow I would like to begin going out. I want us to start with a tour of the city if it isn't raining. We shall take each day as it comes. Now, are you with me?"

"Of course we're with you, Love," Patrick spoke as his arms surrounded her slight frame. "Please forgive me for treating you too fragiley. Fragiley? Is that a word?"

Everyone laughed and they all talked about what they wanted to do in the days to come. As Theresa made her way out of the room to lay down for a rest, she gave them some words that would long live in their hearts.

"We need to thank God for this thing He has brought into our lives. It's a precious gift that He's given us by allowing us to know what's wrong with me. So many die without warning. This way we can have special times and you'll have memories to hold close in the days to come when things look black.

"My prayer is that you'll know how much I love you and that whatever tomorrow brings God will be your all when you need comfort."

Theresa left the room then with a pleading prayer in her heart for wisdom and words. It was time to talk to Marcail of the future.

❑ ❑ ❑

"I started a letter to Loni."
"May I read it?"

Marcail handed the letter to her mother and awaited her approval. She was in her father's lap on the settee in the room she shared with Kaitlin, all snuggled into her nightie and robe. Theresa had told her husband of her plans to talk with Marcail at bedtime and he'd wanted to be with them. Now that the moment had come, Theresa was thankful for his presence.

"You did very well. Are you really cold all the time like you said in this letter?"

Marcail nodded almost apologetically and her mother leaned to kiss her cheek. "We'll have to get you some warmer clothing."

"But what will I do with the warm clothes when we go back to Hawaii?"

This question from an eight-year-old might have surprised some, but Patrick and Theresa both knew their daughter was very bright.

"Do you miss Hawaii so much?"

"Well, not really Hawaii, just Loni. There's no one here to play with."

"We'll find you some playmates as soon as we can, Marcail, but right now Mother and I have something to tell you." Patrick took a deep breath and asked God to give him the words.

"You know why we live in Hawaii, don't you Marcail?"

"Because you work there, preaching and baptizing and helping people in the village."

"Right. And I do that because I believe that God's Son died for everyone and I want the people there to know Jesus Christ." Marcail nodded in complete understanding.

"Marcail, do you remember last year when Loni's grandfather was very sick and I went and talked with him?"

"He died."

"Yes he did, but before he died he understood how much he needed a Savior."

"I remember. He asked Jesus into his heart." A smile lit the little girl's face.

"Yes he did, and we know where he is, don't we?"

"In heaven with Jesus."

"How do you know that, Honey?" her mother wanted to know.

"Because the Bible says if you believe on the Lord Jesus then when you die, you go to be with Him."

"And how do we know we can believe what the Bible says?" Theresa pressed her further.

"Because it's God's Word." This statement was made with such confidence that Patrick felt his throat clog. Clearing his throat, he asked his daughter another question.

"Can you tell me a verse that promises us a home in heaven?"

"'I go to prepare a place for you.' Do you mean that one?"

"That's a good one from John 14. Verses one through six go like this: 'Let not your heart be troubled: ye believe in God, believe also in me. In my Father's house are many mansions: if it were not so, I would have told you. I go to prepare a place for you. And if I go and prepare a place for you, I will come again, and receive you unto myself; that where I am, there ye may be also. And whither I go ye know, and the way ye know. Thomas saith unto him, Lord, we know not whither thou goest; and how can we know the way? Jesus saith unto him, I am the way, the truth, and the life: no man cometh unto the Father, but by me.'"

"Those words are very special to me right now, Marcail." Theresa spoke gently when Patrick stopped. "You see, a doctor was here last week and I told him about how I've been coughing and not feeling well and he told me I have tuberculosis. He also told me that people with tuberculosis don't live very long. So the verses are special to me because I know when I die I'll be with the Lord."

It didn't take very long for the full import of Theresa's words to hit Marcail. Her parents watched as a single tear slid down their daughter's cheek. Marcail was the most heartbreaking person to watch cry because she made no sound.

Theresa reached for her and Marcail buried her face in her mother's neck. Theresa could feel tears against her skin along with the occasional shudder running through her daughter's small frame. Theresa thought her heart would break.

It was some time before Marcail could speak and when she did, there was a torrent of questions. Patrick and Theresa did their best to explain all that had transpired. For some reason, Marcail's young mind centered on Doctor Weston.

"I wish he'd never come here."

"Marcail, Doctor Weston's visit changed nothing. I'm thankful he was able to tell me what I have and how serious it is. That way my time with you can be extra special."

The little girl looked unconvinced and Theresa wondered if maybe she needed someone to blame. Marcail needed a little time right now to face all she'd been told. She was usually so grown up and had always been so intelligent that it was easy to forget she was still a little girl. Soon after, Theresa was tucking Marcail into bed and settling down to sit with her until she was deeply asleep.

Patrick let himself out of the bedroom to find Kate in the hall. The rest of the house was very quiet.

"How is she?"

"Pretty shook up. She blames the doctor. I suppose she needs someone to point a finger at and he's become the center of her blame. I'll talk to her in the morning."

They were quiet for a moment and Kate watched her father stare past the door that stood ajar to the bedroom. She knew he was watching his wife as she knelt by Marcail's bed. Kate's hands clenched at her sides and she turned away to keep from crying.

What would Father do without her? What would they all do without her? Oh God, her heart prayed, *You could do a miracle, You could heal her.* But even as the words came they were pushed away by others, *Your will, God. Your will, not mine.*

This is how Jesus felt at Gethsemane, only worse. With this thought Kate knew an aching desire to read those verses and she moved down the hall to her brother's door.

"Sean, it's me," she said as she opened the door. "Can I borrow your Bible?" Sean nodded toward the nightstand that was lit by an oil lamp. Kate lowered herself to the edge of Sean's bed where he lay looking at the shadows on the high ceiling.

He heard the rustle of pages for a few minutes and then silence. He broke it with words spoken in a whisper, "Read it to me, Katie."

"Luke 22:39-42: 'And he came out, and went, as he was wont, to the Mount of Olives; and his disciples also followed him. And when he was at the place, he said unto them, Pray that ye enter not into temptation. And he was withdrawn from them about a stone's cast, and kneeled down, and prayed, Saying, Father, if thou be willing, remove this cup from me: nevertheless not my will, but thine, be done.'"

Kate turned slightly on the bed to see her brother. His eyes were filled with tears.

"She's really going to die, isn't she Kate?"

Kate could only nod and hold the hand that her brother thrust toward her. They stayed together on the bed for a long time, neither one speaking, and both trying to understand their mother's illness and the thought of life without her.

nine

The day after Theresa made her stern speech to the family and told Marcail of the illness, the entire clan set off to see San Francisco in Aunt Maureen's open buggy. The morning fog had burned off and, with the sun climbing into the sky, Maureen gave everyone a grand tour of the city.

They drove past mansions with balconies, widow's walks, columned porches, and towers. A few houses sported windows with beautiful stained glass. Every imaginable style of architecture could be found. The children gaped in awe at the sizes as well as the variations in color. It became very apparent as the day wore on that their aunt's home, grand as it was, was not the biggest nor the finest San Francisco had to offer.

They sat for a time at the shores of San Francisco Bay and looked across the water to Alcatraz Island. The prison on the island had been holding prisoners from the early 1860's, so Maureen informed everyone.

They finished their morning with Aunt Maureen treating them to lunch at one of the fine downtown hotels.

The coming weeks brought on a pattern of sorts. Most mornings the family would go on an outing and return home for lunch. Theresa spent the afternoons resting or writing letters. Even though she was taking it easy, she was growing worse. Almost daily now she would find blood on her handkerchief, and, try as she might to hide it, the whole family was aware of it.

But her spirits were buoyant and she was very pleased at how normal everyone was acting. Maureen, who was nearly convinced that the children were perfect, had her first glimpse of real family life one afternoon when she was visiting with Theresa in the bedroom.

"Marcail!" Kate, clearly furious, shouted her sister's name. Maureen's eyes grew round as laughter was heard from across the hall and then a furious tirade in a foreign tongue. Maureen, who had been staring at the open door to the hallway, turned to find Theresa's eyes filled with amusement.

"What is she saying?" Maureen almost gasped.

Theresa listened for a moment. "She's going to beat Marcail as soon as she catches her, and Sean had better stay hidden because when he comes out she's going to beat him too."

"But what language is she speaking?"

"Hawaiian. All the children are fluent. And Kate rarely speaks English when she's angry or flustered."

Things quieted down a moment later, and then Patrick let himself into the room. He closed the door and leaned against it, chuckling. The women waited for him to speak.

"Marcail was hiding in the wardrobe wearing a fake beard and a man's hat. Sean put her up to it and Kaitlin plans to get them both."

"I gave that beard and hat to Sean. I never dreamed—" Maureen let the sentence hang, obviously feeling like an accomplice.

"It's not your fault Maureen," her brother reassured her. "And even though Kaitlin is angry, believe me, the children have never had so much fun."

The older woman looked greatly relieved and by the time she saw the children, they were once again the best of friends.

❑ ❑ ❑

Weeks later Father read aloud to the family a letter he'd received from Pastor Graves in Hawaii. The reply had come with remarkable speed after sending word of Theresa's condition. The letter reported that all was well but the Donovan family was sorely missed. Everyone sent their love and said they were praying for Theresa.

Patrick, his heart filled with regret, wrote back to say that Theresa's condition was deteriorating swiftly and that he had no idea when they would be returning. Taking his time, he walked slowly and deliberately to post the letter. His heart, although burdened with his wife's health, trusted God to do His perfect will in their lives.

"This is what Theresa was talking about on the boat." Patrick uttered the words aloud and came to an abrupt stop on the street. "I promised Pastor Graves I'd come back to Hawaii and I'll have to do just that after she's gone, even if only to explain my plans and pack the rest of our belongings."

He sat on a stone wall that landscaped a neighbor's yard for a long time, staring at nothing. The afternoon was quiet and no one disturbed him as he faced the promise he had made. He prayed long and hard and, when he knew what he would do, went straight home to talk with his sister and his children. The letter, at least for the moment, was forgotten in his pocket.

❑ ❑ ❑

"But Father, you were so sick . . . I really think I should go."

"It's out of the question, Kaitlin, although I appreciate your offer."

Kaitlin and Sean looked grief stricken and Father was thankful that Marcail was not here. He knew it was very hard to talk as if their mother were already dead but it was better to know ahead of time what the situation would be. Patrick turned to his sister.

"You're sure, Maureen? I mean, I can make other arrangements."

"Don't be ridiculous, Patrick. Of course they can stay here."

"I'd be happy to go with you, Father."

Patrick's eyes filled with tears over the sincerely spoken words from his son. He knew very well how fresh his son's memory of the trip over was.

"I know that wasn't an easy offer for you to make, Son, and I thank you, but no, I want you to stay here.

"Now, I'm not going to make a promise to you that I'll be right back. I've prayed about this and right now I don't think I can go back as a pastor in Hawaii. I'm returning to settle things and gather our possessions. I'll return to San Francisco as quickly as I can. I want you to understand that I'll be back as swiftly as *God wills*. If something deters me, I trust God to care for you. As your Aunt said earlier, this is your home for as long as you need it."

Everyone went their separate ways when Father was finished. He sat for a long time hurting, but sure in his heart that he'd done the right thing by warning the family of his plans.

Three days later his conviction was confirmed when Theresa Donovan, beloved wife and mother, slipped peacefully and with little pain, from her afternoon nap into the waiting arms of her heavenly Father.

ten

There were few mourners at the funeral and Kaitlin was glad. Never in her life had she wanted privacy more. Not from the family, she was desperate to be near them. But the hardest thing she'd ever lived through was dealing with the undertaker—a stranger coming and taking her mother's frail body away to prepare for the burial. Every time she thought of it she felt ill.

Without warning, all the duties her mother had performed—the washing and cooking, the teaching and loving—rushed into her heart like a tidal wave. And just as suddenly, the weight of being the eldest daughter crowded in upon her.

I'm not ready to be a mother figure to Sean or Marcail, God. Her heart cried out to her heavenly Father and, even though she was looking into the grave, she was very conscious of Marcail's little hand seeking comfort within her own. Sean stood to the other side of her, so close that his shoulder brushed her own. Father had knelt down on the far side of Sean as though lessening the distance to his wife's body might comfort him in some small measure.

Kaitlin watched him rise a few moments later and, out of the corner of her eye, caught the movement of a man approaching.

"I'm sorry, Mr. Donovan," Dr. Weston spoke quietly as he stepped inside the small family circle.

"Thank you for coming." Father shook the doctor's hand and did nothing to hide his tears. Dr. Weston turned and spoke to Sean before moving on to Kate. Kaitlin was thankful for his kindness even as she became aware that Marcail was trying to hide behind her. Kaitlin held tightly to her hand and gave a little warning squeeze. Marcail did remember her manners and thanked the doctor politely when he expressed his sympathy to her but her eyes clearly spoke her distrust. Father had taken time for a long talk with Marcail, as he had planned, but Kate wondered when the nine-year-old would understand that Dr. Weston had nothing to do with their mother's death.

Dr. Weston spoke at length with Maureen, bringing her tears on afresh. The family watched him move toward his small carriage. It seemed the best time to follow suit. Within minutes the family was aboard their own transportation and headed back to the Kent home.

□ □ □

It was with great pain that the children bade good-bye to their father two weeks later. Kaitlin, already feeling as if something vital had been severed from her with her mother's death, was so overcome by Father's leaving that she could not stop crying.

Sean said little, wanting very much to be the man. But his eyes were almost angry, and Father held him tightly in his arms for a long time.

Marcail, having just a week before found out about her father's departure, was so upset she'd vomited twice. Father held her close and mopped her small face.

His heart toyed with the idea of gathering his children and returning to Hawaii for good, but even as the thought came he pushed it away. He didn't think he was in any shape to return and minister to the people there. They had only been in California a week before they'd been made aware of the seriousness of Theresa's illness, so this had not been a restful time as planned.

Father planned to leave very early in the morning so good-byes to his family were conducted at bedtime the night before. No one was asleep the next morning when he left, but everyone stayed in their rooms even as his steps were heard in the hall.

Maureen did her level best to occupy the children for two days before deciding that maybe they didn't need distraction so much as they needed to let themselves grieve. She planned to allow them a few days to themselves and was feeling very good about her decision when she heard heavy footsteps in the entry way. She was walking the length of the library when a tall figure appeared in the doorway. Maureen rushed forward with a joyous cry and threw her arms around her loved one. Percy was home.

eleven

Percival Lawton was immediately captivated with his cousin Kaitlin. In a foul mood he had left Europe on a ship he felt was beneath his station. He'd lost badly at the gaming tables in London. With his best friends still in Europe, Percy resigned himself to a life of boring social rounds with his mother until he could soften her into giving him some more cash. But to his infinite delight he arrived home to find the most beautiful creature he'd ever seen living directly under his roof.

Kaitlin, in her grief, was unaware of the heart-fluttering she was causing within the chest of her cousin. She had been spending many hours reading and talking with her siblings. This didn't leave much time for the other members of the household but Maureen understood, knowing they were going to survive this painful ordeal by those very actions.

Percy, on the other hand, was extremely frustrated over Kaitlin's lack of response to him. He knew he was good looking, and indeed he was, but it wouldn't have mattered if he were Prince Charming himself, Kaitlin was in no shape for a romantic attachment.

The thing that bothered Percy the most was the amount of reading Kaitlin did. He felt it a great insult that she could actually prefer a book to his engaging company.

It was not at all unusual to pass her bedroom on the way out of his own, and see her curled up in a chair reading her Bible. She also read in the library. Not books so much, but the newspapers. And not just the front page stories, as he did, but every page and every word, he was sure.

What Percy failed to see was how starved these children were for current news after living on an island for so many years. Oh, there had been contact, but never this daily fare of words to be devoured at their leisure. And Percy was right, Kaitlin did read every word, even the want ads. Sean was just as bad, and even Marcail could spend an hour with whatever page she'd been allotted.

All of these seemingly simple pleasures, such as reading a newspaper and having time to themselves were working wonders in the hearts of the Donovan children. Daily they felt the pain of their loss and the separation from their father, but also daily, God was their comfort. And not having extra emotional burdens was more beneficial than even they realized, but Maureen saw it and knew she'd handled things the right way. There was a little something bothering her, nagging just at the back of her mind, but she couldn't quite put her finger on it. The children were fairly happy and eating well and she told herself she was worrying over nothing.

Unfortunately the secure world that Maureen had gone to such lengths to create for her nieces and nephew was about to be destroyed.

All four of the cousins were in the library reading one morning; Percy had joined them in an attempt to be near Kaitlin. He held the paper in such a way that he could watch her surreptitiously. He couldn't believe that black hair. It haunted him. And those eyes, deep brown and set in a face with perfect skin. Her skin was a bit darker than he was used to, but all the more beguiling because of that fact.

Even in an unbecoming black dress, Kaitlin had the best figure Percy had seen in a long time. A desire to hold her in his arms was clouding his already poor judgment. He was sure she'd never experienced passion of any kind and he was equally sure if he could just hold and kiss her she would awaken to a love for him that would have her falling at his feet.

Percy really believed on this day that he could wait it out, wait for her to put aside her paper and then invite her to go for a drive with him. But it was not to be. How they could all sit and read for hours was beyond him. When he could stand it no longer he came swiftly to his feet.

"Would anyone care to go for a walk?" His voice was curt but it was lost on the readers.

"Not just now, but thanks, Percy," Sean answered distractedly.

Percy was furious that Kaitlin had not even heard him. He tossed his head to show his irritation but Kate didn't look up until he slammed the door on his exit.

Kaitlin's surprised eyes met those of Sean's, who only shrugged in equal puzzlement. They were both headed back to their papers when Marcail said quietly, "He's in love with you, Katie."

"Who is?" Kate questioned in genuine ignorance.

"Cousin Percy."

Kaitlin waited a moment for Marcail to smile and tell her she was joking but it didn't happen. The little girl was serious. A frisson of alarm shot through Kate and she looked over at Sean to see that he was just as surprised.

"Why do you say that, Marc?" Kaitlin asked cautiously.

"He watches you all the time. Just like Scott used to."

"That doesn't mean he's in love with me." Kate's words didn't convince Marcail who just stared at her older sister and gnawed on her lower lip. In fact, Kate's words didn't convince herself.

There had been a few signs, she realized that now. But the whole idea had been inconceivable to her. They were cousins! When they'd first met she thought he was quiet, because all he did was stare silently at her. But she saw now that she'd taken him by surprise.

Kaitlin put her paper aside and went to her room. She prayed a long time about the situation. When she came down for lunch she was feeling some better and was almost relieved to find that Percy was absent.

Over the next few days Kate was very aware of Percy's actions toward her and knew that what Marcail had seen was true. Her cousin was infatuated with her.

Kate ended up in Sean's room one night talking to him about the way she felt. He'd taken his parents' room upon Percy's return.

"I just feel so bad. I feel like I've done something to encourage him."

"I don't think you have, Kate. I mean you're nice to people and he must have thought you liked him, well you know, in *that* way."

"But I don't and even if I did Sean, Percy and I are cousins!" The thought was so clearly distasteful to her that Sean laughed.

"Does it feel strange to be in this room?" Kaitlin asked when the laughter died down.

"A little. But in some ways I feel closer to Mother. Her clothes and things are still in here and I kind of like seeing them."

Kaitlin nodded in understanding and walked around the room. She reached out to touch a handkerchief that lay on the dresser. The small scrap of cloth still held their mother's fragrance. The scent brought tears to the young woman's eyes. She took a moment to gather her emotions and then told Sean she was headed to the library to get her book and then to bed. Sean lifted the handkerchief after she left and his own tears came as he held it tightly in his hand.

❑ ❑ ❑

"If you would just talk to me. Maybe I can help."

"Just leave it, Mother. You know I don't like to be nagged."

"But Percy—"

Mother and son were in the library in a heated discussion as Kaitlin came down the stairs. That their voices were agitated did not register with her until she was close enough to hear every word.

"I mean it, Mother. Now just leave me alone."

"It's Kaitlin, isn't it?"

"I don't know what you're talking about." Percy's voice was strained, belying his words.

"Yes, you do. You're in love with her," Maureen accused.

Percy's chin jutted out on those accusatory words. "And what if I am?"

"Oh Percy, Percy, no. Don't I give you everything? Don't I let you have whatever you want? Kaitlin's your cousin. She's in mourning; please leave her alone."

"Honestly, Mother," the young man said with an offended sniff. "You'd think I was some ogre trying to throw myself at her."

"Percy, you're cousins!"

It was on those words that Kaitlin fled back up the stairs. Marcail was a very heavy sleeper so Kaitlin didn't attempt to wake her before scooping her up and heading across the hall to Sean's room. Sean was down to his pants in his preparation for bed and watched in surprise as his sister flew into the room and shut the door.

"Kate, what is the matter with you?"

"Sean," she panted as she lay Marcail on the bed. "Try to wake her while I find that newspaper you had earlier."

"Katie, what—"

"Just do it!" she commanded sharply, but Sean just stood gaping at her. Kate turned the lamp high and sat on the floor beside the bed. The rustle of papers was loud in the still room. "Here it is!" Kate finally said.

Santa Rosa—Schoolteacher
Wanted Immediately
For Remainder of School Year
Apply Burt Kemp Real Estate, Santa Rosa

Kaitlin looked over at Sean in triumph. Sean stared at her in complete confusion, which reminded Kate that he hadn't heard any of the conversation downstairs. She took a deep breath and told him the whole story.

"Kate, I think you could get that job but I don't think we need to move away. I mean Percy hasn't really done anything, and you told me you keep your distance."

"So you think I'm overreacting?"

"Yes, I guess I do."

Kate's shoulders slumped. "When I realized I'd caused an argument between Aunt Maureen and Percy I felt terrible and then when Percy practically said he loved me, I panicked."

"It's okay, Kate." They were silent for a moment and then Sean tried to encourage his older sister. "I guess it's kind of nice to know that you could get a job if you needed to. Santa Rosa is that nice town that Aunt Maureen told us about, isn't it?"

"She said she used to have friends there and she talked like it wasn't too far away."

Marcail had slept through the entire episode as well as Sean carrying her back to her bed. He spoke to Kaitlin before he took himself off to bed.

"I can see why it would upset you, Kate, but I think you'll be okay. If you want, I can sleep in here with you."

"No Sean, it's all right. I'm probably just too tired."

"Okay. Good night Kate."

"Good night Sean, and thanks."

It was some time before Kaitlin could sleep but as she prayed she became totally convinced that she had over-reacted, which only made the incident that happened the next day even more upsetting.

twelve

"I've been wanting to talk with you, Kaitlin."

"What about, Percy?" Kate smiled kindly and stood expectantly several feet in front of her cousin, in the library.

Percy was suddenly tongue-tied. Both of Kate's black dresses were being pressed and so she'd slipped into a light-weight spring fabric of green and yellow. Percy found her enchanting.

The warm expectant smile slowly died on Kaitlin's face as Percy's gaze grew intense. Kate's brain was telling her to get out of the room but she was so surprised she reacted too late. In the next instant Percy's arms were around her, attempting to pull her close. Kate's hands were on his chest pushing with all her strength.

"I've wanted to hold you from the moment I saw you," Percy whispered. "Please don't fight me, Kaitlin." Percy's head came forward and he tried to kiss her.

"No, Percy!" Kaitlin gasped as she twisted from side to side. She opened her mouth to call for help when a voice spoke in the doorway.

"Get your hands off my sister." The voice was deadly cold and Percy froze in surprise. It was enough. Kate took advantage of the loosening of his arms and twisted free. She had just arrived at Sean's side when Maureen and Marcail stepped through the door.

Maureen's gaze went from her white-faced disheveled niece and furious nephew to her stone-faced son. Something clutched around Maureen's heart and for the first time in her life she truly saw Percy for the immature, selfish and spoiled man that he was. Before she could say anything, Sean made a quick decision and spoke.

"Aunt Maureen, we appreciate all you've done but we'll be moving to Santa Rosa. There's a possible teaching position there for Kate. We'll be leaving in the morning."

Sean could see he'd shocked his aunt speechless. But he wasn't finished. He turned to his cousin and spoke in a voice so like his father's that both his sisters and aunt could only stare at him.

"If you ever touch my sister again, I'll thrash you to within an inch of your life." Sean did not wait for an answer before he ushered his sisters from the room.

He'd seen a flicker of fear in his cousin's eyes and knew he'd been taken seriously. The truth was that he'd never hit anyone in his life, but he also knew, with the way he was feeling right then, that he was more than capable of carrying out his threat.

□ □ □

"Who will we live with?" Marcail wanted to know.

"We'll figure that out when we get to Santa Rosa," her brother told her. The Donovan children had been talking for over an hour. They had all three prayed and tried to think of what their father would have done in the same circumstances.

"The problem is that this would never have happened if Father had been here," Sean stated logically. "I am really sorry, Kate."

"Stop apologizing."

"But if I'd listened to you last night—"

"It's all right, Sean. We just underestimated the way Percy would act. We're also causing problems between Aunt Maureen and Percy so I think it's best this way."

"Is it my fault that he did that, Katie?" Marcail wanted to know. "Because I said he loves you?"

"No Marc, it's not your fault. Percy is a grown man and he knew better than to try and hug me when I didn't want to be hugged." Kate was surprised at how normal her voice sounded. Every time she thought of Percy a shiver ran through her. She folded her arms across her chest and tried to push the whole episode out of her mind.

"Now, we need to take a vote. Do we leave for Santa Rosa in the morning and pray that God gives me a job? Sean?"

"I vote we go."

"Marc?"

"I want to stay with you and Sean. But mostly I want Father to come back."

Kate hugged her where they sat on the floor of the girls' bedroom. A few minutes later there was a knock at the door. Sean answered it.

Aunt Maureen stood on the threshold looking pale with strain and worry. Sean held the door wide and she entered wordlessly.

"Is there anything I can say, Kaitlin?" The older woman came straight to the point.

"It's not your fault, Aunt Maureen."

If only that were true, the older woman thought, but said in a voice that shook with emotion, "Are you really going to leave?"

Kate went to her. "Aunt Maureen, I have to tell you something. When I came downstairs last night, I heard you and Percy talking. I panicked when I heard how he felt about me because I thought I'd done something to cause that."

"Oh no, my dear, please don't think that."

"Well, I'm feeling better about it but the thing I need to tell you is about the ad I saw for a teaching position. You said Santa Rosa wasn't too far from here."

"About a day's ride on the stagecoach."

"Well, yesterday morning I saw this ad and for some reason I couldn't get it out of my mind. At first I just thought it was because I knew I could apply. I think I was feeling prideful about being an experienced teacher but then after I eavesdropped and panicked, I told Sean I wanted to go and have a try for that job.

"Last night we figured I was overreacting but now we've talked and taken a vote. We'll check the fares and time schedule this afternoon and leave tomorrow morning."

"What will I say to your father?" Tears appeared in Maureen's eyes and Kate put her arms around her.

"I'll write Father. I'm not saying that he won't be furious with Percy but he also trusts Sean, Marc and me to do the right thing. When he gets back here and if I'm still teaching, he can come to Santa Rosa. If not we'll go wherever he wants."

"You sound very confident that you'll get the job," Maureen commented.

"Well, I guess I'm not *that* confident but I'm headed that way to find something and we'll have to wait to see what tomorrow brings. The thing I want you to remember, Aunt Maureen, is that we know God will take care of us."

Maureen nodded and went with them to check the stagecoach timetable. Feeling as though she were living a bad dream, she watched her brother's children pack their things that afternoon. The following morning Maureen drove them into town for the nine o'clock stage. She'd given them extra money for the trip and knew the line was a dependable one . . . but the papers were always filled with stories of robberies. It was tempting to call them back, but they were handling it all so well she knew she needed to leave well enough alone.

Percy made himself very scarce until after Maureen had returned to the house, whereupon he asked for more money to return to Europe. Maureen was more than happy to comply and Percy was surprised at how generous she was until he looked at his mother's face. It told him he would never get another penny from her.

❑ ❑ ❑

Two hours later the Donovans were wondering about their decision. Nothing they had ever experienced had come close to preparing them for stagecoach travel. Their dark clothing was covered with dust, and it was so stuffy inside the coach that Marcail felt sick. The colorful language of their driver made their eyes open wide on more than one occasion. Well, they'd paid the fare to Santa Rosa, so Santa Rosa it was going to be.

Please God, Kate prayed as she looked at the strained face of her sister, *please let our money hold until I can get work. And Lord, if we've made a mistake, show us, so we can go back to Aunt Maureen's.*

She had much more she wanted to say to her heavenly Father but Sean was thrown almost on top of her when the coach dropped into a rut in the road. He came so hard against her she knew she'd have a bruise. Her last coherent thought before her mind refused to think any longer, was that she hoped Santa Rosa would be worth all of this.

thirteen

Santa Rosa, California—March 1871

"Hey, Rigg, I thought you were headed to Burt's office."

"I am. At one, like we decided."

"It's quarter to two."

Marshall Riggs looked at the regulator on the wall and shook his head. "I tell you, Jeff, these accounts for the store are going to be the death of me."

Jeff laughed unsympathetically and the two men headed down the office stairs. Marshall, Rigg to nearly everyone, was the darker of the two with black hair and startling gray eyes that turned almost black if he was upset. Jeffrey Taylor, Rigg's half brother, stood just short of six feet, whereas Rigg was just over. Jeff's hair was a medium shade of brown and his eyes were light blue and usually smiling with mischief.

The stairway took the men down to the floor of one of Santa Rosa's mercantiles. It was a good business with every imaginable type of ware. There was even a row of chairs along one side for the men to sit in and chat when they brought their wives in to shop.

The brothers were passing those chairs now and, as always, Rigg felt a bit of envy. He wished his own wife was shopping somewhere in the store. But Rigg didn't have a wife. He believed that if he was to have a wife,

God would provide one. But the fact that God was in control did not change his desires, the deepest of which was to have a family.

"I thought I told you to get rid of those hats Rigg," an elderly farmer spoke in a gruff, good-natured voice, causing Rigg and Jeff to smile. "They're costing me a fortune." As if on cue, the man's wife appeared with a hat on her head and one in each hand.

"I can't decide," she spoke before she saw the young men. "Oh, hello Jeff, hello Rigg."

"Hello, Mrs. Wallace," Rigg spoke. "I hope you're finding what you need."

"Well, I just can't choose between these hats. You always have such nice hats, Rigg."

"You could take all three," Rigg said with exaggerated innocence.

"Rigg!" sounded the gruff voice from the chair. Laughter was heard as the younger men chose to exit on that note.

The men were headed to Burt Kemp's office to check with him on the vacant teaching position. On the way, the teacher they'd just lost became the topic.

"Mom told me to look you over today and see if you're losing weight."

Rigg laughed. "I will admit to you that I miss Marty's cooking."

The last four schoolteachers had all been men, and Rigg's large home, situated two blocks from the school, had been the perfect place for the men to live. Rigg had gotten along very well with all of them, but he hadn't enjoyed anyone's company as much as the last one, Marty Wright.

Marty's hobby was cooking and Rigg hadn't eaten so well since he'd turned 23 and moved into his grandparents old home three years ago. But two weeks ago Marty had come down with a severe case of pneumonia. Rigg experienced the scare of his life at how quickly the younger man had gone down. School had been called off for a week, but it became clear even after it was no longer a life-and-death situation, that Marty was not going to be able to finish the school year. His parents, who lived in nearby Fulton, came and took him home to recover.

Thus, the ad was put into papers as far away as San Francisco. So far the response had been poor.

Burt Kemp was head of the school board and a kind man. He welcomed Rigg and Jeff into his cluttered office and told them no applications had come in.

"I really wish this had been settled. But I've talked with Greg Carson and he's agreed to take over for me when I leave. In fact he's coming over in a while to make sure he knows what to do."

"When do you go?" Rigg wanted to know.

"This afternoon, late." Burt said the words apologetically and shrugged.

"Don't be sorry, Burt. You need this time with your daughter. I'm sure Greg can handle it." Even as Jeff said the words, Greg's one fault came to mind. He was extremely tightfisted. It didn't often affect his position on the school board but it always made Jeff a little uncomfortable.

The men broke up later and Jeff made his way back to the shipping office that his parents, William and Mabel, May for short, ran. It was actually his father who was on the school board but he'd been tied up and asked Jeff to go with Rigg. He would fill him in after the next stagecoach was unloaded. It was due any time.

❑ ❑ ❑

The stagecoach, with its weary travelers, slowed and came to a complete stop near the shipping office.

On the trip Marcail had fallen asleep and was now revived to full energy. Even Sean had dozed off and didn't look very tired. Kaitlin, on the other hand, was not sure her legs were going to hold her. Every muscle in her body ached and her mouth and throat were so dry they felt as if they had been stuffed with an old rag.

A young man who should be in school, Kaitlin thought vaguely, helped them with their bags and when Sean asked directions to Burt Kemp's office, he gave them politely.

"Who was that?" Jeff approached, as the Donovans walked away.

"I don't know," Nathan Taylor answered. Nate was Jeff's youngest brother. "They're headed to Burt's. I hope he's not a schoolteacher."

"I'll bet you do," Jeff laughed, knowing how much his 15-year-old brother was enjoying this time without a teacher. "Well, I wouldn't worry about it if I were you. He looked a little young to teach school."

"That's true," Nate said with relief.

The boys were joined then by the next brother, 18-year-old Gilbert, and all three of them went back to work.

❑ ❑ ❑

"I can see I've surprised you, Mr. Kemp, and I know my appearance right now is rather a dusty mess, but I *am* qualified to teach your school."

Burt and Greg both stared in disbelief at the lovely young woman, dressed in widow's weeds. It took a few moments for Burt to recover.

"Please be seated, Mrs. Donovan. I'm sorry we—"

"It's Miss Donovan."

Burt blinked in surprise thinking that he'd misunderstood her when she'd introduced herself. He looked at her dress and Kaitlin knew she had to explain.

"My mother died recently." Her voice told of her grief. "I've never been married, although my brother and sister will be living with me."

The meeting, off to a poor start, came to a wonderful conclusion. The men had been hesitant to hire a woman

but within a few minutes they were more than impressed with Kaitlin Donovan. The only cloud on the horizon was Kaitlin's lack of a teaching certificate. Greg was
very bothered by this and came right out and said so.

"We can't very well give you a trial period since this is
the end of March and school ends in two months but I do
think we, as a school board, need to consider this. Maybe
the best route to take would be a lower wage for the first
month, you know, until you've proven yourself."

"That's fine, Mr. Carson." Kate assured him in her
gentle way. Burt felt very guilty about such a move but
the time was moving on. He didn't want this interview
to make him late in leaving—he and his wife were going
to see their eldest daughter, who was about to have a
baby. He'd take up the matter with Greg, when he returned.

Sean and Marcail were ushered into the office and
introduced. The next thing Kaitlin knew, they were
being led down the street to a hotel for the night.

"Now, Mr. Carson will start first thing in the morning
finding you a place to live." Burt was walking and talking so fast that Kaitlin was straining to catch his words.

"You should be comfortable here tonight." They were
in the hotel now, going up the stairs at an amazing pace.
"That will give you the weekend to get settled, and you'll
be ready to start school Monday. Oh! The school records.
Greg can bring you those. Oh, yes, my daughter...
we're going on a trip but you'll have her when we return."

Mr. Kemp had seen them to their room and opened
the door. He gave a quick look around before bidding
them good-bye and nearly running from the room.

The door closed and the children stood still in the
middle of the room. A moment went by, and then Kaitlin
walked toward the only chair in the room and sank into
it. She was nearly trembling with fatigue.

Marcail was fascinated with the idea of staying in a
hotel and she did a thorough inspection of the room.

There was only one bed, but there was a good-sized sofa, and Marcail declared it would be Sean's. Sean was too busy watching his older sister to pay much attention to Marcail.

"Are you going to cry, Katie?"

"I'm too tired to cry."

"Are you happy you got the job?"

"Yes, I'm just a little overwhelmed."

"Why don't I go get us some supper?"

"Would you, Sean?" Kate perked up at the very idea.

"Sure. Marcail and I will go find some food while you freshen up."

Kaitlin did cry then, because he was so thoughtful. Sean never knew what to do when his sisters or mother cried and then he remembered he didn't have a mother.

Please God, his young heart prayed as he moved close so Kate could cry onto the sleeve of his jacket, *please help me take care of my sisters. And please take care of me, too.*

fourteen

The next morning Greg Carson walked with a jaunty step into the hotel dining area to find the new schoolteacher. She was easy to spot because the room was near to empty. If he'd thought her attractive yesterday, he didn't know what to think today. Kaitlin was well rested and in a clean dress.

"Good morning, Miss Donovan." Greg was irritated at the way his voice nearly stuttered, but to his relief none of the Donovan family seemed to notice.

"Good morning."

"I have good news for you." His stuttering was forgotten in his excitement. "I've found you a house. Now, I didn't rent it, because it's up to you if you want it. It needs a little cleaning up but the price is very good. . . ."

Mr. Carson went on to name an amount which caused Kaitlin to blink. This was the very man who had set her salary yesterday and then casually announced to her today that the rent for the house would be swallowing about 90 percent of her monthly income.

Moments before Mr. Carson had come in, Kate and Sean had been discussing the idea of Sean getting a Saturday job. Kate wasn't thrilled with the idea, but if the rents in town were high, they just might not have any choice.

After breakfast they walked to the house that Greg had found. The house turned out to be a one-room cottage. It was quaint, charming even, and painted white. Kaitlin was pleasantly surprised to see a stove and a table with two chairs. She became concerned, though when she saw only one bed.

"It's very nice."

"Then you like it?" Mr. Carson seemed so delighted that Kaitlin smiled.

"Yes, I do." She glanced around and then asked, "Is there any way we could have another bed?"

Mr. Carson looked a little surprised at the request and then looked at Sean as though seeing him for the first time. He'd been given no authorization from the school board to furnish the house and the thought went against his grain, even if he had.

"I forgot that there were three of you," he said almost absently and then a smile lit his face. "The male school-teachers usually stay with Marshall Riggs. I'll bet he'd let Sean stay with him!"

Kaitlin felt her breath leave in a rush. Have Sean live somewhere else, with some man they hadn't even met yet? Kate didn't know what to do.

She asked cautiously, not wanting to complain, "Mr. Carson, when you were checking, did you see any places for rent that were a little bit bigger?"

"Not in this price range," he told her, not unkindly.

"Well—" Kaitlin began, but really couldn't think of anything to say. Greg took it as an agreement.

"Fine, fine. I can go over right now and explain the situation to Rigg and then I'll show you the schoolhouse. Can you find your way back to the hotel?"

"Yes, thank you." Kate's voice was strained but Greg didn't notice. With a quick wave he was gone.

"Are we going to go back to Aunt Maureen's?" Marcail wanted to know. "Katie, are we going to go back to Aunt Maureen's?" The little girl tugged on her sister's dress and Kaitlin finally looked at her.

"I don't know—"

"No, we're not," Sean interrupted in a strong voice. Kaitlin just looked at him. "We're staying here and giving this a try. I can go live with this Riggs fellow and you guys can stay here. You got the job, Katie, and I take that as an open door for staying here. I would rather that we were together but I still think we're going to be okay."

Kate stared at her brother and wondered when he had gotten older than 14.

"All right, Sean, we'll give it a try."

They made their way back to the hotel to pack and wait for Mr. Carson. He was knocking at their door soon after they'd closed their cases and once again all of the Donovans accompanied him, only this time to the schoolhouse.

For Kate, it was love at first sight. The school was painted white with flower boxes beneath the windows. Once inside, she smiled as her eyes caressed the dark wood on the rows of small desks and then the larger one up front for herself. A large flag hung on one of the side walls flanked by a picture of George Washington.

Whoever had come before her had been meticulous because everything was spotless. The blackboards covering the entire front wall were scrubbed clean. On the teacher's desk sat a globe of the world. Kaitlin moved it to a library table against the side wall. She continued to move around touching this and moving that in a way that reminded Sean and Marcail of their mother.

Mr. Carson was very solicitous and had all the school records with him. Kaitlin looked through them with great relish. That she loved to teach was written on her face and her every movement. She would have sat all day in that schoolroom planning for Monday, but Mr. Carson brought her quickly back to the present.

"I think Sean and I should go get your things at the hotel. We'll stop at your house first and then go to Rigg's, so Sean knows where it is."

Kate was quickly learning that when Mr. Carson had a plan, he executed it almost immediately. Before she could say yea or nay, he was gone with her brother in tow.

"Where will I sit, Katie?"

Kaitlin looked at her younger sister and thanked God for her. Marcail had a way of bringing Kate down to earth with her questions.

"Well, Marc, I don't know. We're going to have to wait and see." Kate watched her expressive face and smiled. Marcail was worried and trying not to show it. "What's bothering you?"

"I miss Loni and I wish I knew which desk was mine."

"Does it matter?"

"I don't know, I just wish I knew."

Kaitlin didn't try to sort through this. She just listened and went over to sit beside her sister on the long bench that stretched across the front of the schoolroom.

"Everything is so different here Katie, and I don't want to get a spanking."

"Why would you get a spanking?"

"Because we left Aunt Maureen's without asking Father."

Kate slipped an arm around the nine-year-old. "Marc, who is in charge when Father's not here?"

"You are."

"That's right. So if Father is angry about our move, and I don't think he will be, I'll be the one in trouble."

"Who will be in trouble?" A good-natured voice spoke from the doorway of the schoolhouse and two men came in with easy familiarity.

Kate had been startled to have someone speak so suddenly. Both she and Marcail had jumped up and spun around to see them approaching. That they were father and son was more than obvious as they came closer.

"I'm William Taylor and this is my son Jeff. I'm sorry if I startled you." He didn't look the least bit sorry and Kaitlin couldn't help but smile at the charming display of teeth he was giving her.

"It's nice to meet you both. I'm Kaitlin Donovan and this is my sister, Marcail. I was hired yesterday as the new schoolteacher."

The younger man, who Kaitlin had only glanced at when introduced, mumbled something about Nate being lucky, something Kaitlin didn't understand. But then Mr. Taylor was asking her a question and she didn't have time to pay any further attention to Jeff.

"We were staying with our aunt in San Francisco when I saw the ad for this job."

"How was the trip up?"

"Well, it was different," Kate tried to put it delicately. "You see, we'd never ridden in a stagecoach before and we were unprepared for the dust."

"Where are you from?" Jeff asked, as if Kaitlin had just sprouted wings. Kaitlin was not offended, in fact, she laughed and Marcail answered.

"We live in Hawaii."

"Hawaii? As in the middle of the ocean, that Hawaii?" Again Jeff was incredulous.

"One and the same," Kaitlin said with great amusement, even as she thought that Jeff Taylor was very nice looking.

Bill watched his son's face as he spoke to the new teacher. He doubted Jeff knew he was staring rudely, but then Bill was also compassionate. Kaitlin Donovan was a beauty, as was her little sister. May was going to love these girls.

"What I've come about is to ask if you would come with us to church Sunday morning and then join our family for dinner. And you can't tell me no, because my wife is already planning on you."

Kate was so pleased she took a moment answering. "We'd love to. Oh, my brother, that is, he's here, too, and—"

"The invitation includes all of you. Jeff will come by with the wagon Sunday morning about ten."

"That would be wonderful. My brother is living with— what was his name Marc?"

"I don't remember his name but I think he's the Marshall."

Bill and Jeff shouted with laughter over this, much to Kate and Marcail's confusion.

"I think you mean Marshall Riggs."

Marcail nodded.

"Marshall is his name and he happens to be my stepson. Rigg, as we all call him, lost his father before he was three. I married his mother the next year, the woman you'll meet Sunday. Actually I hadn't thought of it before, but if your brother is staying with Rigg then you can just all come to church with him. I'll ask him about it. Either way someone will be at your house that morning."

"I'm not sure how to tell you where our house is."

"We just saw Greg Carson," Bill assured her. "He told us where you're living."

"Oh, well, thank you, Mr. Taylor. We'll be looking forward to Sunday then."

"Anytime and if you need anything, I run the shipping office where the stage came in. Just come down and if I'm not there, someone will know where to find me."

Kate once again thanked him and then decided she'd best get to the house and get settled. She wondered, as she and Marcail walked to find Sean, if he was getting along.

fifteen

"Two evenings a week and Saturdays."

"Thanks, Mr. Riggs!" Sean felt overwhelmed as he answered. He couldn't believe he was actually being offered a job, something he'd never had before, and by the man with whom he would be staying.

"I think, Sean, that if you're going to be living in my house, you should call me Rigg. Everyone does."

Sean nodded and took a bit of bread. He had a strange look on his face and Rigg noticed.

"Is anything wrong with the food?"

"No, it's fine. I just feel funny eating without Kaitlin and Marcail."

"I've got plenty here. When you're done, we'll take the rest over."

The young man thanked him in awe, finding it hard to believe how generous he was. Sean, quite frankly, had been terrified at the thought of going to live with this stranger, but he hadn't wanted Kate to know. She was a good teacher and even though things were going to be tight, Sean believed they could make it.

He'd come to this house with Mr. Carson expecting the worst, and before he knew what was happening, he was being shown a nice bedroom and given a plate of food.

And Marshall Riggs, well, Sean couldn't stop watching him. He was as tall as Father but Sean didn't think he'd ever seen such a powerful chest and upper arms on a man. Maybe he wasn't a very good judge, but Sean thought Rigg could break a man in two if he wanted.

But even as he thought of it he knew it would never happen. Marshall Riggs' powerful build was not from fighting, not with those beautiful white teeth that flashed at you when he smiled. And his eyes, they spoke of a deep kindness whenever he looked at you or when he offered a couple of strange girls the rest of his lunch. No, Rigg was not the fighting type.

When Rigg spent the next few minutes explaining to Sean what his duties would be, it wasn't hard to figure out how he'd built up his body.

"I get shipments of goods from all over, just about every day of the week. Anything that comes in on Sunday stays at the shipping office until Monday, but everything else I like unloaded right away. How much can you lift?"

"I'm not really sure." Sean was afraid he'd take the job away, but he had to be honest.

"Well, the important thing is that you don't overdo. Whoa, look at the time! I've got to get back to the store. Here, gather all of this up and take it to your family. I'll meet them some other time. Oh, and Sean, can you start this Saturday?"

"Sure!" Sean's expression showed all the enthusiasm he felt. Rigg put his hand out and Sean's smile nearly split his face as they shook.

Sean watched Rigg head out the door and move in a long-legged stride down the street. Watching until Rigg was out of sight, he bolted out the door to find his sisters, the bundle of food in his arms.

❑ ❑ ❑

"You really got a job?" Kate asked around a mouthful of cheese. Sean laughed. It wasn't like his sister to be unladylike, but he knew how hungry she was.

"I start Saturday."

"That's wonderful. What's Mr. Riggs like?"

"He likes to be called Rigg."

"You don't call him Rigg, do you?"

"He told me to."

Kaitlin's brow furrowed with disapproval and Sean shrugged. Nothing more was said on the subject but it continued to bother Kate. She was a bit leery of such familiarity with strangers.

Of course, she told herself, *you agreed to have a meal at a home when you'd never before laid eyes on the man who'd asked you.* Kate took time right then to pray for God's protection and not to listen to fears that were groundless.

□ □ □

Some hours later the house was settled and clean but Kaitlin's battle with the stove had been a losing one. After an hour of trying she could not get it lit and Kaitlin looked like she'd been in a war. Her face was smudged with soot and her hair was coming out of it's bun and hanging around her face. The front door stood open for air because she could only get one of the windows open. The family was sitting down to a cold supper.

Kate had found two cans of beans on the shelf which she'd opened and put into the one pot the house sported. There were no dishes or bowls. She'd discovered two spoons and a knife in a drawer. Sean had moved the table up to the bed to provide a third seat. Marcail sat on the bed and Sean and Kate took the chairs.

The pot was passed around and the girls shared one of the spoons. There had been a bit of bread left from lunch but that had been devoured earlier and now the pot was passed from person to person in an attempt to satisfy the appetites they'd built up cleaning the cabin.

This was the scene Rigg came upon. As the afternoon wore on, he realized he didn't know if Sean was coming back to the house for supper, so he'd gotten the address from Greg Carson to the schoolmarm's house. The picture before him was one he would not forget.

Rigg's frame, stealing all the light from the doorway, was the first indication to the Donovans that they were not alone. Sean immediately recognized their visitor and got up to welcome him.

"Hello, Rigg, come on in."

"Thanks, Sean. I don't want to take you from your supper." Rigg had spoken to Sean but he hadn't taken his eyes off Kaitlin. Kate was acutely aware of his scrutiny and equally aware of the way she must look. She came out of her chair in one graceful movement that belied what she was feeling inside, to meet their guest. Her hands fluttered around her face and hair before she forced them down to her sides.

For some reason she was overcome with uncharacteristic anger at being caught by this man in such disarray. Unfortunately, Rigg was to suffer the brunt of it. It didn't help that Sean was looking at his sister strangely as he made the introductions.

"Rigg, these are my sisters, Kaitlin and Marcail."

"Katie, this is Rigg."

"It's nice to meet you Mr. Riggs. We certainly appreciate your letting Sean stay with you." She had to mentally stop herself from flying off into Hawaiian.

"It's my pleasure, and please call me Rigg."

"Thank you, Mr. Riggs, but I'm afraid I don't approve of such informality. Sean, Marcail and I will call you Mr. Riggs." Kate knew she sounded like a terrible snob, even Marcail was staring at her.

Rigg was not the least bit offended, only fascinated by this beautiful, if disheveled woman. That she wasn't normally so snippy was obvious in the looks her siblings were casting her. That she was exhausted and embarrassed would have been evident to a blind man. Rigg also knew that his staring at her didn't help in the least, but he was finding it hard to look away.

Rigg nodded in her direction and then turned to his housemate. "I just stopped Sean, to check on you. I'm headed home now and I'll see you when you get there." Rigg turned toward the door.

"Thanks, I'll see you later."

Rigg was not ten steps away from the house before he heard Sean's voice raised in anger. "Kaitlin, what is the matter with you?" It confirmed his suspicions about Kaitlin Donovan's actions of the last few minutes.

He had no desire to eavesdrop so he picked up his pace and was quickly out of earshot. Back at the house Kate was trying to make amends.

"I'm sorry, Sean."

"Why, Katie?" Sean's faced showed his keen disappointment. "I thought you would like him."

"I don't even know him." Kate began to feel defensive all over again as her mind pictured those beautiful gray eyes leveled so intently on her. "But you're right, my actions were inexcusable and I'm sorry."

Sean forgave her and helped her clean up the few dishes. He told his sisters he would see them in the morning and then took himself off to Rigg's.

sixteen

Sean let himself quietly into the house and when he would have gone straight into his room, Rigg hailed him from the kitchen. Sean came only as far as the doorway and leaned against it with his hands in his pockets.

"I'm sorry about the way my sister acted tonight. I don't know if it helps, but I've never seen her like that and I know she feels bad."

"Moving is hard work; I'm sure she's tired. How about some supper?" Rigg asked kindly and Sean was rather glad for the change in topics.

"I've eaten, thanks."

"I remember being hungry all the time at your age. Are you sure you wouldn't like something?" Rigg's mother had brought over a large kettle of stew and the aroma was floating from the stove straight in Sean's direction.

"Maybe I'll have a little."

Rigg turned away to hide his smile and filled two large bowls. There was fresh bread and butter on the table and a bowl of fruit. Rigg prayed for the food and the men ate without conversation for quite a spell.

"I normally stay out of my employees personal lives Sean, but would you mind if I asked you a question?"

"No, not at all." Sean seemed genuinely surprised and Rigg wondered at his first impression that all was not well for this new family in town.

"What brings you to Santa Rosa?"

"We saw the ad for the job and came, hoping that Kate would get it."

"Where are your folks?"

There was no mistaking the pain in those young eyes and Rigg waited in silence as Sean took a moment to answer.

"My mother just died and my father is in Hawaii."

Rigg didn't know what to say to this but he didn't have to speak because Sean was ready to talk. He came close to telling Rigg his entire life story—how he had been born and raised in Hawaii, when he'd made a decision for Christ, and right up to the trip to San Francisco, including his mother's death. He ended by explaining why his father left and that he was coming back soon.

"Did your aunt change her mind about your staying with her?"

Rigg considered the question a mild one in the light of all that Sean had shared but the change that came over the boy was startling. Tension radiated from Sean and again Rigg waited. He watched Sean move from the table to the window. He thought he might be calming down but when he turned from the window, his eyes showed deep anger and pain.

"I don't think it's right that a man forces a woman to do something against her will."

The hair stood straight up on the back of Rigg's neck over the image Sean's words created. One woman's face stood out in his mind, a woman he'd seen for so brief a time that it was unusual he would even remember her. But remember her he did, and he was surprised at the emotions flooding through him at the thought of someone hurting her. He worked at keeping his voice level.

"I certainly agree with you, Sean. Did you want to tell me about it?"

"I don't know. I don't want you to think badly of her. That is, I don't know why you would but it's just been so hard here. No one in Hawaii ever looked at my sister the way they look at her here. She told me that she even had to wear her cloak all the time on the ship because the sailors stared at her. And then our cousin grabbed her and..."

Sean could not go on, but then, he didn't need to. The picture was now quite clear to Rigg as to why they were no longer living with their aunt. He didn't think it had gone as far as rape but then it didn't need to, evidently, to leave lifelong scars.

Rigg chose his next words carefully. "Sean, is your sister all right?"

"I think so. She hasn't talked about it so maybe it didn't bother her as much as it bothered me."

Rigg didn't believe that for an instant, but kept the thought to himself.

"I'm glad I came into the library when I did or I don't like to think what would have happened." Rigg knew great relief with those words but also realized that even though the worst didn't happen, this was very serious.

"Sean," he finally spoke. "Are you afraid that your cousin will show up here?"

"I've thought of that but no, I think he's a coward. He won't come here."

"Then I'll tell you what you probably already know. You've got to forgive this man." Sean clearly did not want to hear those words and he sat back down in his chair with a dejected thud.

"Don't be discouraged by my words, Sean. God can help you to that end. I believe that with all of my heart."

"I believe it too," Sean admitted quietly.

Rigg could see that he'd said enough. Silently he decided to look up some verses on forgiveness in his Bible and share them with Sean when the time was right. The life of Joseph came to mind, as recorded in Genesis in the Bible. Joseph was a man persecuted by his family and yet, when he was given the chance, he forgave them.

The men cleaned up the kitchen and Rigg, checking on Sean less than 15 minutes after he'd gone to bed, found him sound asleep.

One street away Kate wished for sleep. She'd confessed her actions to the Lord and knew that in the morning she had to make it right with Mr. Riggs.

Outside of that, the only reason sleep wouldn't come was because she was freezing. After sundown the temperature had plummeted. Now in bed with only the lightest of blankets to cover them, the only warm spot on her was where Marcail was snuggled up against her.

She felt Marcail shiver and pulled her a little closer. She sighed in the darkness. It looked like it was going to be a long night.

seventeen

The next morning Rigg awoke with a start. With everything Sean had told him, he'd completely forgotten to ask about the Donovans' financial state. It had been greatly on his mind when he left that small house where he'd seen two people sharing a spoon and all three of them eating from the same pot.

The next thing Rigg thought of made him sit up and reach for his pants. Santa Rosa's nights were very cold and he hadn't noticed any blankets.

Rigg was glad to see Sean up when he walked into the kitchen from his own room. He came right to the point.

"Good morning, Sean. I wanted to ask you something last night and it completely slipped my mind. Do you and your sisters have enough money?"

Sean felt uncomfortable about the question, as though answering would be hinting that he wanted a higher salary from the mercantile.

"Well, Kate and I really haven't started to work yet. We'll be fine as soon as payday comes."

Rigg began making coffee and thought how nicely he'd evaded the question. But Rigg was not to be put off.

"What about right now, Sean? Do you have enough money for right now?"

"We have a little."

"How much?" Rigg asked and was thinking, *When you*

*break your rule about other people's business Rigg, you break it
good.*

Sean could see that he wanted an answer but still he
hesitated. Rigg's chest, just as tan as his face, became the
focal point of Sean's unseeing stare as he tried to think of
what to say. Rigg was silent for a full minute.

His hand moved over the hair on his chest and he
smiled. "Sean, buddy, what are you staring at?" The
amusement in Rigg's voice brought Sean's attention back
and Rigg tried another tactic.

"Do you know how much money you have, or does
Kaitlin keep track?"

"I know."

"Is it enough to get you through until one of you is
paid?"

"No sir." The voice was quiet and resigned.

Rigg nodded. "What I'd like you to do, Sean, is run
over and ask your sisters to come for breakfast. You don't
need to rush them because I haven't even shaved. That
way your sisters will have a meal and I'll have some time
to think."

Rigg gave Sean no chance to question him as he put
the coffee pot on the stove and returned to his bedroom.

Sean found Kate and Marcail still in bed. He let himself in quietly and called Katie's name.

"Oh, Sean, we must have overslept. It was cold in here
last night."

It still is cold, Sean thought and knew they would have
to do something to make this house a home.

"Hi, Sean," his little sister spoke up from her place
beneath the covers.

"Hi, Marc. Listen you guys, Rigg sent me over to ask
you to breakfast."

Kaitlin hesitated.

"He's got hot coffee."

The covers were whipped back and Kate jumped out

of bed wearing both nightgowns and her robe. Sean stepped outside so they could dress.

□ □ □

Kate thought Rigg's house was beautiful. It was a rambling two-story painted a pale yellow. The front door put them directly in the living room, without an entry way or foyer. At the far end of the living room was an archway that showed a large dining table. Off the bottom of the stairs was a door and Sean led his family in to see his room. It was spacious with a full bed and dresser, a washstand and small table with a lamp.

Kate looked with some envy at the lamp. They didn't have one, so when the sun left the sky and darkness descended, Kate and Marcail were plunged into blackness. Kate had joked with her sister that they would have to wait for a full moon before they could move around without stubbing their toes.

When they again passed the stairway to exit Sean's room, he told them that the upstairs was closed because Rigg never used it. Back into the living room and through the dining area, Sean took them to the kitchen.

There were several doors leading off the kitchen, one was a pantry, one took you to the backyard and one led to Rigg's bedroom. But Kate didn't see any of these because her attention was centered on the man standing at the stove.

Rigg's pants were black and his shirt was snow white with a black string tie at the collar. His features were almost severe with his hawk-like gaze and aquiline nose. He would have been a little frightening if those beautiful gray eyes hadn't been so kind.

"Good morning," he greeted the newcomers. "Coffee?" He held the pot toward Kate.

"Please." Kaitlin wanted to say more but he had come very close to hand her a mug and after the way she'd acted the night before, she was embarrassed.

Rigg prayed for the meal and Kate knew in an instant that he was a believer. It took such a load off her mind about Sean staying in this house that she wanted to weep.

Rigg had made a large pot of cooked cereal and heated a half a loaf of bread in the oven. It wasn't fancy, but very filling. Sean put away enough cereal for three and even Marcail had seconds on cereal and toast. Kate's hard night was catching up to her and the only thing she wanted seconds on was coffee.

Rigg refilled their cups and let himself really look at Kate for the first time that morning. She was in the chair nearest his. Her black dresses must have been in the wash because she was in a dark blue skirt and white blouse that accented her dark hair and eyes to the extent that Rigg could not look away. Kaitlin's face began to warm under his regard and she knew she had to apologize now or she never would.

"Mr. Riggs, I'm very sorry about the way I acted last night when you were at our house. I hope you'll forgive me."

Rigg smiled in a way that made Kate's heart thunder. He wondered how long she'd rehearsed that in her mind before gaining the courage to voice it.

"It can't be easy moving and adjusting to a new job. I promise you, it's forgotten." Rigg reached out and touched Kate's hand where it lay on the table. It was a mistake. Kaitlin's face registered shock and Rigg pulled back swiftly, feeling almost as though his hand had been burned.

Rigg was a physical person, in the sense that he was not afraid to touch a person to help convey his feelings. He hugged his parents and brothers often and it wasn't at all unusual for him to touch the arm or shoulder of the person to whom he was speaking. Most people responded well to his warmth.

But, Rigg reminded himself as he began to clear the table, *it would be easy to give the wrong impression. And that is the last thing you want to do with Kaitlin Donovan.*

The first thing he wanted to do, and knew that he couldn't, was to touch her hand again to see if it was as soft and warm as he'd remembered.

eighteen

Not until the dishes were ready to be washed did Rigg notice how quiet Marcail had been throughout the meal. His heart softened at the sight of her; she was so small and vulnerable. The family resemblance could be seen in all three of them but where Sean and Kaitlin had a very sturdy look about them, Marcail was almost frail in comparison. Rigg had a soft spot for children and set out to charm this little girl, whom he guessed to be maybe six or seven.

"Marcail," he asked her, "if I get you a chair would you dry these dishes for me?"

"Sure," was the congenial reply.

They worked for a time in silence as Sean and Kate continued to clear the table and straighten the chairs. Kate offered to wash but Rigg refused.

Sean disappeared and when Kaitlin had nothing else to do, she sat down at the table to read the newspaper. But it felt strange not to be working, and her eyes continued to move toward that broad back bent over the wash basin. Kate finally gave up on the paper and listened to the conversation between her sister and her host.

"Do you think you'll like having your sister for a teacher?" Rigg was unaware of how patronizing his voice sounded, thinking he was addressing a very young child.

"She was my teacher in Hawaii, too."

"How about Santa Rosa, do you think you'll like it here?"

"I think it's nice. I wish I had someone to play with. Do you have a little sister or brother?"

"I have three younger brothers but they're all a good deal older than you."

"We met your brother Jeff and your father. He stared at Katie an awful lot."

"My father?" Rigg's voice was surprised and Kate broke in from behind them in sharp Hawaiian.

"Marcail, you deliberately let him misunderstand you!" Whenever Marcail's siblings spoke to her in Hawaiian she always followed suit.

"Well, he thinks I'm just a baby because I'm small, and I'm not." Kate gave her a stern look but kept silent.

By now Rigg had turned from the countertop with dripping hands to stare at the females in his kitchen. Sean came in just then, and having heard the conversation, was smiling at the look on Rigg's face. He also took pity on the older man.

"You'll have to watch Katie, Rigg. She tends to forget that everyone here speaks English. And by the way, Marc is nine."

Rigg was still silent. Kate turned a disapproving eye on her brother for a moment and then glanced back at Rigg to find him studying her intently. He seemed to be waiting for something, so Kate apologized.

"No, don't be sorry. I'm just waiting for you to do that again."

Aunt Maureen had done this once so Katie was not totally taken aback. Of course, Kate was a good deal more comfortable with Aunt Maureen than she was with this man. She searched for something safe to say and after a moment spoke in soft Hawaiian.

"I'm not sure if I thanked you for breakfast and for letting Sean stay here, but please know that we're very grateful for both."

Rigg's eyes immediately swung to Sean who translated. A huge smile broke out on his face and he turned back to Kaitlin.

"You're welcome."

Kate answered with a smile of her own and Rigg went back to the dishes grinning like a fool. This woman captivated him, there was no getting around it. A plan had been forming in his mind and as soon as he was finished with the dishes, he was going to bring it up. As he worked he prayed for the right words and for the proper way to approach this young woman, this enigma, who'd landed so unexpectedly in his life and who was causing his heart to do the strangest things.

◻ ◻ ◻

"So you see Miss Donovan, Sean is welcome here for as long as he needs, but for now I think you girls should go to my folks. We can make the announcement Sunday at church that you need blankets and dishes and things. I'm sure by next Sunday you'll have all you can use and more, and then you'll be able to move back to the little house."

"But Mr. Riggs, you haven't even checked with your mother. She's already having us for lunch on Sunday and we can't—"

"Yes you can. She would love to have you. What you can't do is go on freezing the nights away and sharing spoons. The other idea I have is that I'll move home until school is out and you can have this house." Kate stood up so fast she nearly fell.

"Put you out of your home? We couldn't possibly!"

Kaitlin moved away from the living room sofa where she'd been sitting with Rigg and began to pace the room. Putting some space between them helped her to think more clearly.

Didn't this man know he did crazy things to her insides? Kate was not what anyone would term petite, but while on the sofa next to him she'd felt like a little girl.

Rigg watched Kaitlin in silence, as did Sean and Marcail. When she stopped by Sean's chair and finally looked at Rigg, he spoke.

"You don't have to tell me right now what you want to do. But think about your options; there are advantages to both. Here you have everything you need but you'd have to relocate when school was out. The little house is more work because you're starting with nothing, but it might feel more like your own home and you won't have to move."

Kaitlin could only nod, understanding his logic but unable to fully concentrate with him in the room. She was silent for a long time.

"Have I upset you?" Rigg's voice was deep and soft, his gaze watchful.

"No," Kaitlin wished she didn't sound so breathless. "I'm just surprised and not sure what to do."

"I can understand that. You're more than welcome to stay here and discuss it." His look encompassed Sean and Marcail too. "I need to get to the store, it's nearly eight." He stood up and continued, "In fact, why don't you come down to the store today? It's the one you pass when you go from Burt Kemp's office to the schoolhouse. If I don't see you, well, just come up the stairs to my office."

Rigg left and Kaitlin felt like she'd been mowed down by a runaway stage. Marshall Riggs could be a bit high-handed, but he was also compassionate and kind. Kate couldn't believe he had actually suggested that they gather their things and land themselves at the door of the Taylor home.

Well, they had to do *something;* but what that something was to be, at the moment, she didn't have a clue.

nineteen

Kate took a two hour nap on Sean's bed and by ten-thirty she was refreshed and headed with her family to Riggs Mercantile. It was easy to find and one of the nicest stores she'd seen.

Large windows faced the street and the front doors were open wide. A variety of sights and smells assailed their senses, as they walked through those doors—leather goods, paint, bolts of new cloth and ready-to-wear clothing, the apple bin, a pickle barrel—Kaitlin tried to encompass everything.

Things were fairly quiet and Kaitlin took her time touring the aisles where high shelves were stocked with canned foods, sewing supplies, cooking utensils, pots, pans. And again it was almost too much to absorb.

Sean had gone off to find Rigg and Kate assumed Marcail was beside her as she looked at the wall full of beautiful bolts of cloth. Kaitlin was fingering a lovely blue gingham when a commotion started out front. She had no interest in the problem but it caused her to notice that Marcail was no longer at her side.

Looking calmly, then frantically down the aisles Kate then ran to the door. A crowd gathered and a woman's high voice, raised to almost an hysterical note, was accusing someone of stealing her handbag. Not until the woman shouted, "I tell you she stole it!" did Kate see

Marcail being held by a man in uniform. Her heart leapt to her throat as she rushed on the scene.

"Where is it?"

Marcail's upper arm was being held by a short, square built man in a black law officer's uniform. The little girl's feet were nearly dangling due to the angle at which he was holding her. Every so often he gave her a shake.

"You'll tell us who you are right now. Where are you from? Who're your folks?" Each sentence was punctuated with a shake that was none too gentle and would have gone on all morning if Kaitlin's voice, so hurt and distressed, had not gained the attention of the officer.

"Please, you're hurting her."

The officer, who took his job very seriously, looked from this beautiful young woman addressing him to the child in his grip and slowly released her. Deep shame for his actions was bitter in his mouth as he realized that he'd let a screaming woman cloud his good judgment and that he had hurt a child. He had children of his own at home and he'd have challenged any man who dared to do what he'd just done.

When Marcail felt his hold loosen she ran into Kaitlin's embrace. Kate pulled her close and then watched in alarm as her little hand came up to cover her mouth. Rigg came on the scene just as Kate was holding Marcail at the edge of the boardwalk so she could vomit into the street.

There was some conversation behind Kate but the crowd had quieted. That a man had come forward, proclaiming Marcail's innocence and claiming to have witnessed the whole episode, Kate was not to know until later. She turned, seeing no one but the officer and spoke directly to him in a shaky voice.

"I'm sure there has been some mistake. My sister would never take something that didn't belong to her. I'm taking her home now."

His voice was a bit strained as he said, "That will be fine, miss."

Kate held her sister in her arms and was nearly to the house when Sean caught up to them. Once inside, she gave her sister a dipper of water and then held her as tears streamed silently down her face. She was so upset she vomited again.

"It's all right, Marc," Kate crooned softly, as she cleaned her up and tried not to be sick herself. "We know you didn't take anything. It was all a big misunderstanding."

Marcail sat trembling in Kate's lap when someone knocked at the door. Rigg and Jeff were standing there.

"Is she all right?" Rigg wanted to know straight away.

"I think so," Sean answered.

Jeff and Sean watched in silence as Rigg knelt down next to Kate's chair and spoke to Marcail. "You're kind of young to be in trouble with the law," he teased softly.

"I didn't take her purse," Marcail hiccuped.

"Of course you didn't. There was a man on the street who saw the whole thing, came forward and said it was some boy. Did you see a boy, Marcail?"

"No," she answered with some surprise.

"That's all right."

"Is that man going to come and take me away?" Her voice shook and Kate spoke with more confidence than she felt.

"I wouldn't let that happen, Marcail."

They talked a little longer and then Rigg took the frightened nine-year-old into his arms. Kate was a little surprised at how easily she went and watched her sister cling to the big man. He stood and spoke down to Kaitlin where she sat.

"I want you to collect your things now, Katie." Kaitlin was too surprised to notice his use of her name. "Sean can help you get everything, even your laundry. You and Marcail are going to my folks'."

"I really don't think it's your place, Mr. Riggs, to order us about." Kate had stood suddenly and was looking like an angry hen guarding her chicks. She opened her mouth to say more but Rigg, holding Marcail with one arm, reached with his free hand and cupped her chin.

"Marcail is so upset she's trembling in my arms." His eyes held hers with steely determination, his voice equally resolute. "And you're white as a sheet and look ready to collapse. Not to mention, there is absolutely nothing in this house to eat or to eat with. Now gather your things, Kaitlin, because you and Marcail *are* going to my folks'."

His hand slipped to her shoulder until the anger drained from her and she gave a small nod. Kaitlin still believed his actions were rude and overbearing but she was too tired to fight. Aside from all of that, Marcail was more upset than she'd ever been. And that was saying quite a bit in light of all they'd been through in the last several weeks.

twenty

At any other time Kaitlin would have been thrilled with the farm on which the Taylors lived. The surrounding land was not owned by the family, but three of the acres, the house and barn were all theirs, including a small wooded area where the creek meandered through.

It was a wonderful place to grow up, as Rigg or any of the Taylor boys would have told her. There was always something to do as long as the sun was shining. Even on rainy days there was hide-and-seek in the barn, with its hayloft and numerous nooks and crannies.

Jeff had gone ahead to see his mother at the shipping office and explain to her all that had transpired at the mercantile. That he knew all that had occurred was by sheer accident. He'd simply come to give Rigg some papers at the time of the incident.

There had been no hesitation or irritation when Jeff told his mother that Rigg was bringing the schoolmarm and her sister to stay at her house. Normally she would have left it up to Rigg to settle this family, knowing she would meet them at supper, but when Jeff described what had happened with the woman's purse, she dropped what she was doing at the shipping office and had Jeff take her straight home.

Rigg plucked Marcail off the wagon seat as soon as he'd jumped down and then turned to reach for Kaitlin. Her cool fingertips in his palm made his heart race as he helped her from the wagon. Sean had taken his hat off when he saw a woman approaching and stood quietly, holding it in his hands.

All three of the children watched Rigg bend low to kiss his mother's cheek before he made the introductions.

"Mom, this is the Donovan family. Kaitlin is the new schoolteacher. Sean is going to work some evenings and Saturdays for me and this is Marcail. She's nine."

May Taylor beamed at the children before her. Her hair was liberally shot with gray and the corners of her eyes had many seams, as though smiling was something she did all the time. Her figure was full and the gray eyes, now smiling at everyone with warmth and welcome, were so much like Rigg's it was uncanny.

"It's so good to meet you, please come in." May was about to say more but she could see that Kate was hesitating.

"Mrs. Taylor, this is such short notice. Maybe we should come back another time."

May could see that Rigg was about to step in so she lightly touched his arm to stop him.

"I promise you, Kaitlin, it's wonderful to have you. God has blessed us with a large home and we've always opened it to anyone who might have a need."

Kate didn't know what to say to that and actually she didn't have time because Rigg was moving everyone toward the house. May watched her son with some surprise.

This was far from the first time Rigg had sent someone over to stay. In fact the last time a young woman needed a home there had been quite a misunderstanding. Rigg had spent a few uncomfortable hours explaining that his intentions had not been romantic. But this time, well, May was sure she'd never seen him so determined to see someone stay with his family.

They had gone in through the back door and Rigg was heading to the back stairway. You could also get upstairs from the living room but since they'd come in at the kitchen, it was the logical way to go.

Sean headed up first with Marcail behind him. May was given a chance to watch her son, as Kaitlin followed her brother and sister. She had given up believing that she would ever see that special look on Rigg's face. She wondered if he, as yet, could define what he was so obviously feeling. May's eyes swung to the spot that Kaitlin had just vacated on the stairs. Rigg was a wonderful man and May, not knowing her, couldn't help but wonder if Kaitlin Donovan was worthy of him.

□ □ □

Kate sank down into the bathtub with a heartfelt sigh. It didn't matter that it was Friday afternoon and not Saturday night; the water felt heavenly.

Kaitlin sat up and looked around the room. It was just off the kitchen and below the back stairway. By the size it had obviously been a storeroom, but someone had ingeniously converted it into a bathing chamber. The tub that Kate sat in was against one wall and from where she was facing she could see the stove on which the water had been heated. A huge pot was still in the middle of it, steam rising from the hot water within. There was a commode and even a bench to sit on. Kate relaxed a little deeper into the water and decided it was the most wonderful room she'd been in.

Coming downstairs from her bedroom, an hour later, Kaitlin was very self-conscious of her wet hair. But the only people in the kitchen were Sean, Marcail, May and a young man that Kate didn't remember seeing before, but thought he had to be Jeff's brother.

"Feeling better?" May wanted to know.

"Much. Thank you."

"Sit down here and have some lunch. Nathan, this is Miss Donovan, your new teacher."

"Hello."

"Hello, Nathan." Kaitlin smiled kindly and watched as Nate blushed to the roots of his hair. She took pity on him and turned her attention to the plate that May had set in front of her. Kate made short work of a slice of beef, potatoes, sliced carrots and a large helping of applesauce.

Marcail was sitting near her with a cookie in her hand and the other people in the room were talking about the farm. Kate, not wanting to embarrass her sister, spoke to her in soft Hawaiian.

"How are you doing?"

"I'm okay."

"If you want, I can fix you a bath. Believe me, it felt wonderful."

"That sounds nice." Tears came to the young girl's eyes. "Katie, I hate it when I get sick to my stomach."

"I know you do." Kate reached a hand over and stroked her sister's hair. "But I think your way might be easier, you know, just to get sick and get it over with. I hold things inside and then they bother me a lot longer."

Sean had heard part of the conversation and turned without thinking away from May and Nathan to ask his sister a question. The Taylors would have thought nothing of this at most times, but the Donovan children all continued to speak in a foreign tongue, completely forgetting they were not alone.

"Katie, did you have a chance to get writing materials to write to Father?"

"No. I've got to take care of that soon. Actually Sean, tomorrow is your first day at the mercantile, maybe you could just take our dollar and see what you could find. Maybe Mr. Riggs can show you what he's got. We could write tomorrow night and mail it before school Monday."

"Okay. How are you doing Marc?"

"I'm fine. I'm going to have a bath and change my dress."

"You don't smell very good," Sean teased her with a smile. Marcail had just made a face at him when they became aware of their audience.

"Mrs. Taylor," Kaitlin was red-faced and ashamed as she quickly changed to English. "You're going to think that we haven't any manners at all. Please forgive us."

"You've done nothing that needs forgiving. I only hope if something is wrong you'll let me help."

"I was just asking Marcail how she's doing and if she wanted to clean up."

"We also need to write letters," Sean added, sensing a genuine offer of help from this woman.

"No problem. Why don't you come with me, Marcail, and we'll see about your bath. And Nate can show you where you can write your letters."

May certainly had a gift for hospitality. She was so matter-of-fact about everything that no one was given a chance to feel like an intruder.

May disappeared with her littlest house guest and Nate showed Kate and Sean to a desk that sat in the huge living room. Kate took a seat and tried to gather her damp hair to lay it over one shoulder. She certainly hoped the rest of the young men in her class wouldn't stare at her as Nathan was doing.

But in a few moments she was oblivious to everything but the paper in front of her. She was rather glad she wasn't going to be there to see her father's face when he found out why they'd left San Francisco.

twenty-one

May's heart, which had begun to melt when she met Marcail Donovan, was now a puddle in her soul. She was the sweetest little girl she'd ever known. May guessed that her bone structure was very small by looking at her face, but when Marcail undressed, bone structure was the last thing on May's mind.

There was a bruise, gigantic and already black, nearly covering the little girl's upper arm and spreading across her shoulder. May saw that she was safely in the tub and then had to force herself to walk to find Kaitlin. She found her at the desk.

"Kaitlin?" Kate looked up from her letter in expectation.

"Marcail has a huge bruise on her arm. I've never seen one so bad. Maybe I should send for the doctor?"

Kate came to her feet. "I'll look at it, Mrs. Taylor, but I think you should know that Marc bruises easily and that man, well he had quite a hold on her."

May could only nod her head as she visualized Marcail being hurt. "Would you like me to stay here?" she asked when Kate rose from the desk.

"No, you can come. You could have talked with Marcail about it, she's had them before."

The women walked through the kitchen and Kate knocked gently before entering.

"Hi, Marc. How's it going?"

"Fine."

"You gave Mrs. Taylor a scare."

Marcail looked at the older woman in surprise.

"Your bruise," Katie informed her.

"Oh, it doesn't hurt unless I press on it."

May looked instantly relieved and said with a small laugh that she had been ready to get a doctor. The smile left Marcail's face and she nearly came out of the tub. Kate didn't miss her panic.

"It's all right, Marc. She was only kidding."

"I'm sorry, Honey," May said quickly. "I wouldn't do anything without asking Kaitlin first."

The little girl nodded and looked uncertainly at her sister. Kaitlin smiled. She figured something like this might happen remembering the hard time Marcail had with Dr. Weston in San Francisco.

Kate took her leave a minute later in order to finish her letter. Sean and Nate had been in the living room the entire time she was writing and Kate was pleased at how well they were getting along. Sean needed a friend.

"How's the letter coming, Katie?" her brother wanted to know as she came back into the room.

"Pretty good. Why don't you read what I've got?"

Brother and sister traded chairs and Kate found herself once again scrutinized. She tried to ignore it.

"How old are you, Nathan?"

"Fifteen."

"You're tall for 15. Do you like school?"

"Most of the time."

Kate grinned. "That was an honest answer."

Nathan grinned back, turning only a little bit red this time. Sean spoke from the desk. "I added a little to what you have Katie. Are you going to tell Father about what happened today?"

"I don't know. I don't want him to worry about us because I really do think Marc's going to be fine. What do you think?"

"I'd leave it out," Sean said and then thought, *Father is going to be upset enough when he finds out why we left San Francisco.*

The rest of the afternoon sailed by in a lazy fashion. Kate had gone to her bedroom for a while to read her Bible and then joined everyone else in the living room where they were poring over the newspapers. She was so intent on the article she was reading, that she nearly tore the page in two when Rigg startled her by sitting down on the sofa very close to her.

twenty-two

"You look better." Rigg's voice was soft and deep and his eyes were intent on her face from his close position beside her. Kate didn't want to know what he meant by better, so she lowered the paper only to find the room empty.

"Where did everyone go?" Once again Kate's voice was breathless and she wanted to pinch herself.

"They're all in the kitchen; supper's almost ready."

"Oh, my!" Kaitlin exclaimed, "I should be helping." Kate quickly folded the paper and hurried to rise but Rigg caught her arm and kept her in her seat.

"Do you always do the proper thing?" He sounded amused.

"I don't know what you're talking about."

"Don't you?" There was still a smile lurking behind his eyes.

"Mr. Riggs, if you have something to say to me, I'd appreciate you simply coming out with it."

"I do have a capacity for making you furious, don't I Katie?" He had changed the subject in midstream and Kate was having a hard time keeping up with him. She decided not to try.

"If you'll excuse me, Mr. Riggs, I think I'll go into the kitchen to see if your mother needs help."

"She doesn't," Rigg said as Kate tried to rise and found he'd sat on her skirt. That he was equally aware of his position became clear as soon as Kaitlin turned her head to look at him. His look was almost angelic.

They sat looking at one another for a long moment. Kate could see that Rigg was enjoying himself and even though she was frustrated with him, she had to admit that he was the best looking man she'd ever seen.

Very softly, so Rigg had to lean to hear her, Kaitlin said, "You, Mr. Riggs, are a flirt."

Kate was very satisfied with the look of shock that registered on his face. In the next instant she had tugged her skirt free and was headed toward the kitchen.

◻ ◻ ◻

"And heavenly Father, we thank you for the family that has come into our midst. Please bless them and take care of them, and use all of us to Your good pleasure. In Christ's name I pray, Amen."

Mr. Taylor's prayer worked wonders at calming Kaitlin's nerves. It was a classical farm kitchen, the kind she'd only read about, with a very large table and plenty of chairs. Her place was between Jeff and Sean and unfortunately, across the table was Rigg. He was very solicitous to Marcail who was beside him, holding the bowls of food and anything else she needed to serve herself. But even though his attention was centered on the youngest Donovan, he was more than able to make Kate feel self-conscious with his intense glances and warm smile.

That Rigg was the only one staring at Kate, was thanks to Bill Taylor. He had arrived at the house with Jeff and Gil not too long before Rigg, only to find Nate staring at Kate as though he'd never seen a woman before. That his older boys followed suit the moment they arrived, had been a source of great disturbance to him. Kaitlin, intent upon her reading, did not see the father of these young men signal them out of the room to inform each of them that they knew better and to please not do anything to make their guest uncomfortable.

Sean had been an unwilling observer to the whole episode and every time he looked at Kaitlin he wanted to cry. His heart ached for Hawaii where Katie was just Katie and not the object of every man's attention, or where Marcail was not shaken and bruised by some man who never saw her steal a thing.

Maybe he was too young to understand all the ways between men and women but he told himself he was not ever going to stare at a woman as though she had two heads, or blush and stutter when spoken to, no matter how pretty she might be. After all, a person's true beauty was beneath their skin. He might be only 14 but Sean Donovan believed that with all of his heart.

Rigg watched the emotions scoot across Sean's face and wondered what was tormenting his housemate. Surprised at how paternal he felt toward this young man, he hoped they'd have a chance to talk on the way home.

Rigg would have been really surprised to know that he was the only person Sean didn't mind looking at his sister.

After supper Kaitlin volunteered to do the dishes and Jeff helped her. They worked quietly for a time and then began to talk like old friends.

"Is it normal to have your purse snatched here in Santa Rosa? I mean, it was right in front of all those people and well, I realize this is a big city, but I'm surprised."

"We certainly have our fair share of crime but please don't let today paint a black picture for you. Santa Rosa is really very nice. It's growing fast so there is a lot of opportunity here. There's also a good deal of community involvement if you're so inclined.

"Nearly everyone in my parents' generation is very concerned for the education of our generation and it shows in the schools they build and the teachers they hire."

"Was I just complimented, Jeff?" Kate smiled at him.

"No, I'm just trying to butter you up so you'll help me dry some of these dishes when you're done washing."

"Not a chance. If you remember, I gave you a choice."

"So much for chivalry. Next time I'll rope Rigg into doing this.

"Why did you do that?" Jeff said after a second.

"Do what?" Kate asked cautiously.

"Stiffen up at the sound of Rigg's name."

Kaitlin didn't answer and when she held out a dish to Jeff he just stood looking at her without reaching for it. Kate sighed and looked him in the eye.

"Jeff, I know you love your brother but the truth is, he's very high-handed and a flirt to boot."

"*Rigg!*" Jeff was astounded.

"I shouldn't have said that Jeffrey. Please forgive me. He's your brother, I had no right to speak ill of him."

"Kaitlin," Jeff's voice was serious now. "I don't know how to say this, but Rigg isn't what you think." He stopped when her look told him she was more than a little skeptical.

"I mean it, Kaitlin. Rigg is the nicest guy on earth and very much a man of God."

"I can see why you think that way, Jeff, but you did ask me and I thought I could be honest with you."

"You can be. I'm sorry I jumped on you." He dried a few more plates and then asked carefully, "Why do you think he's high-handed?"

"You were standing there, Jeff, when he ordered me to get my things and come here. Please don't get me wrong. I really appreciate your family, but your brother could have been a little more diplomatic.

"He also thinks I'm a rag doll. Telling me he'll put me in the wagon and nearly sitting on me when he thinks I'll move from the sofa.

"Whether or not you want to hear this Jeff, the fact of the matter is, your brother is very accustomed to getting his own way."

Jeff could think of nothing to say. All that Kate had mentioned was true. Also true, was the fact that Rigg wasn't normally like this. In fact Jeff had never seen him so forceful or intent on a person. Kaitlin would never believe it, but Rigg was a little shy around the women at church.

When Jeff said nothing Kate was overridden with guilt. "I don't know what came over me just now, Jeff. But I'm so sorry to talk to you that way. Rigg has been very kind to Sean and I know he wants to help us. I hope you won't hold this against me."

"It's all right, Kate, really." He gave her his most engaging grin and they finished the dishes over a discussion about the church the Taylors attended.

twenty-three

Kaitlin and Jeff had been seated in the living room with Bill and May for just a few minutes when Rigg, right on down to Marcail, came in from outside where they'd been seeing the barn.

Marcail sat next to her sister on the sofa and Rigg took a place on Marcail's open side.

"You should see the barn Katie!" her sister told her with enthusiasm. "They have four horses but one is old and tired; they use him for burning hay."

Kaitlin laughed along with everyone else at Marcail's description. "I think what they meant was that he's too old to work so all he does is eat. That's a hay burner."

"I think Loni's brother must be a hay burner, but he's not that old."

The Taylors watched as Sean and Kaitlin exploded with laughter. The brother Marcail spoke of was 19 and very lazy. They had never heard it put that way before but it was very fitting.

When the laughter subsided, Gilbert asked a question of Marcail.

"Who is Loni?"

"She's my best friend in Hawaii."

"And how old is her brother?"

Marcail looked at Kate.

"Nineteen I think," Kate supplied the expected answer.

"May tells me you sometimes talk to each other in—"

"Hawaiian." Sean supplied for Bill, who was speaking to Katie.

"Right, Hawaiian. Maybe you could give us a sample." His voice was coaxing and Kate could see he was fascinated, but before she could answer him, Sean spoke up.

"There's a sure way to get Katie to speak Hawaiian— just get her mad or upset." Kaitlin threw her brother a warning look but kept silent.

"I know some songs in Hawaiian," Marcail said.

"Please sing one for us, Marcail," May entreated from her chair near the fireplace.

In the next instant the room was filled with the sweet, high sound of Marcail's singing voice. Kaitlin and Sean joined her after a moment and the family with whom they were staying was transfixed at the beautiful words of the song and the perfect blend of the Donovan voices.

No one spoke after the song ended and when the silence continued, Kate told them in a soft voice what the words meant.

"Praise to our God who does save us, Praise to our God who is Lord. He is the Maker and Creator, we know Him better from His word. Praise Jehovah, Praise the Master, praise the Father and Holy Ghost, Praise with all your heart and being, here on earth and heavenly host."

May had tears in her eyes and Bill leaned forward in his chair. "Kaitlin, would you consider singing that for our church on Sunday?"

Kaitlin couldn't have been more surprised if he'd thrown something at her.

"Bill," May spoke softly. "Maybe you should give them a chance to get to know the people at the church. I mean, it doesn't have to be this Sunday, does it?"

The relieved look on Kaitlin's face told Bill his wife's insight had been correct.

"No, but you will do it sometime?"

Kate glanced at Sean who was looking as surprised as she was. "I think we could do that. If your church is very big though, I'm not sure our voices will carry."

"It's a small building." Rigg spoke for the first time. He realized how content he was just being in the same room with Kate. But something was on his mind and he thought that now might be the time to bring it up.

"Will you do me a favor, Marcail?"

"What is it?"

"Well," Rigg put an arm around her and brought her gently to his side. She snuggled against him and he continued. "If it wouldn't bother you, will you please tell me what happened in front of the store today?"

Rigg's peripheral vision told him Kaitlin had started at his request. He raised his arm from around Marcail and reached to touch Kate's shoulder. "You don't have to tell me if you don't want to, Marcail."

"No, I'll tell you. I can't remember everything, but Katie was taking a long time in the store and I heard a dog bark, so I went out front to see where it was. I don't remember seeing that lady or that man but then she started to yell and he grabbed me."

"You mean the officer?"

"Yes."

"And you didn't see anyone run away with the purse?"

"No."

"Okay, Marcail, go ahead."

"Well, he grabbed my arm and it hurt and the lady kept yelling and then he shook me and that hurt and then Katie was there and I got sick. That's all I remember."

Kaitlin bolted from the couch then, and Rigg, after giving Marcail a quick squeeze, went after her. May came over to sit with Marcail and Sean stood, gripped with indecision. He looked toward the kitchen where Kate had run and then back to Mr. Taylor, who smiled at Sean in understanding.

"Don't feel like you have to go out, Sean. I think Rigg will handle it." Sean looked relieved and sat back down. Jeff reached for the checkerboard and all in the living room were glad for something else to do besides wonder what was going on outside with Rigg and Kaitlin.

❑ ❑ ❑

Kate had hit the backyard at a run and was almost to the barn before Rigg caught her. Running in front of her, he turned and gently brought her to a halt. Rigg watched as she buried her face in her hands and cried. He hesitated for a moment before tenderly pulling her into his embrace. Kate came without resistance and sobbed against him.

"I don't know how to be a mother to Marcail." Her voice was broken. "It's my fault she got hurt; I should have kept better track of her."

Rigg let her cry against him. He could tell that Marcail's story was hurting her and he'd honestly never given a single thought as to how *she* might react. His attention, when he asked the question, had been solely on Marcail. By the time he realized his mistake, he could only pray that his hand on Kaitlin's shoulder would be enough. But it hadn't been.

"We need our Father, doesn't God know that? I feel like we've been deserted." Her voice was growing calmer but Rigg still held her in the protective circle of his arms.

"Marcail doesn't blame you, Katie, and neither does anyone else. You're very good with Marcail and I can see she thinks the world of you. What happened today could have happened just as easily *with* your father here. Did you think about that? Marcail was in the wrong place at the wrong time. It's no one's fault."

Kate was still for a moment and then pushed free from Rigg's arms and stepped away from him as though she'd been burned. Rigg watched with some frustration as she smoothed her hair and looked up at him, once again the prim and proper schoolteacher.

"Thank you for coming out with me. I'm feeling better now."

"Are you really? Well, quite frankly I'm surprised since you seem afraid to face that this really happened. You seem hesitant to let yourself feel anything."

Kate had never been so hurt or surprised. He was angry with her and she didn't know why. Her voice told him how hurt she was.

"I've obviously done something to anger you, Mr. Riggs, and I'm sorry. You've been very kind and if I've offended you in some way, I'd be glad to apologize and make it right with you." Kate watched him rake an agitated hand through his hair. When he spoke, his voice was soft in the gathering darkness.

"I'm not angry Kate, but if you should find that you're still upset about what happened today, you can talk to me anytime."

"Thank you," Kaitlin said simply, and tried not to think of how nice his arms had felt and how solid his chest had been. *You've no business throwing yourself at the man that way, Kaitlin Donovan, you really should be ashamed of yourself,* Kate said to herself as Rigg walked her back to the house.

If Rigg could have read her mind he'd have been furious.

Marcail was waiting inside and the anxious look on her face made Kaitlin feel ashamed of the way she'd run from the room.

"Are you all right, Katie?"

"I'm fine Marc," Kate answered and hugged her.

The little girl held on to her sister for a long time, wanting to comfort as well as *be* comforted. When they finally crawled into bed that night, Kate's tears came on afresh when Marcail reached for her hand and whispered that everything was going to be fine.

twenty-four

"Is Katie okay?"

"I think so," Rigg answered Sean as they rode home in his wagon. "She blames herself for today and I really wish she wouldn't."

"Did she tell you that?"

"Yes she did, and even though I told her it wasn't true, I don't think I convinced her."

"Maybe I'll talk to her," Sean's voice was thoughtful and Rigg was further convinced that he was a special young man who cared deeply for his family. Rigg didn't feel that the time was right to ask Sean if anything was bothering him, so he just prayed, asking God to show him the right time.

The next day Sean was awake at a very early hour, brimming with excitement. This was his first day at work. Rigg came into the kitchen to find his young housemate sitting quietly at the table waiting for him.

"How did you sleep?" Rigg's voice was still gravelly from sleep and Sean smiled.

"Fine. How about you?"

"Good. I thought a lot about your sister and I need to ask you something Sean." Rigg took a place at the table and leaned toward Sean, his face serious. "If I were to show interest in Kaitlin, I mean romantically, how would you feel about that?"

Sean answered without hesitation, "I'd think it was okay just as long as Katie did."

Rigg nodded. "She doesn't seem to like me too well, does she?"

Sean found this question embarrassing and didn't know how to answer.

"Don't feel bad, Sean. She's already told me she thinks I'm a flirt."

"Are you?" The words were so quiet that Rigg, who had moved to the stove to start the coffee, almost missed them. He turned to find Sean's heart in his eyes.

"No, Sean, I'm not. I'm not sure if I'm coming or going where your sister is concerned, but this is no game I'm playing." Rigg watched Sean's face to see if he understood and was satisfied with what he saw.

"Come on over here, Sean," he said after a moment. "I'll show you how to make coffee."

❑ ❑ ❑

Rigg walked with Sean to the post office. After Sean posted his letter, Rigg sent him to the mercantile to ask for Joe Crawford, the man with whom he'd be working that day. As he watched Sean head eagerly down the street, Rigg grinned, remembering his first day at the mercantile. He then headed to the shipping office.

His father was in early as he expected. Heading into his office, Rigg shut the door behind him. He took the chair across the desk and looked at the man who'd been a father to him for most of his years.

"Did you see Kaitlin before you left the house today?"

"No, the only one up was your mother."

Rigg nodded and sat quietly.

"I've never believed in love-at-first-sight, Dad, but something is going on. I can't get that girl out of my mind."

Rigg spoke the words sincerely and Bill's heart ached for him. It had been over 23 years since he'd met May but he remembered very well how it felt to watch and wait and wonder. He also remembered befriending a little boy who, if he hadn't responded to him as well as he had, might have kept him from winning May's heart.

But the boy was not three any longer. He was a man, 26 years old—a godly man of faith, with his own business; a man with hopes and desires of his own.

"Do you remember the first time we met, Rigg?"

"My third birthday."

"Yep. I bought you a toy soldier."

"I still have it."

Bill didn't say anything else; he didn't need to. Rigg smiled at what he was thinking.

"Are you trying to tell me that you went through me to get to my mother?"

Bill grinned back at him. "Not exactly, but the fact that you liked me certainly helped my case."

"So you think I should go on as I am, being there for Sean and Marcail, but not pushing Katie?"

"Well, I certainly don't think you should propose—at least not until she relaxes around you."

"I have no one to blame for the way she treats me but myself."

Bill's brows rose in question but Rigg didn't elaborate.

"I guess I'd better get to work."

"All right. Are you coming to the house for supper?"

"I'm planning on it. Are you going to make that announcement about household items for Kaitlin to the congregation in the morning?"

"I'm planning on it."

Father and son grinned at one another and then Bill told Rigg he was praying for him.

"Thanks, Dad, thanks a lot."

❏ ❏ ❏

Kate lay in the bed next to Marcail and knew she should get up. She'd had a very restful night that started almost as soon as her head hit the pillow. Heavy sleeper that she was, she'd been gone until morning.

She had wanted to pray and tell God everything she felt about Marshall Riggs, but her body had had other plans. Now this morning she couldn't think beyond getting ready for school on Monday.

Her mother had always planned for the following week on Saturday, and so that was what Katie planned to do today. She had brought the classification register that Mr. Carson had given her. She said a quick prayer of thanks for Sean's job, and asked protection for him as he worked, and then slipped out of bed. The thought of getting dressed made Kaitlin stop and pray again.

She pleaded with God about wisdom over wearing black for a year. It was easier for Sean, who simply put a black band around the sleeve of his jacket. But for her and Marcail, it was a major wardrobe change. Marcail had one black dress and Kaitlin had two. She also had a dark skirt but only a white blouse to go with it. The rest of her things, as well as Marcail's, were lightweight summer prints.

She stood for a moment, and then the decision was made. She would wear whatever was clean on any given day and sew the lace collars and cuffs back on her black dresses.

❑ ❑ ❑

After having a huge breakfast and exploring the farm with Marcail, Kaitlin was back in the house to work on her lessons. A thrill shot through her as she opened the register and began to read, careful to pass over the percentages of the students. She didn't want any preconceived notions when she walked in that door Monday. Each student would have a fair chance to prove himself.

Kate's eyes skimmed over the names. There were eight students listed under "Upper Form," ranging from age 12 to 17. In the "Middle Form" there were nine children listed, their ages were 10 to 13. At the bottom of the page was the listing for "Primary Form," the ages being from 7 to 11 and totalling eight children. Adding Sean and Marcail to this list would give her 27 students.

Kaitlin went on to study the recitation program, taking note of who recited forenoon and afternoon. In an honest attempt to know as much as possible, she read every word of the teachers' reports. She wanted to ease the transition for this class.

Around mid-morning May came back from the shipping office where she and Marcail had gone with the boys. They didn't disturb Kate in the living room, but it wasn't very long before the unmistakable aroma of freshly-baked cookies floated in to assail her senses.

She worked a bit longer, taking notes on a pad May had given her, and then went to the kitchen.

"How's it going Kaitlin?" her hostess wanted to know.

"It's going well. I'm all set and really looking forward to meeting the class."

"They're normally a good group of kids. I think they'll like you." May smiled. "If they get out of line you can always speak to them in Hawaiian and shock them all speechless."

Kate and Marcail both laughed at the idea.

The remainder of the day was spent doing laundry and baking, and waiting for Sean to come and tell them about his first day at work.

twenty-five

Joe Crawford, the man Sean was to find and work with, turned out to be just a few years older than he was. Rigg had told Joe, who was moving out of town, that he'd found a replacement who would be starting Saturday. Joe was to train Sean and, from the look on the older boy's face, he was none too happy about it. Sean, sensing a hostility in Joe that frightened him a little, tried not to ask too many questions. He found himself wishing that Rigg had offered to show him the ropes.

"That doesn't go there." The words were surly and Sean stopped where he stood, holding a heavy crate. "I told you those go over there! Are you stupid or something?"

Sean said nothing, thinking that, indeed, maybe he was stupid. Never had he made so many mistakes. He couldn't seem to do anything to please his co-worker, but he stayed with it and tried to ignore the angry looks that came his way all morning.

"How is it going, boys?"

Sean watched Joe become a different person in the boss' presence.

"Just fine, Rigg. Sean's a great worker, real smart." That the words were sickeningly sweet, Rigg didn't seem to notice.

"Good. I knew you'd do fine, Sean. Why don't we break for lunch?"

Joe grabbed his lunch pail, went through the store and down the street. Sean stood in indecision—he didn't have any lunch. Rigg was checking the papers he held in his hand so Sean slipped quietly out the back door and walked up the street.

Not able to stop the flood of tears that began to flow, he sped up until he found himself on a quiet street. Ahead of him was the schoolhouse. He moved toward it and collapsed on the steps; his tears intensifying until he was nearly sobbing.

Rigg, who had not been far behind him when he left the store, had followed him when he hadn't gone straight home. From a distance he watched Sean bring his knees up and lay his face on top of them. His arms were over his head, as though trying to protect himself from a blow.

Rigg turned, cut across a few yards and dashed up the back steps of his house. In a matter of minutes he was out again, bearing a loaf of bread, three apples, half a pie and a jug of cider. He whistled as he approached the school steps, giving Sean a chance to know of his presence.

Sean wiped his face on his sleeve when he heard the sound and watched his employer approach.

"How about some lunch?"

"Thanks, but I'm not too hungry."

"Mind if I join you?"

"No."

Rigg sat down on the second step, bit into an apple, and watched Sean's profile. "How do you think you'll like the job?"

Sean continued to stare off in the distance as he answered. "It might take me a while to remember everything. I'll understand if you feel you need to get someone else."

Rigg had never known Joe to be sneaky or underhanded in any way, but Sean's words made him wonder what kind of morning Joe had given him. Joe was not very happy that his family was moving back East. Maybe it had been asking too much to have him train his successor.

"This pie is good, sure you won't have any?"

"I'm not a baby, Rigg. If you need to tell me that I'm fired, please just say it," Sean said with quiet dignity.

"You really have worked yourself into a mood, haven't you?" Sean looked at Rigg for the first time. "I think you're doing fine Sean, and if you're going to do a good job this afternoon, you need some lunch." Sean caught the apple Rigg tossed him and ate it in silence. He didn't refuse any more of the food that was passed his way and, miraculously, found that he did feel better.

Rigg hoped that Sean would share what was on his mind but he didn't. They returned to the mercantile. Sean prayed and took a deep breath before going into the back room. Joe was already there and his first words were a criticism.

"You're late."

Sean said nothing.

"Get that crate unloaded and out with the rest of the sugar—on the shelf where I showed you."

The next hour passed in a similar fashion. Sean said little and Joe reprimanded him nonstop. Sean stopped at one point and simply stared at Joe.

"I said, put that sack over there!"

For the first time he didn't move to do Joe's bidding.

"What's your problem, Donovan?"

"I was about to ask you the same thing."

"Don't give me any trouble Donovan, or I'll clean the floor with you."

"I don't think you will." Sean's voice had gone very soft and, unbeknownst to himself, his look menacing. "Now, I'm going to do my job here for the rest of the afternoon as best as I can. If you've got some problem with that, then you're welcome to go get Rigg. If he's not happy with the job I'm doing then he can fire me, but I want you off my back."

The older boy hesitated. He could see that he'd clearly pushed too far. Silently both boys went back to work. The atmosphere was no more friendly, but at least Sean was able to work in a semblance of peace.

❏ ❏ ❏

"Okay, Sean, here's your pay."

"Already?"

"Every Saturday night at closing."

"Thanks," Sean breathed as he fingered the coins in his hand. Rigg watched him and suddenly felt choked up. To see the boy, you'd think it was a fortune. But this was his first job and Rigg remembered again how good it felt to be paid for a day of work.

Rigg found himself just as choked up when Sean went straight to his sister and turned the money over to her, once they'd reached the Taylor farm. Bill and the boys were not yet back from the shipping office so Kaitlin, Sean and Marcail had a chance to talk with only Rigg and May present.

"How did it go?" Kaitlin wanted to know.

"Fine. I made mistakes but I think I'm getting the idea."

"Good. I prayed for you."

"Yeah, Sean, we remembered you at lunch."

"Thanks Marc."

"Did you have enough to mail the letter?"

"Yes. I put the change with my wages."

"Good. I wrote to Aunt Maureen today. We can mail that letter Monday."

Kate's attention turned from her brother and, even though Rigg was talking to his mother, she had the feeling he'd been watching her.

He had invaded her thoughts at the most unusual

times today. When she'd been working with May and Marcail she had actually wondered what type of cookies he liked. She had stopped just short of asking May and humiliating herself.

The Taylor men piled in shortly after that, and Kaitlin helped May put supper on the table. She decided that feeding this many men was a costly chore. After the prayer Kate watched a huge platter of fried chicken disappear, along with mashed potatoes, green beans, fried biscuits, turnip greens and two pitchers of milk. She had no room for the apple cake that was served with coffee after the meal.

May asked Gil, Nate and Sean to help with the dishes and everyone else moved to the living room. Rigg sat on the sofa and Kate took a chair across from him. She watched as he beckoned to Marcail with one finger. Marcail snuggled into the sofa next to him as if she'd been doing it all her life. Kate was amazed.

"I brought you something."

"You did?" The little girl's eyes grew wide as she watched Rigg draw a snow-white hair ribbon from his pocket.

"This is for me?" Marcail almost squealed, and Kate smiled.

"Yes ma'am," Rigg told her, and watched as she looked to Kaitlin for approval. Kate smiled at her and she hugged the thin strip to herself.

"Thank you, Mr. Riggs."

"You're welcome, Marcail," he answered and then turned a challenging eye on Kate. "I'd like it if you called me Rigg. What do you think about that?"

"That's fine with me, if it's fine with Katie. Is it fine with you Katie?"

Bill had to hold his paper a little higher to hide his smile. Rigg was digging himself into a hole, and fast.

Kate opened her mouth to say something but closed it. That Rigg was testing her was almost more than she could take. He had backed her into a corner and she came out fighting like a teacher. She ended up addressing Rigg as though he were a child.

"I am not used to having my authority questioned, Mr. Riggs. I feel I've already compromised my conviction by allowing Sean to call you by your nickname. As I told you before, Marcail and I will call you Mr. Riggs, and if my sister continues to question me, I might have to punish her."

You asked for that Rigg and you know it, were the convicted man's thoughts. What he said out loud was, "I'm sorry Marcail. Your sister is right; I shouldn't have done that."

"That's all right. I still like my ribbon."

Marcail was off the sofa in the next instant and headed toward the kitchen to show her gift to May. Kate looked over to see Jeff taking it all in as though watching players on a stage. He grinned at her and Kaitlin couldn't take anymore. She mumbled something about needing air and went out the front door.

"Shame on you Rigg," Bill spoke softly when the door had latched. "Why do you bait the girl?"

"I wish I knew," was the tired reply. "I guess I'd better go apologize." Rigg stood up and Jeff couldn't keep from staring at him. He'd never seen his brother like this.

"Why don't you let me go?"

When Rigg's features washed with relief, Jeff followed Kaitlin to the front yard.

She had walked toward the copse of trees that stood tall and green on the south edge of the Taylors' land. Jeff caught up with her just as she reached the creek's edge. His feet broke a fallen branch and Kate started.

"Oh, Jeff, I didn't hear you approach."

Jeff could see that he'd frightened her.

"Sorry to scare you."

"I'm all right."

"It's pretty out here isn't it?"

"Yes, it is. Very nice," Kate agreed.

"It was a great place to grow up. We had such fun in this water. Not every kid lives on a creek. Most people don't know what they're missing."

"You're certainly right, growing up by the water is a little piece of heaven on earth." Her voice was so wistful that Jeff stared at her face and knew she was thinking of Hawaii. He glanced down at the stream of water at their feet and began to laugh.

"What's so funny?" Kate wanted to know.

"Oh, just me with my little creek, telling you how wonderful living by the water is, when you probably swim like a fish!"

Katie laughed with him then. "I do swim, that's true. And your creek is not the Pacific, but it's still beautiful. Actually, it isn't really Hawaii that I miss, but the people, and knowing that my father is there without my mother."

It didn't matter that Jeff had no words to say to that; he knew none were needed. After a moment, they talked of little things and then Jeff mentioned Rigg.

"He certainly enjoys seeing me upset," Kate said, feeling flustered all over again.

"He enjoys you period."

"Sure he does."

"I'm serious, Kate. You can't believe how many women have been interested in Rigg over the years—more than I can count. He's just never met anyone that he felt he could get serious about."

Kate was looking at Jeff with such amusement that he stopped.

"What?"

"Don't you see, Jeff? I am evidently one of the few girls who hasn't thrown herself at his feet and he can't stand it. Somehow that makes me a challenge and it hasn't taken me more than a few meetings with Mr. Riggs to know that he loves a challenge."

"Oh, Kaitlin!" Jeff sounded truly distressed but all Kate did was chuckle. "That's utter nonsense. You can't really believe that?"

"And why shouldn't I? You were sitting in the living room tonight—enjoying everything that went on, I might add. You can see for yourself that I'm just a plaything to your brother." Kate's voice suddenly became very serious. "And if I can speak honestly with you, Jeff, it's the last thing I need. I have feelings and no one likes to be laughed at. My world has come apart at the seams in the last few months. I find myself playing mother to my brother and sister and falling way short of the mark.

"So your brother's actions are just insult on top of injury. You tell me he's a man of God. Well, you can understand why I have a hard time believing that. He brings my sister a present and then challenges my authority right in front of her. If he's such a man of God Jeff, can you tell me why he treats me like that?"

"Jeff can't tell you, but I can."

Kaitlin spun around so quickly that her dress flared. Rigg stood less than ten feet away and Kate knew the time for confrontation had come.

twenty-six

"I heard a little bit of what you said to Jeff, Kaitlin. Is there anything you want to add?"

Kate couldn't say anything. She wasn't really embarrassed, just wary of confrontations. She also knew that the thoughts she shared with Jeff should have been said directly to Rigg. Jeff tactfully left them alone, and the silence between them lengthened.

The sun was beginning to set; it was a little darker beneath the trees and the breeze had picked up, sending a cool draught against Kaitlin's bare arms. Crossing her arms in an effort to keep warm, she finally broke the silence.

"Even though it's hard for me to face you, I'm rather glad you came out when you did, or I would probably never have talked to you.

"I meant what I said to Jeff but I should have said it all to you. You couldn't be more kind to Sean and Marcail, but you treat me so strangely. One minute you're tender and the next you're ordering me about as though you owned me.

"I'm not a child, but neither do I have the wisdom of the ages, and I just don't know how to handle this underlying animosity between us. In another circumstance I would just keep my distance from you, but with Sean living with you and me staying temporarily with your folks, that's impossible.

"If I've done something or am doing something that is offensive to you, I'd be more than happy to clear the air. And I know I've said a lot but there's just one more thing. I hope that anything between us won't affect the way you treat Sean and Marcail. I know they like you and it's so hard to be here without our folks, I just hope that—"

"Kaitlin." Her name, softly spoken in his deep voice, brought her to a halt. He came close enough to touch her, but did not.

"I've been so wrong in the way I've treated you. Will you please forgive me?"

"Yes," she said immediately.

"I'll try not to be so bossy with you, but please understand that you and Marcail gave me quite a scare on Friday. In my mind, leaving you at that house would have been like leaving an infant in the snow. You had no money or food or even sufficient blankets for the bed. I was afraid you would refuse me so I ordered instead of asked.

"As for the other—the teasing—all I can say is that I'm not myself with you. We got off to such a bad start. I mean, right away you didn't like me, and I wanted you to like me. And not just because I let your brother live with me. Am I making any sense to you?"

Kate nodded. "Thank you for telling me. It clears up a lot. So much has happened to bruise my emotions, and my mind never goes more than an hour all day without wondering where my Father is and if he's all right.

"What I need right now is friendship. I hope you'll understand when I tell you I can't handle anything more than that."

"I do understand, and I hope you'll consider me a friend."

"Thank you." The words were whispered sweetly and Rigg watched as tears puddled in those huge brown eyes. Rigg mentally shook his head. He'd just offered to be her friend. *Husband* was much closer to what he had in mind.

Desperately wanting to be the man Kaitlin needed him to be, his heart cried out to God for help. He knew as he looked into those eyes that if it took forever, he was going to try to win this woman's heart. If he had to stuff his own emotions into a place deep within himself in order to do that, that was exactly what he would do.

"It's getting pretty cool out here. Why don't we go in?"

"Okay. Mr. Riggs, may I ask you something?"

"Anything." Rigg wondered how long he could endure being addressed as Mr. Riggs.

"Did Sean really do all right today? Were you pleased with the job he did, or did he get into some sort of trouble?"

"I think he did fine. Why do you ask?"

"He said something he's never said before, something about making mistakes and getting the hang of it. I've never known Sean to have a bit of trouble catching on to anything."

"The young man training him might have given him a hard time this morning. I checked on them several times this afternoon and even though they're not best friends, I think they both know where the other one stands."

Kate thanked him for explaining. She strongly suspected that Sean was putting pressure on himself to work and be the man in the family. She shared her belief with Rigg, feeling for the first time like she could really talk to him.

"And what bothers me the most is his schooling. Sean will be 15 in December. I don't want him getting it into his head to quit school and try to support us."

"I have noticed that he's very conscious of your welfare. I think he'll stay in school and it'll help that Nate is there. But I will keep my ears open and if he says anything to me about wanting more hours before summer, I'll discourage it."

"Thank you. I feel better knowing that you think he should stay in school. Some people think that once you're a teen, you've had all the school you need."

"Well, Santa Rosa certainly has some of those but I'm not one of them."

They were back at the house, Rigg walking with Kaitlin, his heart swelling with joy. She was talking to him like he was a friend. When he'd felt a very definite burden to join her and Jeff, he'd fought it. At the moment he couldn't have been more thrilled that he'd listened to his heart.

All the lamps were lit in the living room when Kate and Rigg stepped through the front door and Bill immediately told Kate they wanted to talk with her. Sean, Nate and Gil were taking their baths. Marcail was sharing Jeff's chair and they'd been reading a story until Kate came in. Kaitlin sat down on the sofa expectantly.

"I've been planning to make an announcement tomorrow morning to the congregation about your house needing supplies. I don't mind doing that, and I can promise you there will be a great response. But Kate, we'd really like you to stay here. That is, we want you to know that you're welcome here for as long as you'd like. We even have an extra wagon and Nate can drive all of you to school each day."

Smiling at the sincere faces of the people before her, Kate's voice told of her gratitude.

"You've been so kind to let us stay with you and I praise God for you. If I knew a little better when Father would be back, I might take you up on it. But I think Marcail and I should go back to the little house as soon as possible."

The Taylors respected Kate's wishes even though their disappointment was evident.

"I'll go ahead with the announcement as planned. May is ready to write down the things you need."

So Kate began, with Marcail and even Rigg adding to the list. Dishes, silverware, hollow-ware, pots, bedding, extra chairs; the list seemed endless.

"Now," Bill said when the list looked complete. "how are you set financially?"

"I got paid today." Sean had come down the stairs in time to hear the question.

"When will you be paid Kaitlin?" Rigg wanted to know.

"At the end of April. Since I don't start teaching until March twenty-seventh, that is, since the month is almost over, Mr. Carson figured he would just put those five days in March onto my April check."

"Has Mr. Carson been handling everything for you, Kaitlin?"

"Yes, he's been very nice."

Bill's face gave no hint of his thoughts, and even though Rigg and Jeff were exchanging a look, Kate didn't notice. None of them were exactly sure when Burt Kemp had left town. They were all hoping that Kate had worked with him, but it looked as if Greg Carson had been on the job.

"So Mr. Carson found the house for you?"

"Right."

"And how about your wages. Did Mr. Carson set that too?" Bill's voice was as smooth as honey, and Kate answered calmly with no signs of offense over such a personal question.

"Yes, he took care of that. You see, I don't have a teaching certificate and he felt it would be better to give me a little lower wage to compensate for that. The rent at the house takes a major part of my salary but we'll get by with Sean working." She smiled with genuine confidence at Sean.

"Kaitlin, would you think me intruding to ask how much your monthly salary is?"

"Oh no, I don't mind. Actually it's kind of nice to have someone to talk to because we've never lived on our own before." Kate went on to answer Bill's question and noticed that the adults in the room became very still. When Rigg spoke his voice was tender.

"Katie, your wages aren't a *little* lower than the usual teacher's pay, they're less than half of what they should be."

"Oh," was all she could say and she looked over at Marcail who had begun to gnaw on her lip, a sure sign of distress.

"Well," Kate said carefully—and maybe a little too cheerfully—her eyes on her sister, "you said the people at the church would be helping us with the things we need, so we just need to buy food."

"Did you have *any* money when you came into town?" Jeff asked kindly. No one had missed the focus of Kaitlin's gaze and all were sensitive to the feeling of security this little girl needed.

"Yes, our aunt gave us some. We used it to pay our rent," Sean supplied.

"And your rent is paid through April?" Bill probed.

"We had enough to pay for about three weeks, so half of April."

"And what had you planned to do then?"

"We've been praying about that."

Bill leaned forward in his chair to make sure he had Kate's attention. "Then will you consider me an answer to those prayers? I would like to give you some money and I would also like to speak with Greg. He needs to be made aware of your financial situation."

"Oh, I don't know. I mean, I don't want him to think I came running to you and complained."

"I can explain everything to him Monday morning, that is, if you agree."

Kate looked over at Sean who told her yes with the move of his head and the look on his face.

"All right Mr. Taylor. And thank you for everything."

"The pleasure is all ours Kaitlin, believe me." These were the first words May had spoken during this talk and Kaitlin would have run from the room if she could have read her hostess' mind. May had just thanked God for a Christian wife for Rigg.

twenty-seven

The next morning found the Donovans and Taylors in church together. A wonderful peace stole over Kaitlin as she entered the house of the Lord; she'd really missed being part of a formal service. Not all of the songs were familiar but they were still beautiful to her ears.

There was one embarrassing moment before the sermon, when Bill made his announcement and asked Kate, Sean and Marcail to stand and be introduced. He told everyone of their situation and that he'd start the list around. He concluded by saying that if anyone had anything to give, it could be brought to the shipping office.

When the sermon began Kate immediately liked Pastor Keller. His eyes were kind and his voice was filled with conviction as he preached from the Word. The morning's text was John 3:14 and 15. He began by reading the verses.

"'And as Moses lifted up the serpent in the wilderness, even so must the Son of man be lifted up: that whosoever believeth in him should not perish, but have eternal life.'

"Let's pray. Our Father in heaven we believe You are the one true God who is able to teach us all things from Your Word. We ask now, Lord, that You open our hearts to Your truth and convicting spirit. In Christ's name I pray, Amen.

"If you remember back in the book of Numbers, God

instructed Moses to make a bronze serpent and raise it high on a pole. The Word says that any and all who looked at the bronze snake would be healed from the poisonous bites of the snakes tormenting them.

"What I want you to think on this morning, is that those who had to look at the snake were condemned to physical death—they'd already been bitten by a poisonous snake. God proved His mercy toward the children of Israel, for when those bitten looked toward the serpent for healing, they were indeed healed.

"Each one of us has also been bitten and received a more dangerous poison: spiritual sin. That old serpent Satan bit all of mankind when he deceived Eve and Adam sinned. We must realize that we are now condemned to spiritual death, and each person must act for himself. In other words, it is *our* personal responsibility to look to Christ, who was lifted up on the cross, as our healing from the spiritual poison of sin, and to understand that without that salvation, we will know spiritual death.

"This is far from the first time I've spoken to you about eternity. Sometimes God burdens my heart so heavily that I know I can't go another Sunday without explaining this precious truth to you. Coming forward will not save you, believing there is a God will not save you. You must be born again by believing in the only begotten Son of God.

"Please, friends, if there is any doubt in your mind, come to me or any one of our elders. We want to see you know Christ in a most personal way."

Pastor Keller closed in prayer and then Kaitlin noticed a man go down front. Pastor Keller embraced him before they sat in the front pew and began to talk.

After the service many greeted the Donovans and told how they had prayed for a schoolteacher. It was a good beginning for everyone. After walking back to the wagon, Kate told Rigg how much she liked the church.

"What?" Rigg asked absently. He had the hardest time concentrating when she looked like she did today. Her dress was a pale pink with every imaginable color of flower swirled all over it. The white lace at her collar against the tanned skin of her face and dark hair was not merely distracting; it was hypnotizing.

"I was just saying that everyone was very nice. I even met some of my students."

"Good."

Kate finally picked up on his distracted attitude and became concerned. "Are you feeling well?"

"Rigg's just having a little heart trouble," Jeff answered as he approached and dropped an arm around Kaitlin's shoulders, as though he were a long lost brother. Kate could see he was having one on her.

"Honestly, Jeff, you'd think I was a hitching post the way you lean on me!" But she wasn't really upset.

Rigg, who had been sending warning glances to his smiling, unrepentant brother, reached up and tossed Jeff's arm away. Rigg's hands went to Kaitlin's waist and he swung her up onto the wagon seat. Jeff looked at the way Katie spread her skirts on half of the seat and then to Rigg who still stood by the wagon.

"I suppose this means I'll be riding in the back?"

"Maybe you can find something back there to lean on," Rigg replied dryly, and Kate laughed.

Jeff grumbled good-naturedly as he boarded and when the wagon pulled away he leaned against the seat back, his legs stretched out before him. He waved at friends and made a few observations as Rigg drove away.

"Hey Katie, have you still got that black dress I first saw you in at the schoolhouse?"

"Yes."

"Maybe you should wear it to church."

"What is he talking about?" Kate inquired of Rigg.

"I think my brother, in his own klutzy way, is trying to

tell you that you were turning heads as we left church today."

Kate turned in her seat to look back at the churchyard and then to Rigg to see if he'd been serious. He had.

"That's ridiculous," Kate said primly. "My skin is much too dark to be considered attractive and my jaw is too square." Kaitlin scowled as both men shouted with laughter.

"I don't know what's so funny about that. Honestly, if any of my class is witnessing this display I'll have my hands full in the morning." But even with her stern words they continued to laugh.

"I wish I'd ridden with your folks," she finally said, and Jeff and Rigg made an attempt to control themselves.

"Are you really mad?" Jeff coaxed from the back.

"Furious!" Kaitlin said, as she smiled and waved at Marcail in the wagon in front of them. Rigg glanced back at Jeff and the two men exchanged a smile.

"And don't you be grinning at each other as though you were actually pleased with yourselves. It's too bad you're too big for a trip to the woodshed. Oh, Mr. Riggs," Kate reached and touched his sleeve, all teasing gone. "Who is that little boy?"

"That's Joey Parker. You'll meet him tomorrow."

"How old is he?"

"I think about nine or ten."

"Why did you ask, Kate?" Jeff piped up.

"I noticed him outside the church but didn't see him come in. I'm glad I'll meet him tomorrow." Kaitlin watched as the boy walked across an open field. His clothes were filthy and his hair hung limply in his eyes. Kate wanted to hold him in her arms forever.

Both Rigg and Jeff refrained from telling Kate what a rough home life Joey hailed from. At the same time, they were both very happy for Joey that a new schoolteacher had been found and he could, at least for a few hours every day, be away from his father.

twenty-eight

"Thank you, Mister...?"

"Hodges."

"Thank you, Mr. Hodges."

"You're welcome, Miss Donovan. You don't know my wife, but when she gets a bee in her bonnet, well, let's just say there's no stopping her."

It was late afternoon on Sunday and one of the men from the church had just arrived at the Taylors' with a wagonload of household goods.

"I know this is quite a pile, so I thought if you'd come along with me and show me your house, I'd deliver it right to your door."

Kaitlin seemed to be in a state of shock so Rigg answered for her. "Why don't we both go with you." He helped a silent Kaitlin into the wagon and they both listened as Mr. Hodges explained why his wife had sent so much.

"Both of our mothers are dead and you always want to hold on to some memories, but we've an attic full of things that haven't been touched in years. The wife couldn't see any point of them sitting there any longer. You might want to air the quilts, but I think you'll find them in good shape."

"I'm sure they'll all be wonderful," Kate's quiet reply caused Mr. Hodges to look over at her on the seat beside him, and then to Rigg. He spoke, after his attention was once again on the road, a smile in his voice.

"I don't suppose there'd be any point in writing to my unmarried son and reminding him that he hasn't visited in a spell."

"No point, Mr. Hodges, no point at all," Rigg answered without hesitation and didn't bother to look at Kate's face—he knew she was smiling. That knowledge made him the happiest he'd been since he met her.

Once at the house the three of them worked steadily to unload the wagon. Quilts, sheets, pillows, pots, a pack of needles and thread, a few dishes and bowls, two vases, a rug beater, cookie cutters and a cookie sheet—Kaitlin wondered when it would stop. When they were finished she flopped into a chair and stared at the pile on the bed and table.

"Mr. Hodges, please thank your wife for me and tell her I'll look forward to meeting her next Sunday. Thank you for bringing us to the house but you don't need to stay. I'll walk back to the Taylors'."

"I'll stay too," Rigg spoke up, and smiled at the twinkle that came into Mr. Hodges eyes. He walked him to the wagon where Hodges gave Rigg another box, and told him briefly who it was from.

Rigg left the front door open and set the box on a chair. He then went about forcing open the windows while Kate tried to sort through the piles. All the kitchen supplies went on the shelves near the stove, and then Kaitlin, who found everything fresh smelling, made the bed with the sheets and all three quilts.

While Kate organized, Rigg attacked the stove. He had it going in about 15 minutes, much to Kaitlin's delight. Rigg showed her a few tricks and then Kate noticed the box he'd brought in earlier.

"What's this?"

"Mr. Hodges said it was for Marcail. It's from his

brother-in-law, who just happens to be the officer who was in front of the mercantile."

Kate looked surprised and then very pleased. Rigg watched as she lifted the lid. "Oh, my," she breathed as she brought forth a lovely doll dressed in an adorable sailor suit. It stood about 18 inches tall and the white suit, including the hat, was completely trimmed in plaid. The shoes and socks were removable and when Kate lay the doll back and brought it forward, the eyes opened and closed.

"Look at these." Rigg brought Kate's attention away from the doll to show her what he'd found in the top part of the box, wrapped in paper. He held up one of six tiny teacups and saucers. There was a matching teapot, sugar bowl and creamer. They were intricate in detail and all appeared to be hand painted.

"She's going to love these."

"I imagine she will. Are you ready to start back? Mom has probably started supper."

"Sure. Let me repack this doll and I'll leave it here for Marcail. She likes surprises."

They walked quietly for the first half of their journey. It was a comfortable silence, and Kate was newly impressed at how gentlemanly Rigg was. He had reached to take her arm several times when the path dipped and once, when a large dog came at them with teeth bared, Kate stepped instinctively close to Rigg, who slid his arm around her. He shooed the dog away with a shout and they were again on their way.

"I've been meaning to tell you, Katie, that I'm sorry about the loss of your mother."

"Thank you. I take it that Sean shared with you?"

"He was in a mood to talk our first night. I imagine it must be hard to have your father leave so soon afterward."

"In some ways his leaving is harder than Mother's death. I know where Mother is, but with Father I can only guess. On our trip over, both he and Sean were so seasick they could hardly stand up. Mother and I took turns tending them but this trip, with him being all alone—" she didn't finish and Rigg knew she was fighting tears.

"If everything went according to plan, is he in Hawaii now?" Kate saw the question for what it was, a chance to collect herself.

"Yes, he should be there. His plans when he left were to gather our belongings and return to San Francisco as soon as he could. If things really go smoothly, I'm not sure he'll get the letter. It could arrive after he's started back."

"You really miss it don't you?"

"Not Hawaii so much as the people."

"Is there someone special waiting for you in Hawaii?" Rigg didn't know where the question came from and wished he could take it back. "I'm sorry, Katie, that's none of my business."

"Don't be sorry, I don't mind." Kate hesitated and Rigg's heart sank. "There was a young man there, still is, who wanted to marry me, but I just never felt that strongly about him. He would make some girl a wonderful husband but I couldn't possibly marry because it was convenient. Could you? I mean, I'd have to be in love."

"I couldn't agree more. Even though it hurts the person whose feelings are stronger, it would be even worse to pretend you felt something that you didn't." Kate looked askance at Rigg as they talked.

"What did I say?"

"Nothing, you're just different than I first thought."

"I hope you mean it's an improvement."

"Now that would be telling." Kaitlin grinned impishly and side-stepped when he reached for her. The farm was in sight and she took off at a run. Rigg caught her in 20 strides and they walked toward the house.

"You didn't really think to outrun me did you?" he asked, with his hand on her arm. She laughed up at him and he desperately wanted to hold her, but must have kept his thoughts hidden because Kate was still smiling at him as if they were old friends.

"You'd have never caught Marcail. She's like lightning."

"I'll keep that in mind when she starts to follow in the sassy footsteps of her sister."

"Sassy!" Kate was outraged and it was Rigg's turn to run. They charged in the back door to find May grinning at them and telling them to wash for supper.

twenty-nine

If Kate looked in the mirror once, she looked 15 times, to see if she'd picked the right outfit for the first day of school. She was downstairs an hour before it was time to leave, pacing and biting her nails. May watched her push her breakfast around and reached out and touched her arm.

"Is there anything I can do to help you relax?"

"Thank you, Mrs. Taylor. I guess I'm just excited. I've never taught without my mother. It feels strange."

"You'll do fine. And I'm sure if your mother knew, she would be very proud." Kaitlin's eyes grew moist and May bent over the table to give her a hug.

Nathan drove the wagon when they finally left the farm. Marcail sat in the back holding the lunch tin that May had packed for everyone. They stopped quickly at the post office to mail the letter to Aunt Maureen and then were, of course, the first to arrive at the schoolhouse. As soon as Kate saw the building her nervousness disappeared. Nate noticed the change in her and smiled. She was in her element now and everything was going to be fine.

"Katie, where will I sit?"

"I don't know. Maybe Nathan can help us with that." They were inside now, and Kaitlin opened the windows next to her desk for some fresh air. The morning was nippy but she didn't even consider lighting the pot-bellied stove; she had always loved crisp morning air.

"Nathan, will you give me a quick rundown of where everyone sat when Mr. Wright was here?"

"Sure. I sit back here with the older kids. The Middle Form kids are around in here and the little ones are in the front rows. Mr. Wright kept these two desks empty for any of the older kids who stepped out of line. He sometimes used the bench in front for the same thing." Nathan blushed suddenly as if he'd said too much, but Kate thanked him and gave him her warmest smile.

"Nate, were there any empty desks?"

Taking a moment to reflect, Nate thought he could remember three. He pointed them out. One was in the middle of the room.

"Well, Marc, it looks as if you might be right here. Why don't you sit down and if no one claims that desk it's all yours."

The little girl look thrilled and Nathan smiled at her. When he'd first heard that the schoolteacher and her sister were coming to live with them he nearly groaned. But Miss Donovan hadn't turned out to be anything like he thought she would be. She was really nice and sometimes even looked a little lost. He figured that was probably why Rigg was acting so funny. Rigg was a sucker for lost kittens and such.

Nate looked over at Marcail and smiled again. She was nice, too. Not at all a brat like he'd expected. It was like suddenly getting a sweet little sister.

A moment later Sean walked into the school. Kate asked him about his night and he said it was fine. She told him that she and Marcail were going to be moving back to the little house the next day. This was news to everyone, but she very logically explained that they had just about everything they needed, plus the money Mr. Taylor had given them for food, and that she felt it was time.

Kaitlin was at the door when the children began to arrive. Asking all of them their names, she introduced herself and then instructed them to sit in the desks they'd previously occupied.

No one was late and Kate noted with satisfaction that all but one of the children were smiling at her. Joey Parker was the exception. His hair was a mess and his clothes filthy. But for some reason, and Kate believed it was of the Lord, she was more drawn to him than any of the other children she'd just met.

The front rows were filled with little girls, mostly ages 7 and 8. Kaitlin looked with compassion at Drew Barsness who was 8 and the only boy in the Primary Form.

She'd checked her register that morning to find out Joey's age. He was 11 and was seated behind Marcail. Sean was a little further forward than he should have been. The desk at the front of his row was empty so Kate had Sean stand while everyone shifted down. His new seat put him where he was supposed to be.

"I've written my name on the blackboard for anyone who can't remember it. It's Miss Donovan. You have probably noticed that there are also two new students in school today. Their names are Sean and Marcail Donovan and I hope you'll make them feel welcome." There was no need to have them stand—it was obvious to all who they were.

"How many of you know where Hawaii is?" Kate surprised most of them with the sudden question.

Nate, Sean and Marcail's hand went up but Kate called on an older girl in the back row. She answered correctly and the class was given the chance to ask many questions concerning their teacher's background. It took most of the morning.

Kaitlin told them they could go to lunch a little early and then had to bite her lip to keep from laughing when one very snippy ten-year-old informed her that it was too early.

"Thank you for telling me, Leslie, but I'm hungry right now. If you're not, you could always eat your lunch during our afternoon break." She winked at the little girl and caught Sean grinning like a fool.

It was very clear to Kate that most of the students had never considered that a *teacher* would experience hunger. So no one would see her smile, she turned to the board to write the time she expected them back in their seats.

After lunch she again caught the students off guard when she called on them, one-by-one, to come forward and tell what they did during the four weeks without school. She had listened to six reports when Leslie raised her hand almost frantically.

"Yes Leslie?"

"You're writing something down. Are we being graded on this Miss Donovan?"

A few of the children snickered over this question and the class was given its first taste of disapproval from Miss Donovan. She stood up and scanned the room with a very stern look. No words were necessary, but a few of the older children looked to Sean, who was giving Kaitlin his complete attention. His look told them she would brook no disobedience.

"No, Leslie, you're not." She spoke when she was sure her point had been taken. "I'm just trying to get to know all of you a little bit better."

The little girl looked so relieved that Kate knew she had an over-achiever on her hands. She smiled at her before calling the next name, which happened to be Joey Parker.

Joey, Kaitlin noted, refused to look at the class. His hands were stuffed in his pockets and his head was bowed. When, after a full minute he didn't speak, she coaxed him in a quiet voice.

"You don't need to give us a long speech, Joey, just share a few things that you did."

"I went to the creek and I hung around town." The boy beat a hasty retreat back to his desk and Kate thanked him as if he'd just shared great pearls of wisdom.

The remainder of the day flew by and Kate could hardly believe it when it was time to dismiss. Nathan and Sean went to get the wagon; Marcail tagged along. Katie was straightening her desk when Rigg walked in.

"How did it go?"

"Oh, it was wonderful. They're all so bright and respectful and fun. I mean we really had *fun*."

Rigg had never heard her talk so fast and was sure she didn't know that she was switching back and forth between Hawaiian and English so fast that he could hardly keep up.

"I take it you had a good day?" Rigg smiled and asked when she came to a breathless halt. He noticed her eyes were sparkling with joy and knew it was a waste of time to hope that the intensity of his feelings for her would abate.

At that moment he found it hard to believe he'd only known her a few days. It just didn't seem possible that he wanted to marry this girl who was almost a stranger. But he did want to marry her and maybe, just maybe, Lord willing, someday he'd be able to tell her.

"Oh, I wanted to tell you," Kate spoke, as though she'd just thought of it, "Marcail and I are going to move back to the little house tomorrow. I'm ready, and if we have to do without a few things, well, I don't think we'll notice."

"You know there's no hurry. My folks meant it when they said you were welcome for as long as you like." Rigg said the words almost casually but he was feeling a little alarmed. Knowing that Kate was at his folks gave him tremendous security. Not that he expected something to happen, it was just nice to know.

"Oh, I know we could stay and it's comforting to know that they're there for us, but my mind's made up. And to tell you the truth," she whispered, "I'm a little excited about it. It's such a cute little place, and we'll be much closer to the school and to Sean."

Rigg's smile was very tender. She was flying high all right, and was probably going to be exhausted later. He didn't stay any longer but told her that he'd invited himself out to supper at the folks and that he'd see her then.

thirty

Rigg's prediction had certainly been correct. Kaitlin fell sound asleep in the Taylors' living room after supper. Nathan and Marcail had already gone to bed and it was a few moments before anyone noticed that Kate was no longer with them.

She was in the rocking chair by the fire and Rigg moved toward her when her body began to slide forward. Surprised that she didn't wake up when he touched her, Rigg looked to his mother for help.

"Lift her gently Rigg, and I'll follow you upstairs."

Rigg did as he was told and expected Kate to wake at any moment, disoriented and upset over being carried to bed. But it didn't happen.

Marcail was already asleep and Rigg gently laid Kate on the bed. He exited quickly, and his mother shut the door behind him. He and Sean, who needed to get to bed himself, waited until May returned to the living room before getting ready to leave.

"Did she ever wake up?" Rigg asked.

"No." Sean supplied the answer before May could. "Once they're asleep, my sisters are like dead people. I've actually held Marcail upside down before and had her sleep through the whole thing." Everyone laughed at the idea. Sean and Rigg bid everyone good night and left a few minutes later.

Kate woke in the morning, refreshed and ready for the day. She didn't remember falling asleep in the living room so she made no inquiries about how she got to bed or why she'd slept in her shift and not her nightgown.

They left a little earlier for school that day so that Kate and Marcail could take their things back to the house. Nate helped them unload and then they were off to the schoolhouse.

The day flew by in a flurry of lessons and recitations. Kate promised a special treat the next day if the weather was nice. Right after school, Kate, Marcail and Sean, who was scheduled to work at the mercantile, made their way in that direction to buy supplies for their house.

Rigg was upstairs in his office which resembled a large indoor balcony at the back of the store. A railing allowed him to look out on the entire floor. When sitting at his desk, which was situated in such a way that he had a clear view of the front door, he could, if he were looking, see anyone who entered the mercantile.

To his great delight he saw Kaitlin enter. He was able to watch her for a time without leaving his desk. When she stepped out of his view, he moved to the railing. He noticed that Marcail stayed right at her side. Kate appeared to be a careful shopper and it was a few minutes before Marcail looked up and noticed him. She waved and Rigg signaled to her to come up.

He watched and listened as Marcail asked, and then as Kate looked up at him. She looked very surprised to see him standing above her, but she gave Marcail permission to go and Rigg watched her skip toward the stairs.

He was back at his desk when she arrived, so she took a chair near him and they talked like old friends.

"Did Kaitlin show you my doll?"

"Yes, she did. She's very pretty."

"I think so, too. Want to know what I named her?"

"Yes."

"Charity."

"That's very pretty."

"Aunt Maureen has dolls. Nice ones. She has a big house too, in San Francisco. We don't live with her anymore because cousin Percy tried to hug Katie." The nine-year-old's hand went to her mouth in surprise. "I'm not suppose to tell anyone that."

"It's all right Marcail, I won't tell anyone." Rigg was thankful that he already knew the details.

"What are you doing?" Marcail was looking at the books in front of Rigg now.

"These are the accounts for the store. I have to keep records of all the things I sell." His voice told her he didn't enjoy it.

"This line is wrong."

"What!" Marcail had been looking at the figures as he spoke and now Rigg spun the book around to check. He was flabbergasted when he rechecked the column to see that she was right.

"Katie's even better in math than me. You should ask her to do it."

"Ask me to do what?" Kate had come quietly up the stairs behind Rigg, carrying her supplies.

"Mr. Riggs doesn't like to do math and I told him you were good."

"Thank you, Marcail. Did you also tell him how well *you* do in math?"

"It's my best subject," Marcail told him. "Are we going now, Katie?"

"Yes. I have everything we need. We just need to pay."

"Where are the rest of your things?" Rigg finally said.

"This is everything."

Rigg didn't say anything but Kate could see his mind working.

"You don't think this will be enough?"

"I think the supplies will last you a while, but you're going to get a little tired of biscuits, beans and rice." Rigg noted that all of the items were the most inexpensive he carried.

He also noticed that Kate was looking very unsure of herself. He was torn between a desire to hold her and another to scold her for leaving the protective care of his parents. He opted for something in between.

"Come here Katie, and sit down." She obeyed him without question. He watched her put her few selections on the edge of his desk. Reaching for paper and a pencil he asked Kate how much money she had. She drew her coin purse from her pocket and emptied it on the desk. Rigg did a quick count and then began to write.

> 4 packages Garland-brand yeast cakes .. 14 ¢
> 1 one-pound can Garland-brand baking
>   powder .... 21 ¢
> 1 8-oz. bottle Iris-brand vanilla .... 30 ¢
> 1 five-pound box Thompson seedless
>   raisins .... 44 ¢
> 1 five-pound sack Matoma-brand rice .. 33 ¢
> 2 cans red kidney beans .... 47 ¢
> 1 five-pound box Garland-brand soda
>   crackers .... 35 ¢
> 4 bars Garland family soap .... 14 ¢
> 1 three-pound package Garland-brand
>   washing powder .... 36 ¢

Kaitlin watched Rigg write swiftly and was surprised at how complete the list was when he handed it to her. He only gave her time to read through half of it. There was everything from yeast to soap. Of course this *was* his business.

"Okay, I think this will help. It's a list of items and what they cost. Head back down and pick up all of these. You have more than enough money and don't forget that Sean will be paid Saturday."

Kate searched for the right words to express her thanks but before she could open her mouth Rigg pushed a large woven basket into her hands and headed her down the stairs. When he sat down again at the desk, Marcail spoke.

"You like Katie, don't you?"

"I like all of you."

Marcail looked almost insulted and Rigg knew he'd underestimated her again.

"Does it bother you that I like Katie?"

"No, there's always someone who does, but I think I like you better than the others."

Rigg wondered how many more there had been besides the young man in Hawaii and cousin Percy. "How did you know, Marcail, that I liked Katie?"

"Sometimes you look at her the way Father used to look at Mother."

Rigg pushed his desk chair back and reached for Marcail's hand. He pulled her out of her chair and into his lap.

"You think I'm a baby, don't you?" The little girl was obviously disappointed.

"No, I don't. I just wanted to hold you."

Marcail let herself be snuggled against him then and Rigg kissed her brow. They were still cuddled together talking when Kate came back up with all the things on the list. Rigg walked them out of the store and they were even able to wave to Sean who was dusting shelves.

"I'll bring the basket right back to you, as soon as I unload it."

"Just keep it for now."

"If you insist, and thank you, Mr. Riggs."

He watched them until they were out of sight and then went in to see the clerk who had taken care of their sale.

"Do me a favor, would you, Cal? Before you leave, fill a sack with the same things the Donovans just purchased.

Oh, and, put in a few special things too. Just leave it under the counter there and I'll get it later."

Cal exchanged a look with the other man who clerked for Rigg. It had taken a while, but it finally looked as though the boss had found someone special.

thirty-one

"How is it?"

"I think I like poi better." Marcail phrased it as delicately as possible, by referring to one of the native Hawaiian dishes she'd grown up on. The result however, was the same—supper tasted awful.

The rice was no longer in tiny individual grains but had congealed into one slimy, tasteless mass. The potatoes were hard as rocks and ice cold. It actually hurt Marcail's teeth to bite into a biscuit. Kaitlin watched her nibble on the edge of one.

Kaitlin didn't know what was the matter with her. She cooked fairly well, although always with her mother. Maybe tonight she was just a bit panicked. Her mother had handled so much of the meal preparation, giving her and Marcail the job of preparing the fish, which they had practically lived on. Kaitlin could serve fish every night for a week and never fix it the same way twice.

"Oh, well," was all she said as she reached for her coffee, remembering as she did, that her mother had always prepared that too. She guessed she'd had worse.

That night both girls slept soundly in their warm bed. In fact, they were almost late for school in the morning.

"Is it almost ready Katie? We're going to be late."

"Almost." Kate was trying her hand at a big pot of cereal like the one Rigg had made them. She decided she must have added too much water because the stuff refused to thicken.

"What will we eat for lunch, Katie?"

"Oh, no!" Kate spun from the stove in dismay. "I completely forgot that I have to pack us a lunch. Look at the cans on the shelves Marcail. See if anything looks good."

Kate had not taken time to make bread and the cheese at Rigg's store had been too costly. If it had been a weekend, Kate would have tried for a regular meal.

She saw Marcail putting things into an old flour sack as she dished cereal into the bowls. The cereal had done a complete turnabout in the pot, going from watery to something so thick it would not come off the spoon.

Watching Marcail grimace over the taste, Kate spread some sugar on the cereal. After so little to eat last night, they couldn't possibly go until lunch with nothing in their stomachs.

"Do you have the lunch?" Kate asked, as she slipped into her sweater.

"All set."

They headed out the door and Kaitlin gave a prayer of thanks that Rigg was taking care of Sean. He'd surely waste away on her cooking.

❑ ❑ ❑

"That was fine reading, Thomas. You may take your seat. We'll break for lunch now and afterward go for that walk I promised you."

As the students dispersed, Marcail came forward and sat on the front bench. Katie pulled their lunch sack out from under her desk and joined her. The first thing she pulled out was a package of yeast cakes.

"Marc, don't you know what these are?"

"Little cakes."

"Yeast cakes. They're used for baking."

"Oh. Sorry."

"That's all right we won't starve." Next came a can of molasses.

"I didn't know what that was either, but the man on the front looked so happy I figured it must taste pretty good." Kaitlin dissolved into helpless laughter while she tried to explain what was in the can. The last item in the bag was a huge package of raisins. Kate didn't even say grace before she began to tear it open.

Marcail's little hand shook as she raised a fistful to her mouth. They ate in silence until Kate laughed again about the molasses and choked on her raisins. Every so often she would go to the door or window and check on the children, but most were eating with no time for mischief.

Sean wandered in when he'd had his fill of what was in his lunch tin and asked the girls if either one of them wanted his last piece of fried chicken. Kate found herself grabbing for his tin like a woman starved, and then remembered that some of her class were eating at their desks.

"You eat it Marc." Kaitlin stood then and took a big drink from the dipper at the water bucket. When she sat on the bench again Marcail was waiting for her. She hadn't touched the chicken.

"We'll share this."

"Thanks Marc," Kate said gratefully, and had to stop herself from swallowing before chewing.

"Rigg told me you bought a lot of supplies. Why are you so hungry?" Sean had stayed close due to the strange behavior of his sisters.

"We do have food, I'm just not used to cooking and packing a lunch. We'll be fine." Kate laughed again when she thought of the molasses and Marcail had to explain. Sean did his own share of chuckling before reaching over to mess his sister's hair.

Offended by his rough treatment, Marcail would have started a wrestling match if Kaitlin hadn't stopped them.

The afternoon found the entire school on a walk. The older children had been put into specific charge over the younger and they ventured forth in small groups to find items that were on their spelling list.

When one was spotted, the find was reported to Miss Donovan and she marked it off the list. Nearly everyone found at least one item and the outing must have been a huge success since the children begged to make it a weekly trip. Kate, in her soft voice, restored order and said that she would consider it.

After school, the moment Kaitlin hit the door, she began supper preparations. She was a woman with a mission and in less time than she expected her efforts paid off. There was no butter for the biscuits or meat for the beans and rice but it was all pretty tasty and she and Marcail were able to eat their fill. Feeling proud of herself, she packaged up the leftovers for lunch the following day.

That night was prayer meeting and even though Kate did not feel up to the walk, she and Marcail started out in time to be there. Rigg, who told her she should have waited for a ride, brought her home. She told him in all honesty that it hadn't occurred to her and realized she hadn't thought of Sean all afternoon.

With her head so fuzzy, she figured the best place for her was bed. As usual she slept soundly. Breakfast was another fiasco and this time it did make them late to school.

"I'm sorry I'm late this morning, class. I'll certainly make an effort not to let it happen again. I want to thank you for all being in your seats. I'm proud of the way—" Kate stopped talking in mid-sentence because Joey Parker had come in late and put an apple on her desk, causing her to look at her desk for the first time that morning.

Her actions in front of a few of her students yesterday at lunch came sharply to mind as she stared at the array of food covering her desk top. Cans and boxes of food, baskets with napkins hiding treats within, two casserole dishes and a few fresh fruits. Tears filled her eyes at the tender hearts of her students. She took a moment to get herself under control.

"If I could choose any class, anywhere in the world to teach, I would pick this schoolhouse with you. Please accept my thanks and also pass it on to your parents for their generosity."

The faces of the children before her told Kaitlin she'd said the right thing. Smiling, her gaze encompassed the room.

"Good morning, class."

"Good morning, Miss Donovan."

Another school day had begun.

thirty-two

It was mid-morning and Rigg sat at his desk, fidgeting with the sack of dry goods he had not yet delivered to Kaitlin. He was concentrating on the conversation he'd had with Sean over breakfast.

"I sort of wish Kate and Marc had stayed at your folks'."

"Why?"

"I'm just afraid that they'll starve to death. I mean, Kate is a great teacher but she's never had to do everything before. Marc is trying to help, but when she packed the lunch yesterday, she took molasses, yeast cakes and raisins."

"So all your sisters had for lunch yesterday was raisins?"

"I had an extra piece of chicken that I shared with them." Rigg noted that Sean looked very guilty. Rigg tried to choose words to help ease that guilt.

"Kaitlin could ask for help."

"She probably never even considered it. She thinks of it as a challenge that she's never met before and thinks she should jump in and do it."

"Why don't you ask them to supper here tonight? I'm not a gourmet, but I can ask Kate if she needs me to show her anything." The conversation ended then as both men went their separate ways.

Now Rigg sat at his desk, his face almost brooding, praying about a way to help Kate without overstepping himself.

"I'm in love with a woman who can't cook." Rigg spoke softly even as a smile came over his face. He froze when he heard steps behind him.

"It's not like you to talk to yourself Rigg," Jeff said quietly. "Want me to leave?"

"No, come on in." Rigg watched as his brother folded his long frame into a chair. He dwelt briefly on the fact that the young ladies at church were very attracted to Jeffrey Taylor but he never responded in kind. It looked for a time as though Jeff might be headed for trouble where girls were concerned, but something had happened when Jeff was still a teen that seemingly changed him forever.

Rigg knew his younger brother to be as desirous of a wife as he was and wondered how Jeff was feeling about what he'd just overheard. He decided to ask him.

"I think the word infatuation fits a little better than love does, Rigg."

"You think it's too soon for me to be in love then?"

The younger man shifted uncomfortably over the vulnerable look on his brother's face. He, quite frankly, thought the world of his older brother and it was hard to see him unhappy. And then there was Kaitlin. It was not at all hard to see why Rigg believed himself to be in love.

"You started working in this store Rigg, when you were only 14. And then Uncle Leo turned the whole thing over to you at 19. You haven't had any time to date girls or even spend much time with them and now Kaitlin Donovan comes into town and knocks you right off your feet. Naturally you assume it's love. Maybe it is, I don't know."

Jeff felt that he'd said enough and watched Rigg's face

carefully to see if he'd upset him. When Rigg finally spoke, Jeff wished he had made him angry. Rigg was more upset than he was letting on and Jeff didn't want anything unresolved between them.

"Well, I doubt if you came by to discuss my love life. What did you need?"

"Rigg?" Jeff's voice was pained.

"No, Jeff it's all right. I *do* feel like I'm in love. But Kaitlin isn't ready for anything like that, and having to explore these feelings on my own is a hurting thing."

"And I just made it worse by saying you're not even in love."

"It's all right, Jeff." Rigg suddenly smiled. "I'll just make you eat those words at the wedding." Jeff laughed. This was the Rigg he knew; confident and purposeful.

❏ ❏ ❏

"Rigg wants you to come for supper," Sean told his sisters.

"What about all this food?"

"I'll help you take everything home. By the way, Kate, I was telling Rigg that you can't cook so if you need help with anything, you can ask him tonight."

"Sean Donovan! How dare you say I can't cook!"

"Well, Kate!" The young man was equally indignant. "You told me yourself what a mess supper was. And don't forget I stood and watched you and Marc swallowing raisins yesterday without even stopping to chew."

The anger drained out of Kate and she began to giggle. Sean shook his head in mock despair. Neither one noticed that Marcail was very quiet.

"If you would catch some fish Sean," Kaitlin said between chuckles, "we could ask Mr. Riggs to our house instead of him always feeding us."

"He'd probably never believe that you weren't out to poison him."

Sean walked his sisters home and then went to see if they'd received any mail. He then headed to the Mercantile to tell Rigg they would be there for supper at six.

◻ ◻ ◻

"If there's some reason Marcail, that you'd rather not go to Mr. Riggs' for supper, you can tell me."

The girls were nearly at Riggs' and Kate, who'd finally noticed Marcail's behavior, had been trying for an hour to bring her out.

"It's fine if we eat here."

"Marc," Kate said gently, "what's wrong?"

They had come to a stop just short of the porch steps at Rigg's. He had seen them approaching and stood framed in the front door looking down at them.

Marcail looked down at the path beneath her feet and then glanced up at Rigg. When she looked back at Katie, a single tear slid down her cheek.

"I don't know if I can tell you." Her voice was soft but Rigg heard and stepped back as Kate led Marcail into the living room. The girls sat on the sofa and as soon as they were settled, Marcail turned her face into Kate's side and sat very still.

Kaitlin kept her arm close around her and stared up at Rigg and Sean who looked on helplessly.

"Marc," Kaitlin finally spoke softly, "please tell me what's wrong. Maybe I can fix it."

A few more moments went by and Marcail shifted until her cheek lay against Kate's side. Rigg, seeing the evidence of tears on her face, was surprised. He hadn't been aware that she was crying because she hadn't made a sound. His heart melted at the sight of those tears and he sat down beside her.

"Is there anything I can do, Marcail?"

"No."

"You might feel better if you talk about it Marc," Sean suggested from a nearby chair.

"Someone will get into trouble." Her young voice was almost depressed.

Kate cuddled her closer with new understanding. How many times had history repeated itself over this subject. One child had information over another child's sin and was in torment over whether or not the news should be shared.

"Marcail, I understand why you're upset but be sure to ask yourself if this person will end up in worse trouble if you *don't* tell."

Marcail was silent for a few minutes and the others in the room watched her chew her lip in indecision.

"Joey Parker told me today that he took that lady's purse. He said his father told him to." Marcail's face was once again buried against her sister's side. Rigg looked down and watched a shudder run over the child, the only indication that she was crying again. He looked up to see Kaitlin's face—it was white with strain.

"Would this man really do that?"

"I wouldn't be surprised." Rigg's voice was regretful.

The next hour was spent trying to calm Marcail down enough to eat supper. The food had gone cold but no one really seemed to notice.

Little by little, as they ate supper, Marcail elaborated. She said that Joey had approached her during afternoon recess and asked her if she'd told her sister who took the purse. Marcail hadn't known what he was talking about. When he realized his mistake, he'd become very angry and said it hadn't been his fault to begin with: He was just doing what his Pa had told him to do.

They all knew they were going to have to step lightly around this small boy in the very near future or he would surely know that Marcail had told.

Kate and Marcail didn't stay long after supper but before Rigg walked them home he asked everyone to gather in the living room for a brief time of prayer over what to do and how to reach out to Joey without causing him more hurt.

thirty-three

Kaitlin had told herself on Friday night that she was going to sleep until noon on Saturday. She could tell by the angle of the sun that it wasn't that late but she awoke so rested she didn't care about the hour.

May had sent word through a blushing Nathan the afternoon before, that she and Marcail were invited to the Taylors' for supper on Saturday evening. They were to also plan to take their baths, stay the night and go with them to church in the morning.

Kate shuddered at the thought of tackling Marcail's hair. After visualizing herself washing that thick mass as well as her own in the dish-pan, she decided to accept May's offer. But right now the whole day stretched ahead of them and Kaitlin was going to start it with prayer.

As she remembered her family, her mind returned again and again to Joey Parker. Kate thought he was one of the most precious little boys she'd ever encountered.

She had surmised right away that he was not as well liked as the other children and even though they played with him, he was always on the outer fringes of their special talks. There were certainly other children who didn't really fit in either. But Joey was the only one who appeared to be from a very poor home. And after Marcail explained her tears the day before, well, Kate couldn't even think of the boy without her own tears starting.

Please Father, use me. Help me to help him. I want so much to go to him right now and hug him and ask him to church but it's too soon; I know that. And I also know that You love him and died for him. Please God, make the pathway to this little boy clear so I can tell him of Your love.

Kate prayed for many minutes in this vein, and not until she realized that Marcail was stirring beside her, did she begin to pray for her friends in Hawaii, Mr. Riggs, the Taylors and her other students.

"Good morning, Katie." Marcail's voice was heavy with sleep but she was always cheerful in the morning.

"Morning, Marc. How did you sleep?"

"Good. Are we staying at Taylors' tonight?"

"Yes, I think it's a good idea. It's hard enough to do your hair without you having to bend over for half an hour."

"Maybe we should cut it."

"What would Father say?"

"I don't know." She was silent for a moment. "He is coming back, isn't he Katie?"

"He said that he would and I know that he'll come as soon as he can."

The girls had a leisurely breakfast and then went to the post office. There was a letter from Aunt Maureen and they decided to wait until they returned home to open it. As they walked past the shipping office, Gil hailed them.

"Hi. What are you two up to?"

"We got a letter from Aunt Maureen," Marcail told him.

"Good for you." He smiled at Marcail and touched her shoulder.

Kaitlin thought he was one of the nicest men she'd ever met. Good-looking, too. Of course she believed that Gilbert and his brothers were all handsome, with their light blue eyes, medium brown hair and tall, lean physiques.

"I'm glad you came by. A few things were delivered yesterday from the church folks and I wanted to take them to your house. Are you headed home now?"

"We're going to the mercantile," Marcail informed him.

"But we can go right home if you want to meet us there."

"There's no hurry," he said with a smile. "Why don't you give me a time and I'll meet you then."

"Oh no, Gilbert, we don't want to put you to any trouble—" Kaitlin began but stopped when his eyes told her he was close to laughter.

"What time?" The question was asked again. Kate suggested ten-thirty before turning and moving down the street, a little bemused, wondering what Gilbert must have found so funny.

Gil watched them walk away, his eyes still smiling. *One of these days, Katie Donovan*, he thought to himself, *you're going to understand that the look in Rigg's eyes when he's near you, makes you and your family very special.*

□ □ □

Kate wondered how many times she would be able to walk into Riggs Mercantile and not feel a sense of wonder. It was all so delightful. She loved to look at the farm tools, the counter laden with jars of penny candy, paint supplies—from stove-pipe enamel to paint brushes of every conceivable size. There was a large selection of toys, with baby dolls and tea sets of fine china. You could find sports and fishing equipment and even a selection of ladies intimate apparel.

Kaitlin never stayed in that section for very long, but she was very curious and a little envious of women who wore muslin nightgowns trimmed with lace, or taffeta and silk underskirts with camisoles bordered in scarlet ribbon.

"This is pretty, isn't it Katie?" Kaitlin was brought out of her dreams when Marcail picked up an underskirt piped in pale blue ribbon.

"It sure is." The girls exchanged a smile of understanding. Even if their father were here and working steadily, he would not have allowed such an extravagant purchase.

Watching from his office, Rigg knew exactly what the girls were looking at even though he couldn't hear their words or see what they were holding. Sensing that he might be invading their privacy, he turned and sat at his desk.

Rigg believed it to be totally improper to give clothing to a woman who was not his wife, but the smile he'd seen on Kate's face led him to believe that such a gift would bring her great pleasure.

I need patience, Lord. I can't rush her and I want to do Your will but I can't get her out of my mind. Show me some peace Lord, show me how to be near Katie without scaring her off.

Rigg's prayers were cut short when the object of his every waking moment called from the stairway.

"Mr. Riggs, are you up there?"

"Come on up."

"We just wanted to say hello before we go home. Gilbert is bringing more stuff to us from the church," Marcail informed him. He stood until his visitors had found seats.

"Did you get everything you need?"

"Yes, we were just here for some little things," Kate answered, and noticed for the first time how heavy his beard was. He was clean-shaven, but the outline of whiskers was black against his tanned face. He was very nice to look at and for the first time Kaitlin let her eyes have their fill.

She watched for a moment as Rigg talked with Marcail and then suddenly drew in a sharp breath. He was exactly like the man she visualized being married to one day! Kaitlin had grown up around well-built Polynesian men with black hair and dark skin and eyes. Rigg would never have been mistaken for one of the men from the island, but he did have the looks that Kate found most attractive.

Rigg's peripheral vision made him very aware of Kate's scrutiny but he kept talking with Marcail. He desperately wanted to know what was going through Kaitlin's mind but was afraid to ask.

When a few minutes later the girls said good-bye, Rigg wished he had questioned Kate. She had seemed uncomfortable when she left, almost as if she were afraid of him. For an instant he wondered if he reminded her of her cousin and then frowned at the thought.

After a few minutes he bent back over his account books, wishing as he did, that he had someone trustworthy to do them for him.

thirty-four

Dear Kaitlin, Sean and Marcail,

I've missed you so much and worry day and night over your safety. If you haven't written to me, please do so right away. I don't think I can bear another day without hearing from you.

I haven't heard from your father, but I did write him to explain. I suppose you did too.

There is one more thing I need to tell you—Percy is gone. He departed for Europe right after you left and I believe he's not coming back. Please consider returning to San Francisco. I promise I'll make everything wonderful for you. Please think about it.

Don't forget to write me.

Love to each of you,
Aunt M.

"Are you going to write today?" Marcail wanted to know.

"Probably after lunch."

"Katie, is Aunt Maureen saved?"

"I don't know Marc. Why do you ask?"

"Because she worries so much and she said something at mother's grave about her being gone forever. Mother's not gone forever, she's just gone from the earth."

Kate reached out and hugged Marcail. She, too, had heard her aunt's words and wondered at them.

"Father and I discussed it one night, Marc, and he's sure that his parents were born again. Maureen has always been a great support to Father but he's not sure where she stands.

"I think she believes in God and tries to do the right thing, but I don't know if she's ever confessed to God that she needs a Savior."

"Katie, I miss Sean. We never talk with him anymore."

"I miss him too," Kate answered, thinking how quickly a nine-year-old could change the subject.

"Are we going back to San Francisco?"

"No—at least not right away. I have to teach for two more months and I don't want to make another move until we hear from Father."

"Are you glad Percy is gone?"

"I'm glad for myself but not for Aunt Maureen."

Marcail nodded and then changed the subject once again. "What's for lunch?"

"Oh, I don't know," Kate said, this time relieved at the change in topic. "I thought we might have yeast cakes and molasses."

◻ ◻ ◻

The remainder of the day flew by after Gil came with the wagon. The girls now had more blankets than they knew what to do with. Kate worked on some mending and her school lessons for the next week. Marcail didn't seem to notice how distracted Kate was. About an hour before supper they began walking toward the Taylors'.

"I knew you would do this," Jeff called to them as he brought his wagon to a halt in the road beside the Donovan girls.

"Do what?" Kate asked.

"Walk to my folks'."

Kate looked surprised and both Gil and Jeff grinned at her from the wagon seat.

"How else were we to get there?" Kate inquired after a moment.

"You were supposed to assume that we, being the fine gentlemen we are, would come for you."

Kaitlin laughed, but then surprised them by declining.

"I need the walk, but thanks anyway."

"What are we going to say to Rigg?" Gil let the cat out of the bag as to who had been the *real* gentleman and Kaitlin laughed again.

"Please thank Mr. Riggs for his offer, but I'm still going to walk. Marcail can go with you if she likes."

Marcail climbed into the wagon and Kate put their bag next to her. Jeff sat holding the reins in indecision.

"Will you be all right Katie?" Marcail asked as she leaned over the side.

"I'll be fine, thanks Marc." With those words Kate swung around and started down the road. Without Marcail, her long legs made quick work of the distance. Jeff, Gil and Marcail passed her and not too far from the farm Rigg and Sean came abreast of her. Kate stopped and watched as Rigg handed the reins to Sean and jumped down. Rigg was silent until Sean had pulled away.

"How was your day?"

"Okay," Kate answered quietly and when she stumbled a moment later, Rigg reached to steady her. He knew when she side-stepped his touch that he had to ask.

"Katie, have I done something to upset you?"

"No." Kaitlin answered honestly and with a little frustration. She had thought about Marshall Riggs all afternoon. She had come to the conclusion that she could fall in love with this man, but her life was so unsettled right now she didn't feel they had a chance. He hadn't even met her father. For that matter she didn't even know where her father was. A sudden image of his ship going down sprang to mind and Kaitlin felt a little sick.

"Then what is wrong?"

"What?" Kate's voice was distracted and breathless and Rigg brought her to a halt with a hand on her arm.

"Kaitlin, what is wrong?" His voice and face were a picture of determination and Kaitlin looked at him helplessly.

"I don't know exactly."

"Have I done something?"

"I don't think so." It was a vague reply but Kaitlin was suddenly feeling frightened. Rigg read all of those feelings in her eyes and one vast hand came up to tenderly cup her face. His voice was whisper soft when he spoke.

"Katie, whatever you're running from, run to me."

His eyes, having gone from gray to black, held hers captive and Kate stood mute for a long moment. She didn't know what to say or do. Running to him would be so easy. Being caught and held in those arms would be a haven of comfort like she'd never dreamed of.

But her mother had only been dead a few months and her father had not been in touch, plus the fact that Sean and Marcail needed her to be strong. She said something in soft Hawaiian and carefully pulled free of Rigg's hold.

He released her, longing as he did, to know what she had said. But it was obvious that this perplexed woman needed more time. It was a quiet couple that made their way to the farmhouse for supper.

thirty-five

With Sean in tow, Rigg was at his parents' home bright and early the next morning, asking Kate to ride to church with them. He had been very watchful of her and considered the possibility that she was coming down with something or that she was just plain exhausted.

It never occurred to him that her feelings for him had changed and that that was part of the turmoil he was reading on her face. He assumed that her sudden unease around him was because of Percy. She was obviously remembering the way she'd been treated. In fact her memory had probably been spurred by something her aunt had written in the recent letter.

That Kate had not yet read the letter when her feelings changed, Rigg didn't know. She seemed rested, he noted, as they rode to church and she conversed easily with her brother. Once there, she greeted some of her students and met quite a few parents.

Rigg was turning to ask her a question when she suddenly darted away from him. He looked beyond her to see Joey Parker at the corner of the church. The little boy scooted out of sight when he saw his teacher bearing down on him, but Kaitlin pursued him and Rigg watched her disappear around the corner of the building.

"Joey," Kaitlin called, when he was once again in view. "Will you come here please?"

The little boy came with obvious reluctance. Kate accurately read the look of fear on his face. Fear that Marcail had snitched and he was in deep trouble. Kate ignored the look.

"How are you, Joey?"

"All right." the boy answered without taking his eyes off his dirty bare feet.

"I'm glad to hear that. Joey," Kate said gently, "would you like to come into church with me?"

The little boy's head snapped up, his eyes wide. She could see he was excited about the idea but then his shoulders slumped.

"I ain't dressed for it."

"I'm not dressed for it," the teacher in Kate automatically corrected him. "And I'm quite sure that God doesn't care how you look."

Joey considered this for a spell. "Maybe if I sat in the back."

"That's fine if you want to sit in the back. I'll sit with you. Oh! Here's Mr. Riggs. Mr. Riggs have you met Joey Parker?"

"No, I haven't. Hello, Joey." Rigg's huge hand came out and Joey stared at it a moment before offering his own grubby little hand.

"Joey and I just decided to sit together in the back."

"Great, may I sit with you?"

It took a moment for Joey to comprehend that the question was being directed at him. He couldn't believe this big man was actually waiting for his permission to sit with them in church. Joey muttered something and the next thing he knew he was being ushered into a rear pew.

The service had started and two songs had been sung, but Joey hadn't heard a thing. He was still working through the fact that Marcail obviously hadn't told on him. When they'd come in together and Miss Donovan had propelled him into the pew, he'd seen Marcail sitting with the Taylors. She looked back at him as though there was nothing the least bit unusual about his sitting with her sister.

Snatches of the sermon floated to Joey but for the most part he was too busy sneaking glances at Kaitlin. She looked real pretty, he thought, in her white dress. Sometimes at night Joey would lay awake and dream about what it would be like to have her for a mother. He would dream about her voice and the way she smiled at him. But then he would think about his house and knew that she would never even visit there, let alone come to live.

Thoughts of his house drew his attention to his father. He wondered how much trouble he'd be in if his Pa knew where he was sitting.

"In closing," the pastor was saying and Joey was finally listening. "Please take this thought home with you. God is our heavenly Father. We need never be afraid to go to Him with any need because He loves us like a father does, only with such tenderness and compassion that we can't help but respond."

Up to that moment Joey believed that getting to know God might be a very good thing to do but he'd never before heard God referred to as a father. Suddenly he was not so sure he wanted to know Him.

"Joey, would you like to come back to my folks' place for some lunch?" Joey was brought abruptly back to the present when Rigg spoke to him.

"I gotta get home," he said with some reluctance.

Rigg and Kaitlin walked him outside and Kate told him she'd see him at school in the morning. They watched as he cut across a field in the direction of his house.

"What is his home like?"

Rigg hesitated and Kate pressed him.

"I want to know."

Rigg sighed and spoke. "It's pretty bad."

"Does he actually have a family?"

"A father."

"What's he like?"

"He doesn't work that I know of, and when he does get an odd job, he spends his pay on liquor."

"Maybe I should go for a visit."

"I don't know if that's a good idea, Katie. Parker is not exactly trustworthy." Rigg would never know how he managed to keep his voice so calm. What he wanted to do was grab Kate and tell her she was not to set one foot on the Parker property, not now, not ever.

"You keep calling him Parker, doesn't he have a first name?"

"I've never heard it. Everyone calls him Parker. Of course you'll refer to him as Mr. Parker." Rigg's voice had taken on a patronizing tone.

"Now what did that mean?" Kaitlin demanded.

"Only that you're just a little too prim and proper at times for your own good." Rigg smiled at her outraged face, glad that he'd been able to change the subject as well as get a dig in about her calling him Mr. Riggs.

"There is nothing wrong with being proper and it's fine to be prim as long as you're not a snob."

"Is that a fact?" They were over by the wagon now and Rigg was close to laughter.

"Yes, it's a fact! Do you think I'm a snob?"

"No, I just wish you'd call me Rigg. Mr. Riggs makes me feel like an old man."

"I don't think I know you well enough to call you Rigg," Kate stated firmly with a tone she would have used on her students. In her mind the matter was closed; it wasn't in Rigg's.

"What do I need to do so you'll know me better, Kaitlin, kiss you?" Rigg watched as she blushed to the roots of her hair. He could also see that she was angry.

"If you did I'd slap you."

Rigg thought she might be serious but he was feeling reckless.

"Thanks for the warning. I'll be sure to hold both your hands when I do."

With those words he grabbed Kate's waist and lifted her aboard the wagon, effectively cutting off any reply she might be tempted to make. They made the drive to the Taylors' in silence; Kate wondering why her anger cooled so quickly and Rigg regretting that he hadn't kissed her right on the spot.

thirty-six

Kaitlin and Marcail spent the afternoon at the Taylors' and Rigg took them home when he and Sean were ready to go. His words to her the evening before had told her that he'd noticed the abrupt change in her behavior.

So Kate had made a point of relaxing in Rigg's presence, and she was sure that she'd done a good job keeping her thoughts to herself. She blushed every time she remembered the words she'd said to him on the walk to his parents' house.

It didn't matter that he couldn't translate them—a young lady did not tell a man that she would love him if she could! What if he should ask Sean what she said? Oh! She couldn't bear to think about it.

Dealing with her topsy-turvy emotions all day left Kate very weary. She had thanked May again and again for sending them home with full stomachs and a tin for the following noon. Kaitlin suddenly smiled when she remembered Mr. Carson approaching her at church.

"Miss Donovan, how are things going?"

"Fine, Mr. Carson, thank you."

"I've heard wonderful things about your teaching and I know I told you it would be a month before your raise, but starting tomorrow you'll be paid full salary."

"Oh, Mr. Carson, thank you!" Kate's eyes had shone with gratitude and joy and she wondered over the strange look on the man's face.

What she didn't know was that Mr. Carson, at a hastily arranged meeting, had been told by Bill Taylor and the other men that he would adjust the teacher's salary, including back pay for the days she'd already worked plus a housing allowance. But the stingy monster rose up in Greg Carson and he decided on his own to start things on Monday.

Kate had no suspicions that anything was amiss. She wouldn't have caused trouble even if she had. The family was getting along fairly well now.

Of course, all of Sean's pants were too short, even though Kate had lengthened them as far as they would go. Marcail needed new shoes. In fact, if she wore the old ones much longer, Kate would have to slit the leather so Marcail's toes could move.

As for herself, she was badly in need of undergarments. It was not a matter she discussed with anyone but her Lord, confident that He would provide in His time.

As the days turned into weeks, Kaitlin reached out in a special way to Joey Parker. Whenever he was near she touched him or gave him a tender smile. He did not come to church again and with seeing him every day at school, Kate did not feel led to go to his home. She told herself though, that if on any given day he failed to show up for school, she would go immediately to his house to investigate.

Two more letters came from Aunt Maureen. Even though she hinted that the children should return, she seemed to accept that, at least for the time, they were staying where they were. Maureen had also mentioned coming to Santa Rosa for a visit, but Kaitlin wrote and assured her that they were doing well. Kate was happy to read in her last letter that their Uncle Mitch had come home. She knew that his presence would ease her aunt's loneliness, at least for a time.

One afternoon, when school had only four weeks to go, Kate and Marcail were in the mercantile. That very morning Kaitlin had had no choice but to cut Marcail's shoes. She knew Marcail was embarrassed but payday was not until the following week and she couldn't let her go on this way any longer.

Kaitlin needed some buttons and, even though it could have waited, she wanted to say hi to Sean, who was working that afternoon. It seemed they saw less and less of him all the time. He usually ate lunch with his friends at school and on days he worked, he left for the mercantile as soon as Kate dismissed.

When the Donovan girls entered the store and didn't see him, they made their way to the back of the store where they knew he would be. There was a platform area where the freight wagons from the shipping office could pull alongside to be unloaded. This is where they found Seán and today Rigg was working with him.

Both men were stripped to the waist and Kate saw in an instant why Rigg's shoulders and arms looked powerful enough to lift a draft horse.

Kaitlin watched as he hefted enormous crates without visible effort, sometimes swinging one onto his shoulder and carrying another under his arm. They were almost finished unloading when Rigg told Sean to put his shirt on, make a delivery uptown and then return the wagon to the shipping office.

Sean, Kate noticed absently, was damp with perspiration. Rigg, on the other hand, was not even breathing hard. Kate had not meant to stay as long as she did and was embarrassed when Rigg noticed her. He retrieved his shirt and vest, put them on and then motioned to Sean who was also covering himself.

The men approached and Kaitlin was glad she was standing in the shaded area because she could feel herself blushing.

"We just came by to say hello and to see how you were doing." Kate's voice sounded strained even to her own ears.

"I'm fine. I was going to come for supper tonight."

"Okay," Kaitlin said with a smile.

"I've got to get this wagon back. I'll see you tonight."

The girls bid their brother good-bye and Kaitlin noticed for the first time that Rigg was silently eyeing Marcail's feet. She couldn't tell exactly what he was thinking but when their eyes finally met she thought he might be angry.

"Did you come down today to buy shoes?" The words were said softly, deceptively so.

"No, but I get paid next week and we'll get them then." Kaitlin looked very pleased with herself.

"Marc, why don't you go in and look at the shoes? We'll come in later and you can show us the ones you like."

Marcail looked to her sister for approval and then went in the rear door.

"Kaitlin," he said as he tried to control his temper, "didn't Mr. Carson give you some extra money?"

"No. He told me about my raise though," Kate's smile faded when she saw how upset he was.

"My father told me that you were to get back pay for the money you should have been getting, a housing allowance *and* a raise."

"Well, maybe he's going to get it to me this week. Or next week when I get my pay."

"Either way, that is not what the board decided. You were to get the money immediately." Rigg ran a distracted hand through his hair and spoke as though he'd forgotten Kaitlin's presence. "Marcail's shoes aren't fit to wear and Sean's pants are inches above his ankles." An instant later he glanced sharply down at her feet.

"Let me see your shoes!"

"They're fine." Kate said quietly, but he was so upset that she lifted the front of her dress about an inch, thinking as she did that she would never tell him what was really needed in her own wardrobe.

His eyes were on her dress now and Kate's chin jutted out, daring him to question her further. Wisely he took the warning.

"All right Kate, I won't ask. But if you need something, I want you to go see my mom. Do you understand?"

Kate gave him a curt nod and went inside to find Marcail. Rigg was on her heels, thinking as he did, that he'd have to go to his father with this. He was too emotionally involved to go to Carson himself. He was certain to say or do something he knew would be displeasing to the Lord.

"Look at these Katie," Marcail called to them as they walked toward her. Marcail was holding out a small pair of black leather boots. They laced to the top and had low heels.

Rigg of course recognized them as his best pair of children's shoes so he carefully blocked Kaitlin's hand when she tried to reach for the price tag.

"You really should try these on, Marc. They look to be your size."

"Maybe we should wait until next week. I mean, it might be better—" Kate stopped because no one was listening to her.

"Oh Katie, aren't they pretty?"

Kate nodded lamely, having just checked the price on a pair still sitting on the shelf. How could she ever tell her that they cost too much?

"You know," Rigg was saying, "I don't think there's any reason why Marc can't have these now. Like you said, payday is next week." Rigg said this knowing that between now and then he'd figure out a way to keep her from paying.

Kaitlin was shaking her head and trying to signal him but Rigg continued to lace Marcail's shoe as though he had all the time in the world. In the next instant Marcail was on her feet moving around as if she'd just discovered walking.

"We can't," Kate was whispering furiously as she pulled on Rigg's arm, finally gaining his attention. "We can't afford those Rigg! She should never have put them on! Just look at her! She'll never want to take them off!"

Kate was so intent upon Marcail that she didn't notice Rigg grinning at her.

"Marc, I need to talk with you." Kate's voice was concerned but Marcail didn't notice.

"Oh Katie, can you believe how nice they are? And they don't hurt at all," Marcail said without ever taking her eyes off her new shoes.

"Your sister is so pleased she's speechless." Rigg's arm went briefly around Kate and he gave her a warning squeeze.

Rigg knew that she wanted to argue, but he silently tipped her chin so she had to look at him. With a small shake of his head he told her to be quiet and then went over to scoop Marcail up in his arms. She was so delighted with the shoes she threw her arms around his neck and hugged him with all her strength.

Rigg laughed in delight and turned to see Kate staring, as though seeing him for the first time.

"What's the matter Katie?" Marcail asked cheerfully, finally looking at her.

"Nothing." The answer was rather faint and she tried to smile. She looked at the man holding her sister and wondered if they needed to talk. He was being presumptuous again, but Kate's feelings were different this time and she recognized that fact.

Without really knowing how Rigg did it, Kate found herself out the door and on her way home, a few minutes later. He had assured Kaitlin he'd get rid of Marcail's old shoes. Kate had supper well under way before she remembered she hadn't bought any buttons.

thirty-seven

Kaitlin woke the next morning with an awful premonition that Rigg was going to do something about her salary. She didn't want to get anyone in trouble *period*. Kate was convinced that Mr. Carson must have had a reason for his actions.

Knowing there would be no time to go and see Rigg before school, Kate planned on going to the mercantile immediately after. She was pleasantly surprised when he walked into the schoolhouse moments after she dismissed school for the day.

"Hello." His deep voice and pleased smile nearly made Kate forget what she was going to ask him. "How was your day?"

"It was great." Kaitlin felt herself blushing and wished she had better self control.

"I came by because I wanted to ask you something." Rigg's eyes were watchful. He needed to gauge how she was doing to know how she would respond to his question.

"I'm glad you did because I wanted to tell you something too."

"All right. You go first." Rigg sat on the bench at the front, crossing his arms over his chest.

"Yesterday, well, I got to thinking that you might go to someone about my salary and I don't want you to do that. I know you were upset but I think Mr. Carson must have had a reason to do what he did and I don't want to file a complaint or anything like that."

"I'm sorry you feel that way, Kaitlin, because it's too late. I spoke with my dad this morning."

"Oh no," Kaitlin sighed and sank down into the chair behind her desk.

"Kate, it was bound to come out at some point and Greg Carson knew what he was supposed to do. I promise you that my dad will handle it gently. You'll get the money you've worked hard for and that will be the end of it." Rigg gave her a moment to ponder his words and realized he couldn't have asked for a better lead-in to his question.

"Actually, I'm glad you brought this up. I've been thinking about the fact that school is out in a month and you'll be out of work.

"Now, I think Sean will want to put in more hours and I can certainly use him. I can also use you and your gift for numbers. I would like to hire you to handle my book work."

Kate's mind was working furiously. Just last night Marcail had asked her what they were going to do for money when school was out. Kate had answered honestly and told her she didn't know.

"Would I work right at the mercantile?"

"Up in the office."

"What would I do with Marcail?"

"I don't want you to be upset with me but I've discussed that with my mother. She's been thinking for some time about cutting back on her hours at the shipping office. She told me if the only thing holding you back from accepting my offer is someone to be with Marcail, well, she said she'd be glad to watch her."

Kaitlin could only stare at him. "I've never done any bookkeeping before." It was the only thought that would come to mind.

"That's not a problem. I can show you my system and exactly what I would want you to do. For the first few weeks you'd probably be full time but then on most days, if you're as fast as I suspect you are, you'll probably be ready to go home by two."

How can I possibly spend all day working with this man? Kate asked herself. He had backed way off and had become her friend, just as she'd asked him to, but now her heart was changing just as his must have. Only she was falling for him and he obviously thought better of getting involved with her.

Oh, he was kind to her, really sweet actually, but the intensity he'd shown when they first met was gone. Maybe that was for the best.

"I've never noticed anyone working in your office."

"No, I've never hired an office clerk, but I've prayed a long time about someone to keep books for me, someone I could trust, and I just feel that the Lord sent you my way.

"If you're worried about us working alone in the office, well, it's very open. Anyone in the front-half of the store can look up and see all the way to the back wall. I'll have another desk brought in and, actually, if you're doing my book work, freeing me up for things on the floor, I shouldn't have to be underfoot very often."

In his next breath Rigg told her what he would pay, along with offering an employee discount on items in the store. Kate's mind reeled.

"What about my father?" His face suddenly sprang up in her mind. "I don't have any idea when he'll be back or where he'll want to live. I wouldn't want to leave you without help."

Rigg had already considered this and knew that he'd ask Kaitlin to marry him on the spot before he'd ever let her up and walk away.

"Well, I don't have any help with the books now, so however much time you can give me will surely help.

Don't let that stop you from taking the job. We'll cross that bridge when we come to it."

"May I let you know?"

"Certainly." Rigg stood. "Take your time and just tell me when you've decided."

Kate thanked him and he left a few minutes later.

"You're going to tell him yes, aren't you?"

"Marcail Donovan! You were eavesdropping!"

"Yes, I guess I was," Marcail admitted from her place outside. She poked her head through the window that sat to the side of Kaitlin's desk. Rigg must have known she was there all along.

"What are you standing on?" Kate knew she wasn't that tall.

"A box."

"Well, get down before you fall and don't do that again." Kaitlin tried to sound stern but the truth was she was so pleased she couldn't scold anyone.

A job at the mercantile! It was something she'd never considered. A moment later Kate found herself almost wishing that her father wouldn't return right away and then instantly felt guilty for the thought.

She stopped then and there to pray for her father, wherever he was. As always it was a comfort to know that God knew his location and loved him more than she ever could.

Unfortunately, knowing God was in control did not lessen the pain of their separation. Kaitlin bit her lip even as she wondered if he was still alive. *My thoughts are not your thoughts, neither are your ways my ways*, the verse came softly to Kate and she closed her eyes against a sudden rush of tears.

Oh God, she prayed, *help me to go on without knowing. I wish he was here but I want to trust You.*

"What are you doing Kate?" The question came from her brother, who had entered quietly.

"I was praying and trying to find some peace about Father." Kate was not prepared for the angry look that came over Sean's face.

"Sean, what is it?"

"I just think he should be here! School lets out in a month and Rigg wants me for more hours but it isn't going to be enough to pay the rent on that house and—"

"Sean, he offered me a job at the mercantile," Kate cut into Sean's angry tirade. He gaped at her.

"Doing what?" the boy's voice was cautious.

"The book work, up in the office." Kaitlin watched her brother's shoulders sag and understood for the first time, the pressure he'd been putting himself under.

"Sean," Kate's voice was gentle. "We're going to be fine. God is going to take care of us. He always has."

The words failed to comfort him as they had in past times but he was careful not to show his sister. He nodded and smiled at her and then Marcail came in and they talked, each one agreeing that Kate should take the job. As Kate closed up the schoolhouse, she couldn't help but wonder what the next few months would bring.

thirty-eight

The final month of school went by in a whirlwind of activities. Many of the families wanted to have the schoolteacher to dinner before summer break. Kaitlin, Sean and Marcail went to supper in ten different homes in two weeks. Exhausted, Kate was nevertheless bound and determined to put on an end-of-the-year program. The children were learning songs and poems and even writing pieces to share.

As the children's big night drew near, Kaitlin's nerves were fraying. Rigg was over at their house to finally give them the sack of groceries he'd had on his desk for so long, and Kate looked ready to come apart at the seams.

"What if no one comes?" Kate's voice was on the edge of panic.

"Everyone will come," he assured her calmly.

"You don't know that."

"Yes I do. The people in this district love their children and they'll be there. Kate, try to calm down."

"I am calm."

Rigg nearly laughed out loud. She was working very hard at being her prim and proper self while biting off every one of her nails.

"Why don't the three of us go for a walk right after supper?" Rigg asked the question with real enthusiasm but Marcail had just found some cookies in the bag of food and Kate was staring at the tabletop as though the secrets of life were written upon it.

"Katie, may I have some of these?"

"Sure," Kate answered without even looking at Marcail who was holding up the cookies. Rigg knew in that instant how really exhausted she was. Supper was on the stove and she'd just told Marcail she could have cookies.

"Why don't you wait until after supper, Marc?" Rigg asked softly, and the little girl nodded in agreement. Rigg then proceeded to put supper on.

"Kaitlin," he reached over and took her hand. "You need to eat." He watched as she gave her head a little shake as though trying to clear it. Marcail thanked God for the food and the evening went much better. Kate voiced many of her fears and Rigg did his best to reassure her. As supper continued, Kate relaxed. She even remembered to thank Rigg for the gift of food as he was leaving.

❑ ❑ ❑

The schoolhouse was packed the night of the program, just as Rigg had told her it would be. But even in the crush Kate noticed that Joey Parker was absent. He didn't have a solo part, but Kate felt his absence in a very personal way and realized how much she'd come to love the boy.

The program went off without a hitch—well, almost without a hitch. Some lines were forgotten and there were occasional nervous giggles, but the children were respectful and the parents applauded after each recitation or song, as though seeing and hearing the greatest performers the country had to offer.

Parents and grandparents flocked around Kate to thank her for a job well done. When the formal program was concluded, the older students called Miss Donovan to the front and presented her with a gift. They insisted that she open it in on the spot and the room shook with laughter as Kate peeled back the paper to reveal a cookbook. Kaitlin hadn't realized how far afield the news of her cooking skills had traveled. But she laughed along with everyone else.

A few moments later she had to fight down tears when the younger students presented her with a lush bouquet of flowers. The evening closed with refreshments and everyone confirmed that it was a huge success.

The next day, a Friday, was the last day of school. The children were squirmy and Kate let them all go early. She was, she admitted to herself, a little squirmy too. Monday was to be her first day at the mercantile. She thought it might be rather nice to have a job that you didn't need to prepare for on Saturday. Of course the hours at the mercantile were different because so much of her schoolwork could be accomplished at home but Kate was looking forward to the challenge.

Rigg, Bill, May and all the Donovans sat down together to figure out a schedule for Marcail. It was agreed that on the days Sean didn't work, she would stay with him. The other days, May would stay home or run errands and Marcail would be with her.

Kate was very careful to check with her sister on all the plans, watching her face intently for signs of fear or feelings of being deserted. Kaitlin was relieved to see that Marcail found the whole idea a lot of fun.

With Kate's raise in pay from school and her final check, they were able to buy dress material. May planned to start sewing the very next week for her new little charge and Marcail couldn't stop talking about her new dress.

Kaitlin woke up Saturday morning with her new job on her mind. The day promised to be a relaxing one, with plans once again to go out to the Taylors' for supper and to stay the night. The girls had done so many little things as the day progressed that they didn't get to the post office until they were on their way out to Taylors'.

Rigg was driving them in his wagon and Sean and Marcail waited with him outside. When Kate exited the small building the smile she'd been wearing on the way in had been replaced by a look of worry and almost fear.

Two letters had arrived. One from Aunt Maureen, the other from Father.

thirty-nine

The letter began "Dear Children." Kate read out loud from her place near the creek, where she, Sean and Marcail had gone for privacy.

"There is no way for me to express how helpless and angry I felt when you explained why you had to leave your aunt's. Please know that I'm glad you did. I was just about to write to you in San Francisco when your letter arrived from Santa Rosa. When I looked at the date you wrote, I know that God alone sped that letter to me.

"I wish I could tell you that all is fine here, but in truth we have suffered a major disaster. Two days after my ship landed, the islands were hit by a hurricane. No lives were lost, but the damage is extensive.

If you write and tell me how badly you need me, I'll get on the next ship east, but I feel led to ask your permission to stay on here. I ask this in strong belief that you are doing well in your new surroundings. That isn't to say that we don't miss one another—and if you say the word, I'll leave immediately.

"I fear you'll think I'm telling you to be strong without me—I'm not. If you need me, I'll come straightaway. But if you are well then I'll probably stay on until fall or possibly longer. They need me here.

"Can it only be a few months since we were together? I miss you until I don't think I can stand it. To return here without you or your mother has given new meaning to

196

the word lonely. If you're thinking of coming back to Hawaii, do not. I still believe we're to live there and I want you to wait for me.

"Kaitlin, make sure you are getting enough rest. What will you do for income when school is out? I love you, Katie. Sean, do not put pressure on yourself to take care of everyone. Work together and do not burden yourself overmuch. I love you, Sean. Marcail, be respectful of Kaitlin's teaching without mother. Obey your brother and sister and pray that they'll know the right courses of action. I love you, Marc.

"I'll anxiously await your letters. I've written to your aunt and she knows I'm encouraging you to stay where you are if all is well. But don't hesitate to go back to her. Percy is gone for good. Write me. I love all of you, Father."

Kate thought her head would burst in an effort to contain her tears. Marcail's tears streamed soundlessly down her cheeks and Sean kept his face buried against his upraised knees for a long time. The evening lengthened and even though Kaitlin knew that May would be keeping supper warm for them, she couldn't move to go inside.

It was almost dark when Rigg came out of the house to find them. His heart wrenched at the sight of them huddled together beneath a mammoth willow by the creek. He assumed that their father's letter told them his return would be delayed. He didn't try to talk to them but gently lifted Marcail into his arms. With his free hand he pulled Sean to his feet and then reached for Kate.

He carried Marcail all the way to the house and kept his arm around Kaitlin. He ushered them in the back door to his mother's tender care before he realized Sean had not come inside. Rigg stepped back outside just in time to see him retreating to the barn. With a prayerful heart he followed.

Sean walked into the barn, thinking as he did that it was darker inside of him than it was in the barn. He knew he needed to turn to God but he was so angry that his mother was dead and bitter that his father was gone.

He heard someone come in behind him. Not until a lamp was lit did he turn to see who it was, making no attempt to hide his tears.

Rigg's tall form stood next to the post where he'd hung the lamp. They regarded each other in silence for a moment, then Sean's voice betrayed to Rigg his pain and fury.

"I suppose you've come out here to tell me to be a man! To be strong for the girls!" The words were hurled as an accusation and Rigg stood quiet as a dry sob followed those embittered words.

Sean turned to lean on the door of a stall, his body now shaking with his cries. The older man moved toward him. There was no hesitation when Rigg's arms went around the young man. Sean turned and clung to him.

Rigg let him cry in silence, thinking as he did that 14 was not so very old. Sean was capable and responsible and looked like a man, but it didn't change the fact that at 14 you still need your father very much and Sean's only parent was many miles away.

Rigg thought back on his own life at 14 and how close he was to Bill, enabling him to ask questions about the changes in his body. Why everything felt so strange, as though he were living inside of someone else's skin. Rigg was quite certain that Sean would never be able to talk with Kate about how he felt. It wasn't that she was unapproachable, just a woman who probably didn't understand the transition from boy to man.

A few minutes later Sean pulled away from Rigg and wiped his face on his sleeves. "Are you ready to head home?" Sean's voice was quiet but not embarrassed, a fact for which Rigg was thankful.

"We can go if you want or you can have something to eat first. Mom kept things hot."

Realizing he was hungry, Sean nodded and started toward the door. It was on Rigg's mind to tell him they could talk later, but somehow, holding the boy as he cried was enough for now. It let him know that Rigg was there when he needed him.

forty

Kate had a restful night but stayed home from church in the morning. She spent a long time reading her Bible, the book of James. She then took a leisurely bath, washed her hair and left it down to dry. May had set out some bread and eggs and after Kaitlin was satisfied, she started a letter to her father. As she began to write in the quiet house, she realized how long it had been since she'd been alone and how much she missed the solitude.

Dear Father,

We received your letter yesterday and even though we share your grief over this calamity, we're sorry you're not coming right home. Please stay in Hawaii where they need you so desperately. We are doing very well; please don't worry about us. We too wish we could be with you but understand your responsibility to the mission. Give our love to the people there and tell them we're praying.

School dismissed for the summer on Friday but I have a good-paying job at the mercantile where Sean works. I'll be doing the store's book work.

If you were here, Father, I would want you to meet the man who owns the mercantile, Marshall Riggs. He's the man with whom Sean lives. (Marc and I are settled in our small house. It's really very cozy.) I don't know how I feel about this man, Father, but I feel something that I've never felt for anyone. He is a believer and when we first arrived, I thought he might be interested in me. I'm not sure now. It is, of course, his store in which I'll be starting work on Monday, June 5.

Please don't think he's been threatening in any way. I believe it's very safe to work for him. As I said before, the only thing not settled are my feelings. I know you'll pray for me and I feel better just having shared this with you.

Sean is working hard and Mr. Riggs is pleased with his effort. Marc will be with Sean on the days he's not working or with May Taylor, Mr. Riggs' mother. I am writing from the Taylors' right now. They have taken us under their wing and we usually stay with them on Saturday night and then ride with them to church. The family is William and May Taylor with sons, Marshall, May's son from a previous marriage, Jeffrey, Gilbert, and Nathan. Nate is one of my pupils.

I suspect you'll want to know about the church. The fellowship is good and the preaching straight from the Word. I miss your services though.

I'll encourage Sean and Marc to write this week. Please pray for me as I begin this new job and as I work closely with Mr. Riggs. I love you Father, and remember you're always in my prayers.

Katie

Kate felt drained when she finished the letter and went out to sit in the sun to dry her hair. Her mind strayed to Joey and the chance that he might have been at church that morning. With school out she wondered when she would see him.

The one time she'd mentioned going to his house, Rigg had discouraged her. He had tried to sound casual but Kate had been acutely aware of the tensing of his body so contrary to the nonchalant tone of his voice.

Well, she would have to do what she thought was right. Kate continued to dwell on Rigg and she thanked God for the way he'd gone to Sean the night before. Kate had been so drained, and she just wasn't as close to Sean as she once was. She wouldn't have known what to say even if she had gone to the barn with him.

She and Marcail had just been finishing their own supper when Sean had come in and polished off two large bowls of stew and Kaitlin didn't know how many biscuits. She hadn't seen him this morning before they left for church, but knew he'd be coming back for lunch.

Kate had talked to Marcail as they'd gone to bed and felt she was doing very well. Marcail was good about expressing her feelings. If something upset her, she usually talked about it or cried and then got on the road to getting over it or changing it. Kate envied her that trait.

Kate had a tendency to bury her hurts deep inside and when they tried to rear their ugly heads, she effectively pushed them right back down. Kate gave the appearance of handling upsets well, when in actuality she did not handle them at all.

It seemed there was much to pray about on this sunny morning and Kate's hair was completely dry by the time she left the porch. Once in her room, she scooped the blue-black mass into her usual chignon and went downstairs to peel potatoes for lunch. She had Sunday dinner well under way, much to May's delight, by the time the wagons pulled into the yard.

❏ ❏ ❏

"Did you have a restful morning?"

"Yes, I really did. I haven't been alone in a long time and it felt good to sit and pray when it was so quiet. I also wrote a long letter to Father."

Rigg and Kaitlin were walking across the yard to the swing, where Marcail was sitting. Kaitlin had promised to come and talk with her after lunch. Rigg, not believing how much he missed having Kate with him in church, had followed her.

"It felt good to tell him how we're doing. I want to thank you again for giving me a job. I know it's a burden off his heart to know we're taking care of ourselves."

"You don't need to thank me, Katie. I didn't make the offer out of charity. I need you." Something in his voice, on those last words, caused Kate to turn and look at him. But she didn't see anything out of the ordinary and her heartbeat slowed down.

"Hi Katie," Marcail called to her from the swing.

"Hi Marc."

"Hi Mr. Riggs."

"Hello Marcail. You're holding on tight aren't you?"

"Sure." Marcail looked surprised and Kate chuckled.

"What's so funny?"

"I'm laughing because I still don't think you believe she's nine years old."

"She is small."

Their voices were low and Marcail wasn't paying much attention to them anyhow.

"She's the picture of our mother who was very petite. Sean and I resemble Father. We appear to be stronger and sturdier but in actuality it's Marc who has all the energy. In the morning she wakes up ready to go, and most nights I have to tell her to be quiet so I can go to sleep. Of course once she is asleep nothing could wake her. I'm the same way."

"Yes, I know."

"What?" Kate asked softly, looking at Rigg in open curiosity. Rigg wished he could hide somewhere. He had planned on telling her that he'd carried her to bed when they were celebrating their tenth anniversary and not before.

"How did you know?" Kaitlin pressed him, thinking that she would have to speak to Sean about sharing such private matters without her permission.

Rigg, seeing that she was waiting, took a deep breath and told Kaitlin he'd carried her to bed. He watched her eyes grow very round before she drew herself up in her teacher's stance, finger in the air, mouth open to speak. But Rigg cut her off.

"There you go. Getting all prim and proper on me again. We were getting along just fine and now you're the teacher again."

Kate was so surprised a slight breeze could have pushed her over. But she was quick to recover.

"Mr. Riggs—" she began, only to hear Rigg interrupt again.

"You start at the store tomorrow and I don't want to be addressed as Mr. Riggs." He watched Kate's chin go into the air but he was equally as determined. "You've called me Rigg once. I suppose when you forgot to be your prim and proper self, so I'll expect to be called Rigg from now on."

"I never—"

"Yes, you did."

They stood in stony silence for a moment before Kate saw that Marcail was no longer swinging but standing within earshot.

"Can we go see the barn?" her voice was tentative and Kate drummed up a smile to let her know everything was all right. Rigg joined them and Kate wondered if Marcail could feel the tension in the air. She watched as Marcail touched the velvety noses of the Taylors' horses and then climbed up into the buggy seat. When she moved to the ladder that led to the hayloft Kate called her back.

"It's very safe," Rigg assured them both and Kate gave her permission. She stared up anxiously while standing at the bottom of the ladder. Rigg watched her face as Marcail climbed.

"Now who's forgetting she's nine?" His voice was amused and Kate laughed at being found out. Marcail climbed with no problem and disappeared over the side.

"This really would have been a wonderful place to grow up, Mr. Riggs," Kate said as she looked around. "I almost envy you."

Rigg could see that she hadn't addressed him that way deliberately; it had become a habit. He moved around her and stepped up to the first rung of the ladder. He turned, holding on with his right hand and reaching for Kaitlin with his left. He spoke after he had her jaw in his palm.

"I'm going up to see Marc. And Kaitlin," he paused to make sure she was listening. "If you call me Mr. Riggs again, I'll kiss you." With a look that said he hoped she would, he turned back to the ladder.

Kate's mouth swung open and she stood like a statue as he climbed and disappeared into the loft. She doubted he would do as he threatened—but she couldn't be certain.

"And I have to go to work for him tomorrow." The words were said just above a whisper, as Kaitlin's heart thundered in her chest. Was it fear or something else entirely?

forty-one

It didn't take Rigg more than a second to see that Kaitlin was terrified. He knew it was not what he'd said to her the day before because even though she'd been cautious, she had been fairly relaxed around him for the rest of the day.

No, this morning's nerves must have been the job and Rigg went out of his way to make her feel at ease.

"Here is your desk. And these are the books I want you to start with. Marcail took me by surprise when she found an error in my addition. I want you to check these books for mistakes—January through May of this year.

"This will also help you understand my system. I'm going to be working on an order so if you have questions, just ask."

Rigg went immediately and sat in his desk chair. Kate stood for a moment before doing the same. The extra desk was just a little smaller than Rigg's and he had pushed them so they faced each other. After sitting down, Kaitlin was painfully aware of Rigg directly across from her. She tried to look everywhere but at him and in doing so discovered what a wonderful view the office had of the store.

Kate opened the first book cautiously and began to read, pencil ready. Rigg's handwriting was a bold script, easy to read and a bit like her own in style. Kaitlin mentally congratulated the teacher who taught him the skill.

She worked for almost an hour, correcting some columns and putting a check by all she'd re-added, before she had a question. She loved numbers and once involved, it was an effort to drag her mind away. Rigg had been up and down and Kate, who would have said that no one could distract her, was finding out how wrong she was.

She tried not to stare at Rigg's dark hair and the way it curled slightly on his collar as she stood up with the January book and moved toward him. He looked up immediately, giving her his full attention.

"What do these letters mean?" Kate pointed to the side of the ledger next to the names of the brands.

"Those are my suppliers. H is Hicks, B is for Bates, Br is for Brenner and so on. They don't have any bearing on your work right now, but if at some point I show you the ordering, you'll have to know them. I'll write out a list of my suppliers for you over the next few weeks and give the letters for each one. Then if you need to refer to it you can." Kate thanked him and he smiled at her.

The remainder of the morning went by in similar fashion and Kaitlin was surprised when Rigg told her it was time for lunch.

"I was going to head down to the Binks, would you care to join me for lunch?"

Kaitlin was startled, not because his offer was such a surprise but because she'd once again forgotten to pack something for her noon meal. No wonder she and Marcail had both taken off weight. She kept forgetting to feed them!

"Yes, I would," Kate answered, and a moment later they were walking down the street to the Binks Hotel and Boarding House, the place where Kaitlin, Sean and Marcail had spent their first night in town.

The Binks was one of Santa Rosa's older lodging establishments and it was well managed. The food in the dining room was said to be the best in town. Rigg had gone to school with the present owner's son, Darrell Kolstad. Darrell ran the hotel with help from his wife, Jane. Darrell was on hand to greet Rigg and Kate when they came in and to see that they found a table.

Rigg asked Kate if he could order for them and she readily agreed. She wondered if he'd noticed her weight loss when he ordered the day's special. A mammoth plate of roast pork, mashed potatoes and gravy, brussels sprouts and green beans was placed before her. Kate stared at it and then at Rigg. He grinned at her.

"You don't really expect me to eat all of this, do you?"

"Not if you don't want to. I just thought you might be hungry. There's apple cobbler for dessert," he added, with another grin, and Kate shook her head at him and picked up her fork.

Their conversation was relaxed and when they were finished Kaitlin asked if she had time to go check on Sean and Marcail.

"Sure. Are you worried about them?"

"Not really. I just want to make sure that Sean gave her some lunch."

"I don't think you have anything to worry about—if Marcail is with Sean, she'll eat."

Kate agreed wholeheartedly. "You're certainly right about that. Sean's best friend is his stomach. But I'd like to see them just the same."

As they walked back to her cottage, she told him a little of what her father said in his letter. Rigg was a good listener as Kate shared some of her feelings about how suddenly she had become the main provider for the family.

"I really have been ignorant as to what it costs to house and feed a family. Sometimes I panic about what would happen to Sean and Marc if I got sick. Do you feel that way about the store?"

"I did when I was younger. My father opened the mercantile and he and his brother ran it. They were partners on a very unbalanced scale. Not that that ever bothered either of them, but my father owned around 90 percent of the business and Uncle Leo the other 10 percent.

"When my father died, Uncle Leo naturally stepped in and took his place. I started working there when I was Sean's age. Uncle Leo taught me everything, making it plain from day one that someday the business would be mine.

"It happened sooner than we all thought. I was just 19 when a rich Texas widow came into town for a visit. It was love at first sight for my uncle and the next thing I know he's handing the entire operation over to me. He's never been back, but we get a letter from him and Aunt Ruth at Christmastime each year.

"I told you all of that so you wouldn't be discouraged. In the early days, when I'd just taken over the store, I nearly lived down here for fear something would happen if I was away. Nothing had changed really. Uncle Leo had pretty much handed the reins over to me. I see now that it was the best thing he could have done.

"You're experiencing the same thing I did. The suddenness and the newness can be frightening, but you're doing great. If you're like me, you'll find yourself turning to God more and more about the doubts and fears. He's taking care of everything, just like you knew He would."

They were at the house now and Kaitlin turned before opening the door. "I need to give myself time, something I'm not very good at. Thank you for all you shared, Mmmrr—Marshall." She had come so close to saying Mr. Riggs that she had used the first name she could think of.

Rigg's brows were halfway to his hairline. The only person who ever called him Marshall was his mother and that was when she was getting after him over something. Kate hadn't used his name in an endearing way, but he rather liked the sound of it.

Kaitlin was watching to see how he would respond. She had made an effort all day not to call him anything lest she make the very mistake she dreaded, but it never occurred to her to call him Marshall until that moment and she wondered if he minded.

"Are you going to go in and see if they're here?" Rigg's question propelled Kate through the door and also told her he wasn't upset.

As it was, Sean and Marcail were not there but Kate wasn't really worried. As they walked back to the mercantile, she guessed they were at Marshall's.

The rest of the day went by very well until almost closing time, when Kate spotted Joey Parker passing by the window. She hadn't had time to think about him all day and now as she prepared to leave for the day, her heart ached for him.

That ache continued through the evening and Kaitlin opened her Bible and asked God for comfort. She had just finished reading through 1 Thessalonians. It was on her mind to go on to the next book but she stayed in 1 Thessalonians and reread the first two chapters.

A half hour later Kate closed her Bible. She was surprised at the words she'd missed the first time through. Kate hugged the Bible to her and asked God to give her wisdom in applying the truths she had read.

forty-two

"Are you headed home Katie, or out to Taylors'?"

"I'm going to walk out to Joey Parker's and then to Taylors'. I'll see you when you get there."

It was the Saturday afternoon of Kaitlin's first week at the mercantile and she and Sean had both worked that day. Marcail was with May. Sean watched his sister head out of the store, his heart a little doubtful about what she was doing.

Sean had more work to do and he told himself, as he headed back to the loading platform, that Katie wouldn't do anything stupid.

❏ ❏ ❏

Kaitlin's first view of Joey Parker's home made her wonder if it had been such a smart idea to come. It wasn't the house itself, but the location. Kate knew that the church was not too far away—but no one would be there on a Saturday night. There was a wooded area that bordered two sides of the house, giving it a feeling of being closed off from the world.

She had prayed very seriously about coming here and just how God would want her to handle her relationship with Joey, or if she was even to have a relationship with him.

The event that clinched the decision for her was remembering the way he had hung around the church. He hadn't been back since she took him in and sat with him but Kate was sure he was interested. This little boy needed Christ.

Her thoughts kept her feet moving toward the rundown building. Kate stepped carefully around the junk in the front yard and at one point caught her dress on some rusty barbed wire. Her hand returned again and again to her nose and she tried not to think about what might be causing the dreadful odor that hung in the air.

Her knock at the front door brought furious barking from within. If Kaitlin hadn't been frozen in terror she'd have bolted for her life. She thought she might faint when the door was thrown open and a dog the size of a small horse, stood in the doorway, barking as though he was going to devour her on the spot.

"Stop it Frank, be quiet," Joey maneuvered himself beside the huge animal and was shouting almost as loud as the dog barked. It took Kate a moment to realize they'd been joined by a third person.

"You must be Joey's father." Kaitlin had to shout to be heard. "I'm Miss Donovan, Joey's—"

"*Shut up!*" the man suddenly bellowed, and Kate, Joey and Frank all halted in their tracks. The dog lay down next to the stoop with his head on his paws, looking for all the world like an innocent pup.

Kaitlin's hand had gone to her throat and she was hoping Parker wouldn't ask her in because she didn't think she could move her legs. She was also conscious of Parker's eyes on her, so she tried to collect herself enough to speak.

"I hope I'm not coming at a bad time, but I really wanted to see Joey. I'm his teacher, Miss Donovan, and I've missed him since school let out. I came to see how he was doing." Kate made an instantaneous decision about returning to this place.

"Mr. Parker, would you have a problem with Joey coming to visit me in town?" There was no reply. In fact, Kate was beginning to wonder if he'd understood anything she said.

If Kaitlin thought the yard smelled bad, she didn't know what to think of Parker himself. His shirt had holes in it and was covered with grease and dirt. His boots hung open and Kate could see no socks on his dirty legs. His binders hung down around his knees and she was a little worried he was going to lose the filthy pants he wore.

Most of his teeth were missing and his hair and beard needed trimming. He wasn't that much taller than Kaitlin but looked a good deal heavier, with a stomach that protruded far over the waistline of his pants. His eyes were dark and watchful and they looked Kate in the eye with a keen intelligence she'd not been expecting.

When a full minute had passed and Parker had still not spoken Kate tried again, this time with Joey.

"How have you been Joey?"

"Fine." His voice was carefully neutral but his eyes revealed that he was glad to see her.

"Joey, would you like to come and visit me? I work during the day, but if you want to come any evening during the week, I'd welcome you. Do you know where I live?"

"Yes, Miss Donovan."

"Good! Then all we need to do is get your father's permission." Kate turned with a smile she didn't feel and looked inquiringly at the man. When he still did not give an answer, she managed to stretch her smile a little farther and say with false cheerfulness, "Well Joey, it seems your father has no objections so I'll expect to see you sometime next week." Kaitlin watched as the little boy looked to his father. He must have seen something affirmative because he looked back at Kate and gave a slight nod, his face lighting briefly with a look of yearning.

"I'll look forward to seeing you. It was nice to meet you, Mr. Parker. Bye now."

Kate forced herself not to look back until she was just about to step out of sight. When she did turn around, she saw that they were both as she'd left them—even the dog was still lying quietly. She gave a small wave that Joey returned. A few seconds later the trees hid her from view and her tears began to fall.

"You can't have him, Kaitlin. As much as you want to go back and steal that little boy and cherish him forever, you can't."

Kate cried and walked in the direction of the Taylors', praying as she went that Joey would come next week. She didn't think she could ever go back to that place. But then Joey's dirty little face and yearning eyes swam before her. She told the Lord that she had to reach that boy, that she'd do whatever He asked of her if it would give her a chance to tell him of Christ's love.

❑ ❑ ❑

"Did Kate head home to get her things?" Rigg asked. He and Sean were closing up for the night.

"No, she sent everything out with your dad this morning when he picked up Marc. She went to see Joey Parker."

"Is that what she said?"

"Yeah. She plans to walk to your folks' after." Sean felt uncertain and then fearful at the look on Rigg's face. What was this Parker guy like? Sean didn't ask the question aloud, but followed Rigg as he made a beeline for the wagon.

Kate had her tears under control by the time Rigg's wagon rolled into view. The horses were approaching so fast that Kaitlin thought something might be wrong.

Rigg jumped down almost before the wagon stopped and ran toward her through a cloud of dust.

"Are you all right?" He grasped her upper arms and waited for her to answer.

"Yes. What's happened?"

Rigg didn't answer. His relief was so great that he pulled Kate into his arms and held her almost fiercely. She was too surprised to be upset and looked at him with wide eyes when he once again held her away from him.

"Was Parker home?"

"Yes, he was there."

Rigg's hold tightened and Kaitlin flinched.

"I don't want you to go there again." Rigg's eyes had gone black and he strove desperately to control his voice. "It's not safe for a woman alone and I want your promise that you won't go back."

"I can't do that. I mean, I invited Joey to come and see me but if he doesn't, I just might have to come back out here. So I can't make you that promise, Marshall."

It was more than clear to Kate that Rigg was not satisfied with her response. She watched as he pulled in a deep breath and relaxed his hold on her arms.

"Will you make me this promise—that you won't come out here again without telling me?"

"Yes." Kate was able to answer him right away. The pain and worry in his eyes were very real.

"Please tell me why it's so dangerous," Kate said softly.

Rigg hesitated and then glanced at Sean who had come to stand with the horses.

"A woman was raped in these woods a few years back. There was no proof as to who did it, but the description the woman gave and everything she said pointed to Parker. He was even arrested but the woman was afraid to come in and identify him. Without some evidence they had to let him go."

Kate's hand had come to her mouth and Rigg pulled her into his arms one more time. This time, when he released her, his hand came up and the backs of his fingers stroked feather-light down her left cheek, his eyes once again telling her how frightened he'd been.

They were all a little drained as the wagon moved toward the Taylors' and Rigg found himself touching Kate as they talked.

"Did I hurt your arms?"

"No," she assured him softly.

He leaned forward slightly to see her face better and for a long moment their eyes met. It was Kate's turn to touch Rigg when she saw the caring in his gaze. And he briefly covered the hand she put on his arm with his own, thanking God as he did for this woman and also asking Him to keep her safe.

forty-three

Sunday passed in a relaxed fashion. The next day both Kate and Sean had to work so Marcail stayed with the Taylors. After work on Monday, Rigg asked Kate to join him and Sean for supper. They planned to collect Marcail a little later in the evening.

Kate told Sean that she was going home to clean up and that she'd see them at the house. She was totally unprepared, but thrilled, to find Joey Parker on her front step.

"Hello Joey." Kate's smile was genuine.

"Hi," was all the boy said, but his eyes told Kaitlin he was glad to see her.

"How are you today?"

"O.K."

"Would you like to go somewhere with me, Joey?"

"Sure." He looked confused but agreed—anything to be near his beloved Miss Donovan.

"If you'll just wait right there, I'll go inside for a minute and then we'll go to Mr. Riggs' for supper. How does that sound?"

"Fine." Kate watched his small face carefully lest he be intimidated about going to Rigg's and leave when she was inside. But she need not have worried; he was waiting patiently for her. Within minutes they were standing on Rigg's front porch.

"I brought a guest with me," Kate said to Sean when he opened the door.

"Hi, Joey," Sean greeted the boy and opened the door wide. Rigg was in the kitchen and everyone headed that way. Kate silently thanked Rigg for the way he handled Joey, treating him as though his coming to supper was an everyday occurrence.

"Okay Joey," Rigg instructed him, "wash your hands and you can help Sean set the table."

The adults in the room were quiet and tried not to stare as Joey solemnly assisted Sean. Kaitlin could see that he took his task very seriously and she kept her face averted so he couldn't see the way she was struggling with her emotions.

Rigg and Kaitlin made a nice team as they efficiently put supper together. Two whole chickens were fried—a job Kate tackled. Rigg mixed biscuits for the oven and Kate also made gravy and then sliced fruit for a salad.

"You're a better cook than Sean led me to believe," Rigg commented at one point, when Sean and Joey had gone into the other room.

Kaitlin chuckled. "It's been slow in coming. The only thing I cook well is fish. One of these weekends I'm going to send Sean to the creek and then I'll be able to cook for you and your family for a change."

"Gil and Nate love to fish. I think they'd probably bring back enough for an army."

"I'll have to mention it to your mother when we go for Marc. I can pick up the things I'll need this week."

Rigg didn't answer; he couldn't right then. It felt so right having Katie here, working beside him. He didn't want to get his hopes up but he was sure she was looking at him these days with different eyes. At first her eyes had been almost hostile and then had gone to guarded. And now they were changing from friendly to tender.

At least that's what Rigg thought. But that was the problem, the difference between *thinking* and *knowing*.

He knew he still needed to bide his time or take the chance of destroying everything they had built between them.

Sean and Joey came back in just as supper preparations were complete. As they began to eat, it became apparent that Joey did not use utensils. Kaitlin felt deep compassion watching him dip his fingers in the gravy when his biscuit was gone.

When he picked up his plate, intent on licking it, Kate paid close attention to her own food, as did Sean. Rigg leaned close to Joey to instruct him in a few table manners. Spoons and forks were clearly a new concept to him, but in his eagerness to please, he gave them a try.

When Sean found out there was nothing for dessert at Rigg's, he suggested they go get Marcail and raid Mrs. Taylor's baked goods. Joey was again treated as one of the family and was not even asked if he wanted to go. The little boy stood in obvious indecision next to the wagon. Kate ignored his look.

"Climb in, Joey. Mrs. Taylor is the best baker I know. You don't want to miss out on her cookies."

Rigg swung Kate onto the seat and was pulling himself aboard when Joey jumped in the back with Sean.

Marcail was thrilled to see her sister and talked nonstop for the first ten minutes. It seemed that she and May had done a great many things that day and Marcail had had so much fun that she was determined to tell her oldest sibling about it in one breath.

Joey was introduced to the Taylor family and then followed Sean's signal to help himself to the cookies. Sean and Nathan were used to walking away with as many as they could carry. Joey was more circumspect.

"You may have more than one Joey." May smiled and held another cookie out to the little boy. He was cautious as he reached for it; he captured May's heart in that moment. His hair was hanging in his eyes and his clothes were torn and filthy.

"Gilbert and Nathan were pretty hard on clothes when they were your size, Joey," May began, and Joey looked at her strangely. "But they had occasional growth spurts where they outgrew the clothes before they could ruin them. I have a pair of pants and a shirt just about your size, if you'd like to have them."

As Joey had been doing the entire evening, he looked to Miss Donovan for approval. She smiled and nodded at Joey as though she'd never heard a better idea. May asked Joey to go upstairs with her. When they came down Joey was aglow in his *new* clothes, his old tucked under his arm. His face flushed when Kate made over him and his eyes were shining under her approval.

"Now Joey, I think I'd better get you home. While we're there I can check with your father to make sure it's all right for you to keep the new clothes."

It was quite plain that Kate's plan to take Joey home was news to Rigg. He looked thunderstruck, but Kate was telling Marcail to gather her doll and tea set and get to the wagon. She grasped Joey's hand, thanked May and sailed out the back door.

Nearly everyone followed their progress to the barn, Rigg with his eyes on Kate alone. Joey and Marcail were close to Bill as he hitched up the horses and Rigg was able to get Kaitlin alone. Putting his arm around her waist, he led her just outside the barn door. When they stopped he stood face-to-face in front of her with his hands behind his back, his whole body bent to speak directly into her upturned, attentive face.

"You made a promise."

"I'm not breaking my promise," she told him. Her own hands were clasped behind her back and she cocked her head a bit to stare up into his gray eyes with honest candor. "I said I wouldn't go out there alone and I'm not. You're going with me."

"And if I refuse?"

"I'll ask Jeff." Her chin came up just a bit and Rigg brought one hand out to grasp that chin between his thumb and forefinger.

"I knew the first time I saw this chin, that you would be stubborn."

"I am not stubborn!" Kate denied, but made no move to step away from his touch. "And further more, Mr. Riggs, I feel very strongly that we need to be involved in this little boy's life and not just once in a while. And that is going to involve our going to his house once in a while—"

Rigg had a very strange look on his face and Kate stopped.

"Are you finished?" he wanted to know.

"Yes," Kate answered tentatively.

"You can't say I didn't warn you."

Kaitlin watched as Rigg's head lowered and his mouth brushed across her own. She was too stunned to move.

He smiled tenderly into her eyes when he raised his head. "I've changed my mind Katie," his voice was deep and soft. "You can call me Mr. Riggs anytime you want."

The entire family spilled out of the barn then, with the wagon ready to go. Rigg, Kate, Sean, Joey and Marcail were halfway to Joey's house before Kate realized she was no longer standing outside the Taylors' barn.

forty-four

Parker's dog Frank, bearing down on the wagon, was the needed element to bring Kate back to earth.

"Shut up, Frank!" a voice bellowed and everyone, including Parker standing by the house, stared at the young schoolteacher. The dog dropped to the ground as if by magic and looked up at Kaitlin with soulful eyes.

Kate climbed down from the seat, unassisted, patted the dog and moved toward the house. Knowing Rigg did not want her here, she took matters firmly into her own hands. Not unexpectedly, Rigg's feet had hit the ground as soon as Kate's did. All he could do, however, was watch her.

"Good evening, Mr. Parker. We were out at the Taylors'. I hope we didn't keep Joey out too long." Forging right ahead, Kate continued, "Mrs. Taylor gave Joey some old clothes that her boys have outgrown and I wanted to make sure you didn't have any objections."

Kate had walked closer as she talked and even though Rigg and Sean held their places by the wagon, they were watchful.

Kate stood about five feet from Parker now and waited. She noticed he looked a little better than he had before and wondered at the reason. When her statement went unanswered, she asked straight out.

"Mr. Parker, may Joey keep the clothes?"

The man's eyes moved over his son who stood next to Kate and then back to the men by the wagon. He looked at Kate a moment before speaking in a voice that sounded like it wasn't used much.

"How much did she want?"

"She wanted to *give* them to Joey because her boys can't wear them."

He shrugged after a moment and then spoke again.

"Sure." The answer, although brief, was enough. A smile broke across Joey's face.

"I need to get home now, Joey. I'll see you later. Good evening, Mr. Parker." Kate had all she could take for the moment. This family needed so much and right now she was feeling too emotionally drained to deal with any more of it.

Kaitlin and Marcail waved from their seats in the wagon and Kaitlin was surprised when Sean and Rigg did too. Her heart felt like a heavy weight within her as she left Joey in that run-down home with no warmth or caring. And then the Lord reminded her that Parker had let him keep the clothes.

Kate praised God for this and thanked Him for May's tenderness and generosity. She then began to pray for Parker. Kaitlin was so intent on her thoughts that it took a moment for her to realize when the wagon had stopped in front of her little house.

It was growing late. Both Sean and Rigg got down to help the girls. Sean took Marcail inside and Rigg stood next to the wagon with Kate in front of him.

"You were a thousand miles away just then."

"Not a thousand, only about two."

"Joey," Rigg guessed correctly.

"And Mr. Parker," Kate said softly. Her gaze centered on nothing in particular in the gathering darkness.

Rigg's brows rose but he didn't question her. With Kate's mind on Joey he wondered if she'd even remembered his kiss. He couldn't get it out of his thoughts.

"Do you suppose that Joey has ever told his father that he loves him?"

"I don't suppose he's given the boy much to love," Rigg answered honestly. "He's too young to understand that the drinking his father does is not his fault, and yet, in a manner of speaking, he is the one who gets blamed when Parker is drunk and abusive."

"Are you sure that Mr. Parker is abusive? I mean, I've been to their house and I can see that they're poor. I could tell that just by his appearance at school and how little lunch he would bring. But I'm not sure I believe he's been abused. Neglected, possibly. Abused—I'm not too sure. Do you have firsthand knowledge that Mr. Parker abuses Joey?"

Rigg had never been asked that question before and he had to think a moment. He was a little ashamed to admit to Kate that he wasn't sure if what he'd heard was fact or town gossip.

"I feel rather ashamed."

"Oh, don't feel ashamed!" Kate said, her face wreathed in a smile. "I'm *glad* you don't know if it's true because it changes the way I feel about Joey and his father." Rigg looked confused by her logic and Kaitlin went on.

"I'll admit to you that I have a hard time with Mr. Parker when I think he might have hurt that woman or harmed Joey. But Rigg," both of Kate's hands came up to grasp Rigg's shirt front. "What *I* feel doesn't matter in the least. No matter what kind of a man Mr. Parker is, Christ died for him!" Kate pulled on his shirt a little more, her face and movements telling Rigg how badly she wanted to be understood.

"Please go home and read 1 Thessalonians chapters one and two. Please do that, Rigg, and tell me if we've reached out to him in the nurturing way those verses instruct. Does our love go out as God's does—unconditionally—or are we the type of people who only want to minister to the lovely, to the people who are easy to be near?"

The tears that flooded Kate's eyes were now flowing down her cheeks. "I want," she whispered tearfully, her voice breaking, "for Joey to come to Christ. But I also want Mr. Parker to know that someone loved him enough to die for him."

Kaitlin was utterly spent. Rigg watched her whole body sag before enfolding her in his arms and laying his cheek on the top of her head. He held her that way for a brief moment and then with a promise that he would read the chapters, called Sean to the wagon.

forty-five

The chapters Rigg read that night before going to sleep were familiar to him. But never before had he read them with a person's face so clear in his mind. Parker.

It would be very easy to answer Kate's question after reading 1 Thessalonians 2:7—"But we were gentle among you, even as a nurse cherisheth her children." No, we haven't reached out as we're admonished to—"as a nurse cherisheth her children."

Rigg knew these chapters were describing Paul with Silas and Timothy, and the way they ministered to the people at Thessalonica. Paul stated in 1 Thessalonians 2:2 that a previous experience in Philippi did not keep them away, even though they were treated shamefully. But still they went to Thessalonica because God was leading them to the people there.

Rigg couldn't help but wonder how they'd been treated when they first arrived at Thessalonica. In 1 Thessalonians 1:5 Paul states that it wasn't just lip service on their part, but that they lived among them, in an effort to lead them to Christ, and lead them to Christ they did.

1 Thessalonians 1:6,7—"And ye became followers of us, and of the Lord, having received the word in much affliction, with joy of the Holy Ghost: So that ye were ensamples to all that believe in Macedonia and Achaia."

Rigg went on , going to 1 Thessalonians 2:8, "So being

affectionately desirous of you, we were willing to have imparted unto you, not the gospel of God only, but also our own souls, because ye were dear unto us." If Rigg had any doubts about whether or not he was as burdened as Kate was for the Parkers, this verse cleared them immediately. At some point in Kaitlin's dealings with Joey, her heart had become very burdened for his soul. Now her heart was just as burdened for Parker.

Rigg read the chapters through one final time and fell asleep praying about how he could be involved in the Parkers' lives.

◻ ◻ ◻

The remainder of the week was busy giving Kaitlin and Rigg little opportunity to discuss the Parkers. But when they did talk about it, they decided that the weekend would be the best time.

In the days leading up to the weekend, Joey came to Kate's house three times. She ministered to his physical needs—his elbow when he cut it, his stomach when it was empty, water for his thirst and shelter from the sun that shone down fiercely in the middle of the summer.

And unbeknownst to Joey, his emotional needs were being met as well. In a hundred little ways Kate made him feel special. Her hand on his shoulder, the way she smiled when he talked to her and the most special times of all, when she took Joey's chin in her hand, raised his head to look at her and told him he was so special to her and that she loved him very much.

During these visits Kate had done the majority of the talking. This trend changed on Saturday morning when Joey came to the house just as Kate was finishing with Sean's hair.

"I'm going to be late for work, Kate. Are you nearly through?"

"Yes, I am. Although Marshall will say your tardiness was worth it, now that you no longer look like a gypsy."

Marcail found this highly amusing and Sean made a smart remark to her in Hawaiian. Standing in the doorway unnoticed for a time, Joey listened to the heated discussion in a foreign tongue.

"Hi, Joey." Marcail said in a loud, surprised voice and all conversation stopped.

Kate could see that the little boy was ready to leave and spoke quickly, "Come in, Joey. I just cut Sean's hair. Would you like me to cut your hair?"

Joey's eyes went to Sean's head and Kate had a hard time holding her laughter. Sean let himself be inspected before flipping his cap onto his head. The cap was a brimless number with a visored front. Sean wore it rain or shine, giving him a jaunty look. It had been a gift from a Scottish missionary who'd been visiting Hawaii and Sean cherished it. He looked at Joey for a moment longer before winking at the younger boy, thanked his sister and headed out the door.

It took a little coaxing, but Kate persuaded Joey to sit down. She covered his clothing with a sheet and began to trim. Marcail was busy with her doll and for the first time Joey initiated a conversation.

"My Pa told me to thank you for the bread." Kate had ended up with an extra loaf of bread the day before and had sent it home with Joey.

"You're welcome Joey," she said simply and continued to snip.

"I haven't been to the church lately."

"No, I guess you haven't." Kate tried to keep her voice neutral, even through the surprise she felt that he was talking at all, let alone mentioning the church.

"Is God really like a father?"

"Yes Joey, He is. The Bible describes Him that way many times, but you need to remember that there is a difference between an earthly father and a heavenly Father. We love our fathers here on earth but they're not perfect. God is."

Joey was quiet for a time, as was Kaitlin. She wondered if, in the past, she had done too much talking or if it was because he was faced away from her as they spoke.

"Do you really think God hears when you pray?"

"Yes, I do. The Bible says God hears us and I know He's answered my prayers all my life."

"You always get what you ask for?"

"No I don't. Sometimes God's answer is no."

Again the little boy dwelt on this in silence. Kate was praying with all her heart and knew that she had to ask this child about eternity before he left her.

"I know all about Christmas," Joey shared softly. "I know that Jesus was born. But a little baby shouldn't die for a person's sins so I don't understand what Jesus it was that did that."

Kate was again surprised, this time at his knowledge. "Were you always the size you are now, Joey, or were you once a baby?"

"I was a baby."

"But you didn't stay a baby and neither did Jesus. He grew to be a man and it was that man who died on the cross to save the world. The baby and the man are the same Person, God's only Son."

"Does it say that in the Bible?"

"Yes, it does. Would you like me to show you?"

He nodded and Kate made a few more cuts with her scissors, removed the sheet, brushed him off and retrieved her Bible. She opened to the book of Luke and began to explain.

"In Luke 2, Joey, Christ's birth is told. Do you remember the story?"

"With the angels."

"That's right. In verse 11 it says, 'For unto you is born

this day in the city of David a Saviour, which is Christ the Lord.' And if you keep reading it says that the shepherds came to see Him."

Joey nodded and Kate went on. "Well, if you read even farther down to verse 41 and 42, it says that when Jesus was 12 He went into Jerusalem with His mother Mary and her husband Joseph. So you see right there He's already 12 years old.

"And there's more. The last verse in chapter 2 says 'Jesus increased in wisdom and stature, and in favour with God and man.' Increased in stature means His body grew. The next chapters in Luke tell all about Jesus as a man, the miracles He performed and so much more. Then, if you turn all the way to chapter 23, it tells of Jesus Christ's death. How they nailed His hands and feet on the cross and how He died there for our sins. But Joey, He didn't stay dead. When the people who loved Him went back to His grave it was empty. He even appeared to some of them at their homes and on the road. Jesus is alive, Joey, and He's still alive today, saving all who believe in Him."

Joey's eyes had never left Kaitlin's face—even when she'd pointed at her Bible or read. He took a deep breath and stood. Kate's heart sank as he moved to the door and she exchanged a confused glance with Marcail.

But Joey stopped on the threshold. "Thank you for cutting my hair and thank you for explaining about Jesus. It's not what I thought it was. I gotta go."

Kate was left with those cryptic words and an anguished heart. *How silly you are, Kaitlin,* she said to herself. *To think that the moment he heard the gospel he'd be jumping out of his seat to know Christ. It doesn't always happen that way and you know it.*

Kate prayed and tried to reason with herself but it wasn't working. Tears were just beneath the surface and when Rigg showed up at the door, they overflowed.

He stood for a moment and watched the woman he loved sob into her hands and then he glanced at Marcail. She answered his unasked question.

"Joey was here and Katie witnessed to him and then he just walked out. He seemed so interested and then he thanked her for telling him and left."

Rigg went over and hunkered down beside Kate's chair. "It's all right Katie. You're forgetting the verses in 1 Corinthians 3, where it says that some plant the seeds and some water, but God gives the increase. You remember those."

"I know but I just thought—" Kate was choked up all over again and then felt terrible. "I have no business crying," she sobbed. "It's just my pride. I wanted to see it happen today. He's only been coming here for a week." Even as Kate reasoned with herself, she continued to cry. Rigg reached for her hand and looked to Marcail for help.

"Katie cries easier when she's tired."

"I do not," Kate denied, having heard the softly spoken words.

"She says that too," Marcail stated logically and Rigg's hand came up to rub at his upper lip. Kate, whose tears were abating, saw the movement and scowled at him. The fierce look was spoiled when she sniffed. Rigg grinned at her.

"I came down to see if you'd trim my hair. Sean didn't mention that I'd need an ark." Kate pulled her hand from his. With an indignant toss of her head she wiped her face on the handkerchief he offered her.

"Thank you," she said after a moment, and began to look truly embarrassed. Rigg was immediately sensitive.

"We'll keep praying, Kaitlin," he assured her softly and she thanked him with grateful eyes.

"Did you really want your hair trimmed?"

"If you would."

Kate nodded and Marcail came around to sit in front of Rigg so they could talk. Kate was quiet, her mind on Joey.

She continued to pray as she cut Rigg's hair and an idea came to mind. She decided to keep it to herself for the moment; tonight they were headed out to the Taylors'—that might be the time to mention her idea.

forty-six

That Saturday afternoon Kate and Marcail made their way to the mercantile. Kate hadn't worked that day and even though she enjoyed her day off, it felt a little strange to go into the store where she earned her living.

Kaitlin bought the needed spices for the fish dinner she would prepare at Taylors' Sunday evening. Then she and Marcail waited for Rigg and Sean to close the store so they could all go out together.

May's first comment when she saw the riders in the wagon was praise that both Rigg and Sean had been to the barber.

"Katie cut it," Rigg informed her and May looked at her in surprise.

"I don't suppose you'd care to cut three more heads tonight?"

"Sure," Kate answered with a smile. "But only if they're willing."

"Oh, I can see to it that they're very willing," May joked. "I'll tell them that they won't get fed unless they agree to line up in front of your scissors right after supper."

The first to sit quietly for her hair-cutting skills was Nate. She could see that he was not against the idea, but neither was he jumping for joy.

Once May and Bill had taken care of the dishes, they joined the family on the front porch. When Nate headed

233

in for his bath, Gil took his place. His hair was very thick and lay nicely when cut. He told Kate he liked his a little longer in the front and she was careful to do as he asked.

Kaitlin felt like she was cutting the same head of hair twice when Jeff sat in the chair; it was so like Gil's. Thick and medium brown in color, it had just enough wave to make it a dream to cut and shape.

"Have you always cut Sean's hair, Katie?" May wanted to know.

"No," she answered softly as she finished with Jeff. "Mother usually cut Sean's and Father's hair. She showed me what to do but I can't say as I've had much experience."

"You've had some practice though," Sean commented from his place on the edge of the porch. Kate laughed and Sean explained.

"Mother first showed Katie when she was 17. She was pretty proud of her new skill and decided to practice on Marc and me. Well, my hair had been cut just a few weeks before but she badgered me into sitting for her. I looked like a skinned rabbit when she was done." Everyone laughed, including Kaitlin who was sweeping the porch.

"What happened to Marc?" Rigg asked. All three of the Donovans laughed and then Kate answered.

"I didn't have to coax Marcail—she wanted her hair cut. I thought it would be so simple to just brush it out and cut straight across the bottom—only I didn't cut so straight. I kept getting one side shorter and then I'd have to cut the other side to make it even. We figured that I'd cut about a foot before I knew I had to stop."

"A foot?" Rigg was incredulous and reached over to touch Marcail's hair. He turned her until her back was to Kaitlin. "So it was up to here?" Rigg's hand was almost to Marcail's neck.

"Marc's hair wasn't as long as it is right now. I had her hair above her shoulders."

"What did your parents say?"

"Mother was very understanding but Father wanted to punish me. Mother talked with him; she felt I had tried my best and that I'd probably learned my lesson."

"Mother was always understanding," Sean said quietly. "Remember my boat?" Kate and Marcail both nodded.

"When I was nine my dream was to have a boat. I was going to paddle around the island with a friend and prove to my parents I could take care of myself.

"My friend and I worked hard on that boat, all in secret. The day before we were to set off, two younger boys found our hiding place and took the boat quite a ways offshore. They nearly drowned when the boat capsized in the rough surf.

"I was punished but not as severely as Father wanted. Again, Mother said I'd learned my lesson. She was right."

"I never learned my lesson," Marcail admitted, and her siblings laughed at her.

"What Marcail is trying to say is that she was punished regularly. I'm afraid Loni was not always a good influence on Marc." Kate smiled at her sister before she went on, "along with the fact that Loni's mother is dead, so there was very little adult supervision at their house. But I think even Marc would admit that Mother was always fair."

"She was," Marcail said in a small voice as a tear slid down her cheek. Kate beckoned and Marcail moved away from Rigg and into her arms. Kate talked as she held her sister close.

"I remember when Sean was born. Mother had been so sure it was another girl and they hadn't settled on any boys' names. 'You're kidding me!' Father said when he found out. He actually went and checked under the blanket before he believed that they'd actually had a boy." Kate chuckled and went on.

"And then the name! Father was sure that Mother wanted to name the baby after her father and Mother was sure that Father wanted to name Sean after him and his father. It was a mess. But Mother was adamant and so Sean is Patrick Sean the third.

"Father only agreed, if Mother would name the next little boy after her father. And lo and behold it was a girl! So Marcail is named after her maternal grandmother."

"Remember the surprise party for Father's thirty-fifth birthday?" Sean said with a laugh. "It was a fiasco. Everything that could go wrong, did!"

"You see," Kaitlin picked up the story, "Mother's and Father's birthdays are only two days apart. That year Father's was on Friday and Mother's on Sunday. The logical day to celebrate was Saturday and our parents decided to have surprise parties for each other on the same day. We knew about all the plans but we couldn't say a word. The other family that was helping us plan stayed quiet and made it a dual celebration.

"I remember when we all walked down to the beach to the big luau. Everyone yelled *surprise* and Mother turned to Father and said, 'You don't look surprised.' And he said, 'Why should I be, I planned all of this.' I've never seen my parents laugh so hard."

The last word was said on a sob and Kate buried her face against Marcail's hair. Her body shook and Sean went to join his sisters. They sat huddled together crying and talking in soft Hawaiian. The Taylors stayed on the porch, not intruding, but showing concern with their presence.

Rigg thanked God for their emotional display. He knew from talking to Sean that with their busy schedules and uncertain future, this family hadn't taken time to discuss their mother's death—at least not since arriving in town.

"I can't believe she's really gone. I mean, I know that we'll see her again but I want to see her *now*." The words were Sean's and Kaitlin felt Marcail shudder against her. She didn't want to stifle their grief but it did no good to concentrate solely on their mother's absence.

"At least we know we will see her." Kate's voice was choked as she tried to stop crying. "And she's not suffering anymore like she did with the tuberculosis. I read that it could have gone on for years. God was merciful to take her so quickly."

Kate's words, after a time, had the desired effect and the children's conversation turned to their father—how he was and when they would see him again. The tears eventually stopped and Kate prayed aloud for their Father. She asked God to deliver their letters to him safely and to let them hear soon how he was doing.

The evening was growing long and Kate sent Marcail to have her bath. Rigg and Sean were getting ready to leave when Kate turned to May and Bill with a question.

"I really appreciate the way you let us come every weekend and how at home you make us feel. But this is still your house so don't be afraid to say no to the question I want to ask you."

Bill and May looked at one another and then back at Kaitlin.

"May I invite Mr. Parker and Joey to our fish dinner tomorrow night?"

forty-seven

The only sound was the evening breeze rustling the leaves. Nate, Gil and Jeff were all finished with their baths, so the only person not staring at Kate was Marcail, who was still in the bathtub.

Kaitlin's face began to heat and she was about to apologize for her question but instead her chin came out with steel determination.

"Like I've said, you've always made us feel so comfortable and I don't want to take advantage of that. I've prayed about inviting Mr. Parker to my little house in town . . ." Kate halted when Rigg came abruptly to his feet.

"*But*," she went on, looking straight at him, "I know that would be improper and not a good testimony. I feel so strongly that we're—I should say *I'm*—to have some type of outreach to this family. Right now I can't think of any other way to get close to them." Kate went on and briefly explained what had transpired that morning with Joey and how badly she wanted to keep the door open for further witnessing.

The group fell silent once again. When the silence became too heavy, Kate excused herself to check on her sister; fighting the tears that threatened.

Marcail needed help rinsing her hair and Kate was thankful for the diversion. She decided not to go back to the porch and, after she settled Marcail into bed, she prepared her own bath. The steam rising around her did wonders toward relaxation and this time she didn't try to stop the tears.

"Oh, Lord," she prayed, "I really believed they would share this burden with me. I know they don't like Mr. Parker but You love him and You've given me a love for his soul and Joey's. I can't do this by myself. Please Lord," she sobbed, "show me what You would have me do."

Kate would have put her head beneath the water if she knew that Bill was lingering outside the door, allowing him to hear her prayer. He'd come to tell her that she could invite whomever she wanted, anytime. But he was doing so with a reluctant heart.

He leaned against the wall a moment and then went back to tell his family that they needed to support Kate with their whole hearts. He prayed for a miracle in his own heart; a miracle that needed to take place between now and supper-time the following night, when he would face Parker.

❑ ❑ ❑

"Do you mean it? They said I could ask them over?"

"That's what they decided. I know they felt bad when you didn't come back last night. That's why I'm up here this morning." Sean spoke from his place on Marcail and Kate's bed where he'd thrown himself upon entering the room.

He and Rigg had arrived early, as they usually did, and Bill told them that Kate hadn't come back out, even after they'd left. Sean volunteered to go up and talk to Kate.

"That's wonderful," Kate said softly, silently thanking God for His provision. It took a moment for her to realize that her legs were falling asleep from the knee down.

"Sean, you're putting my legs to sleep."

Sean shifted and they talked for a bit longer before Kate shooed him away so she and Marcail could get ready for church.

As soon as she sat down to breakfast Rigg asked her how she planned to invite Parker and Joey.

"If Joey's at church this morning, I'll ask him then. If not I'll walk over when the boys go fishing."

Rigg's eyes held hers for a moment and Kate remembered his words outside the barn when he'd threatened not to take Joey home. Kate was the first to lower her eyes and defeat washed over her. She didn't want to fight everyone over this; she wanted to think that someone was behind her, otherwise she would doubt her wisdom of getting involved at all.

Kate decided not to ask anyone to accompany her. There were enough men at the table to overhear Rigg's question and if someone wanted to go with her they could just offer. Otherwise, she'd made a promise not to go alone—

The incomplete thought hung in Kate's head and she found herself praying that Joey would be at church so she could ask him and simplify the whole matter. But Joey was nowhere to be seen.

Rigg didn't miss the way Kate reluctantly walked to his wagon for a ride to church. Or, after arriving and taking a seat, the way she looked toward the door time and again, for a glimpse of Joey Parker.

Rigg was learning about relationships. It was obvious to him, in a way it hadn't been before, that even if he and Kate were married, she would still have a mind of her own.

It had seemed to him as he was growing up, that his parents never quarreled about anything. But as he got older, he observed expressions and eye movements which spoke volumes. His parents didn't disagree in front of him or his brothers, but he would never have gone so far as to say it didn't happen behind their closed bedroom door.

And now this thing with Joey Parker. Rigg had no right to tell Kate no, nor was he sure he wanted to. He didn't own her and wouldn't own her even if they were married. But at least if they were married he'd have free rein to go to her the night before and talk about the question with which she'd surprised them. As it was, his father had gone and that was as it should have been. But that didn't stop his frustration, knowing Kate left with things so unsettled and him not able to change that in any way.

Gil, Nate and Sean went fishing as scheduled, just after lunch. Marcail wanted to play in the barn and Kate went with her. Marcail had just disappeared up the ladder to the hayloft when Rigg entered.

Kate was trying very hard to hide her disappointment and believed she was succeeding nicely. Rigg didn't let on that he could read her like a book.

"Have you ever been in a hayloft?"

"No, I guess I haven't."

"Go on up."

"No, I'm fine right here."

"Too prim and proper?" It was clearly a challenge; one that Kaitlin couldn't resist as Rigg stepped lightly up the ladder and then stood above looking at her. He watched as she grasped the ladder with both hands and began to climb. Rigg immediately dropped to his stomach to reach for her and in a few seconds Kate gasped when she found herself standing in hay up to her knees. Rigg still had hold of her arms and walked her away from the edge.

"Hi Katie, isn't this fun?" Marcail was rolling and hopping around, basically having the time of her life and all Kaitlin could do was stare.

She watched birds fly back and forth to their nests in the rafters and felt the temperature contrast from below.

The aroma was wonderful and Kate breathed deeply and took a step. A second later she was flat on her face and could hear Rigg's laughter as he stood above her.

Kate rolled and threw a handful of hay at him but it only blew back in her own face, causing Rigg to laugh all the harder.

"Are you going to help me up or laugh all day?" Kate's voice was indignant. Rigg came down on his knees beside her and helped her to a sitting position.

His voice was soft as he pulled bits of straw from her hair. "Still upset with me?" Kate believed the question related to that morning and not the present. She was right.

"Not upset, just disappointed."

"Why didn't you ask me to take you to the Parkers'?"

"I wanted you to offer. I wanted to feel like someone cared as much as I do."

Rigg was quiet a moment and then sat down facing her. He leaned one hand across her and rested it in the hay so he could bring his face very close.

"I believe the caring is coming but it will never equal the way I care about you. You're so innocent and you talk about going over to the Parkers' as if you're going to see your grandmother. It's not the same. I fear for your safety because you don't. Do you understand what I'm saying to you, Kaitlin?"

Kate nodded. "I won't go if you don't want me to."

Rigg knew what it cost her to say that and his eyes became so tender and loving Kate feared she might be kissed again. She wasn't sure she was ready for that. Rigg's hand came up and with one finger he touched her chin.

"Such a stubborn chin." His voice was loving and Kate watched as his head lowered.

"Katie!" Marcail called and Rigg stopped, his eyes on Kate's.

"I forgot she was up here," he said with a half smile, his voice soft.

"I'm kind of glad she is," Kate answered and grinned at him.

Marcail plopped down in the hay next to Rigg and Kate a moment later. "Look at this." She held the fragile half of an eggshell within her cupped hands, holding it carefully for their inspection.

"What kind is it?"

"Barn swallow," Rigg answered promptly. "We found them all the time as kids."

"Katie!" Marcail said suddenly. "You've got hay all over you!" Clearly the nine-year-old had never seen her sister in such a state.

"Is Katie always so prim and proper then?" Rigg couldn't resist his standing joke.

"Tell him no, Marcail," Kate ordered, but the little girl just smiled.

"Let's go down now so I can show Mrs. Taylor my egg."

"All right but first I want Kate to do something that would *not* be considered prim and proper."

Kate could feel her temper rise. "That's ridiculous. I am not too prim and proper."

Kate rose ungracefully and started toward the ladder but Rigg was faster. He climbed down and stood on the ladder with the upper part of his body showing up in the loft. Marcail was trying to keep from laughing and Kate faced him, arms akimbo.

"I need to get down," she stated.

"Just as soon as you prove to me that you can throw off your 'schoolteacher cloak.' "

"That's ridiculous."

"What shall we have her do, Marc, sing off-key?" Marcail found this highly amusing and couldn't hold her laughter even when Kate's eyes narrowed in her direction.

"Sing us a song Katie," Rigg directed.

"No!" Kate was beginning to see the humor in this and a smile was breaking across her face as she came toward the ladder but Rigg could not be bluffed. She plopped down before the ladder and tried to muster up a glare.

"I'm a man with infinite patience, Kate-love. Sing us a song and you can have the ladder."

Marcail laughed again and Kate could see Rigg wasn't going to budge. She threw back her head and crowed out the silliest song she could think of. Her voice screeched and cracked, causing Marcail to howl with laughter and Rigg to beg her to stop.

"Are you satisfied now?" Kaitlin demanded.

All Rigg could do was laugh.

"Hello."

May's voice came to the three in the loft and Kate and Marcail both leaned slightly over the edge to see her.

"Is everything all right?" Her tentative question started the laughter all over again as they made their way to the ground.

"Your son thinks I'm too stuffy for my own good and I was proving to him otherwise. Oh! Marc, did you bring your egg?"

Marcail displayed her prize once again and then May surprised them all with a question to Kate.

"I was wondering, Kate, if you'd like me to walk with you to the Parkers', so we can ask them to supper tonight?"

forty-eight

Rigg stared at his mother, completely nonplussed. He almost asked if Dad knew what she was planning, something he'd never even thought of saying to her before.

"I can see you're surprised and I don't want you to think I'm going behind your father's back. If Katie says yes, then I'll ask Bill to take us in the wagon. If Katie declines, I'll tell Jeff he's to escort her." May looked almost sternly at her son.

"You've bullied her about this Rigg, and I don't like it. I can understand your anxiety but you need to talk with her, not stomp on her hopes with your disapproving looks."

Kate found herself wishing she'd stayed in the haymow. She told herself she'd made a terrible mistake which had caused May and Rigg to have words. Marcail was equally as uncomfortable and tried to stand as unobtrusively as possible behind Kate. Kaitlin, with Marcail behind her, inched carefully toward the door, not wanting to disturb the conversation between mother and son. But just when she thought the way was clear, Rigg reached for her.

"Is that the way you feel?" His hand was on her upper arm and she could see there was no escape.

"Come along Marcail," Kate heard May saying and glanced over to see them exiting the barn.

245

"Do you Katie? Do you feel I stomp on your dreams?" Rigg's gaze was as intense as his voice.

Kate sighed. How could she explain all the emotions that were swirling around inside of her? She wasn't sure, but she needed to try.

"Rigg, how would you feel if you brought a girl home to your family and told them you wanted to marry her and they were not the least bit comfortable with her? I mean, they didn't warm up to her at all. Wouldn't you wonder if you'd made the right choice? Wouldn't you begin to question your heart—no matter how right things might have seemed at one time?

"Well, that's the way it is with Joey and his dad. I really believe that I'm supposed to reach out to them, but if none of you feel the same way, then I need to rethink my stand. If I was a man or my father were here, it would be different.

"But I'm not a man and I don't have a husband or a father to make going there all right. So if all of you, my closest friends in Santa Rosa, are against this, then for now at least, I have to assume the door is closed. But that doesn't change my heart or my prayers that Joey and his father will come to Christ.

"And now this, today. I've caused you to have words with your mother and that can't possibly be of the Lord. So I think I'd better drop the whole thing before I cause any more problems." Rigg watched Kate's shoulders sag and was overcome with guilt.

"Thank you for telling me how you feel. I owe you an apology, Kate. You didn't cause Mom and me to quarrel; I needed to hear what she had to say. The caring is coming but I'm more concerned for you. Where Parker is concerned I probably overreact. I mean, he'd be coming here to eat and you couldn't be more safe."

"Then you'll take me?" Kate was truly surprised.

"Right now, if you're ready."

"What brought on the change?"

"It's not as sudden as it seems but we've had no time to talk. Those verses in 1 Thessalonians really spoke to me. I've read them over and over and I can't say I've been faithful in the way I reach out to the unsaved in Santa Rosa. And when I have reached out, it was to someone easy, not someone of whom I was suspicious.

"Paul says the people he worked with were 'dear to him' and that's what I've been asking God for in my own heart. A deep compassion that would make Parker and Joey dear to me. As I've said, it's coming."

Kate was so relieved she felt tears sting her eyes. Why hadn't they talked like this a week ago?

"Thanks Rigg," was all she said and he smiled at her before turning to hitch up the wagon.

❑ ❑ ❑

Joey was the first to spot the wagon and Frank, having recognized Kate, didn't bother to bark.

"Hi Joey!" Kate called, and the little boy came close to the wagon to talk with her.

"My pa liked my hair cut." He smiled and Kaitlin was amazed at how he'd blossomed in the week he'd been coming to see her. Their conversation of the morning before came to mind and Kate prayed for an opportunity to question Joey.

"Is your dad here, Joey?"

"Not right now." Joey's look became uncertain and Kate hurried to explain.

"Tonight?" Joey asked. "For supper? Both of us?"

"Right. We're having a fish dinner and you should be at the Taylors' about six. Don't forget to tell your dad."

When the wagon pulled away, Kate looked back to see Joey waving furiously. She returned the wave feeling absolutely buoyant.

The guys had returned from their fishing spot up the creek with their creels overflowing. Marcail was an old hand at the procedure and she and Kate enlisted the help of Rigg and Jeff. Kaitlin wanted to do this for May so she sent Bill and May on a walk.

The men stood back and watched the girls attack the fish on the back porch. The fish were cleaned in record time and then cut in perfect strips. Neither one was the least bit squeamish and the job was done neatly and efficiently.

The men, sure they were being pressed into service to clean the fish, were fascinated. Once the fillets were ready, Rigg and Kate worked together over a bowl of what Kaitlin said held secret ingredients. When the fish had been dipped, Jeff was put to work frying.

"What is that for?" The question came from Rigg who was watching Kate prepare May's large roaster to go into the oven.

"This recipe is best when the fish can bake after they've been fried. It also gives us time to finish the rest of the meal."

"Us?" Rigg and Jeff chorused.

"Of course," Kate stated with absolute calm. "Rigg, you can start the rice and when you're done at the stove Jeff, you can shred that lettuce. Marc and I will fix this sauce and cut up the rest of the vegetables."

"Marc," Rigg asked, wanting to know, "has she always been this bossy?"

"Don't you answer that Marcail Donovan!" her sister warned. "It could get you into a lot of trouble."

Rigg gave Marcail a conspiratorial wink and a giggle escaped before she could stop it.

The table was set with two extra places and Kate fluttered around in a nervous dither as six o'clock drew near. The smell of fish wafted its way through the house and if Nate said he was hungry once, he said it a half-dozen times.

Kaitlin had been pacing the living room when she glanced out the window and froze. Tears filled her eyes as she watched Joey walking beside his father toward the house. Bill came out of his chair and gave Kate's cheek a kiss before going to greet their guests. May smiled and followed her husband.

"Use this Kate," Rigg held his handkerchief out to Kaitlin. She quickly wiped her face.

"How do I look?"

"Beautiful," Rigg answered sincerely.

"No, really, do I look all right?"

"You look fine." Rigg shook his head at how satisfied she was with the word fine but Kate didn't notice. She was headed to the kitchen to check on supper.

"Katie fixed supper tonight. Come on in and find a seat." It was Bill's voice coming from the living room as he led Parker to the kitchen where Kate stood by the table.

"Hello Mr. Parker."

His head bobbed in her direction and before too many minutes passed the whole family was seated and Bill was returning thanks for the food. The meal passed in mild pandemonium with everyone talking at once, or so it seemed.

Kate's cooking was a great success and she was complimented many times over. She acknowledged those compliments absently because she couldn't take her eyes off Parker. His manners were impeccable. He'd brushed his hair away from his face and buttoned his shirt to the neck. Kate had fully expected him to eat as Joey had the first night, but other than his hands shaking occasionally, his manners were flawless.

And he was talking! He sat to Bill's right and the two men conversed like old friends. Parker declined dessert and he and Joey didn't linger long after dinner.

Kate wanted to hug May when she extended an invitation to join them again for the following Friday night. Parker accepted graciously and then he and Joey took their leave.

Kate felt emotionally and physically drained. She was drying the dishes that Gilbert washed but she kept coming to a stop in the middle of the kitchen and staring at the dish in her hand without really seeing it.

"Are you all right?"

"What?" Kate had finally heard Gil's question.

"If you're tired Katie, I can do this," he offered kindly.

"No, I can help you." Kaitlin wasn't aware of how her every movement and even her voice, spoke of how exhausted she was.

"You must be glad that the Parkers came." Gil watched in helpless surprise as tears filled Kate's eyes.

"I am glad Gilbert. I can't think why I would need to cry about it."

"I think I understand." Gil looked with desperation at his mother who entered the kitchen just then.

"Why don't I help?" May said cheerfully.

"You don't need to." Kate's voice caught as she continued to dry the dish she'd had in her hand for five minutes. May didn't answer, recognizing her fatigue and praying that Rigg would come in and rescue her.

He did just that a few minutes later. Marcail was staying the night because Sean had to work in the morning and Rigg, as gently as he could, shepherded Kate to the wagon.

Kate didn't know when anything had felt as wonderful as crawling into her bed. She fell asleep before she could thank God for the tender hearts of the Taylors and that He was still holding the door to Joey Parker wide open.

forty-nine

The clock in Rigg's office on Monday morning read eight forty-five and Rigg debated what to do; Kaitlin was late. He'd half expected her to be late because of her weary state the night before, but there was the remote chance she was not well and for that reason, Rigg couldn't rest. He stood up, having decided to go check with Sean when he saw her rush through the front doors.

She was flustered and apologetic when she arrived in the office but she also looked well rested. Rigg told her that her rest was important and that he wasn't at all upset. Kate didn't believe him and continued to apologize and berate herself.

"All right," he said quietly. "You're docked a day's pay."

Kate halted and stared at him. He was dead serious and she told herself she'd asked for it.

"Do you feel better now?" Rigg asked quietly and Kate felt like an utter fool.

"Katie," his voice was gentle and without rebuke. "I tease you at times but I think you'll agree that I've never played games with you. I also know you well enough to know that you take your job seriously. I *really* don't mind your being late."

"Thank you." Kaitlin's cheeks were still heated. Thankfully Rigg had work to do downstairs and Kate was given a chance to calm herself.

Her pride had been involved this morning and it had made a fool of her. She'd been horrified to awaken and see how late the hour was and rather then come in and apologize, she'd carried on until she forced Rigg to threaten her. She didn't think he would dock her but she had no business backing him into a corner that way.

Kaitlin prayed and was able to put the incident behind her. She could feel that she and Rigg were getting closer to one another every day but that didn't change the fact that he was her boss and he had a business to run. She told herself that starting immediately she was going to show new respect to him.

Kate was making fast work of the account books for the year and Rigg was pleased with her progress. The morning flew by and Bill came over to say he'd treat at the hotel. Kate popped into the post office and found a letter from Scott Harper in Hawaii. She tucked it away to read after work.

Sean surprised Rigg and Kate by offering to fix supper that night, so as soon as he was finished with his work he left for home. Rigg had some last minute things to do, so Kaitlin passed the time by reading her letter. She sat on a bench by the back door, knowing Rigg would want to go home that way.

Dear Kaitlin,

Hawaii has not been the same since you left. I told myself that I would not carry on in this letter about the way I miss you. At the same time, I want you to know that it took a while for me to accept that you're not coming back. I still think of you every day.

The work here prospers and we're thankful to have your father with us, even temporarily. So much damage occurred during the hurricane that I believe God must have known we would need him. In spite of the losses there is a bright side, and I'm talking about the hearts of the people. History repeats itself and it's exciting to see the revival that has begun in the wake of this disaster. Please continue to pray for us.

When I asked for your address I was surprised that you're no longer in San Francisco. Why aren't you? I thought you were living with your aunt?

I hope you'll write to me but I'll understand if you don't. I'm praying this finds you well. My folks send their love and please tell Sean and Marcail I said hello.

As ever,
Scott

Kate had effectively put Percy out of her mind for weeks. There was no one here like him and that certainly helped. But the guilt she felt, that she had somehow been the cause for the way he'd treated her, continued to plague her. And now, a simple question in Scott's letter brought the whole ugly episode back to mind as though it were happening all over again.

A shiver ran over Kaitlin when she remembered the way Percy had pulled her toward him. Her hand went to her throat when she pictured the way his head had bent toward her before Sean's words had stopped him.

"Katie?" Rigg's voice caused Kate to start violently and then pull away from the hand Rigg had placed tenderly on her arm. She looked up into his confused face and thought she could never explain. He wouldn't want anything to do with her if he knew.

"Katie," Rigg questioned her perceptively, "what is in that letter you just read? Is your father hurt?"

"No."

"Your aunt?"

"No. No one, I'm just—" *Just what?* Kate asked herself, knowing that Rigg was waiting for an answer to his question.

Rigg watched the emotions run over Kate's face. He was glad they were still inside the store because he had the strong impression she was about to run from him. After a short period of silence Rigg spoke softly.

"Who is the letter from?"

"Scott."

"Who lives in Hawaii?"

Kate didn't even hear his question.

"He wanted to know why we aren't living in San Francisco." Kate hadn't meant to say that out loud.

If Rigg had been unaware of the reason she'd left San Francisco he'd have had no idea why Scott's question was so upsetting. As it was, he believed he knew exactly what was going through Kate's mind.

"Katie, there's something I want you to know. Sean told me why you left your aunt's." Rigg's words, though gently spoken, had a traumatic effect on Kaitlin. Most of the color drained from her face and her eyes dilated with hurt and betrayal.

"He had no right." The words were choked out.

"He needed to talk. He was very upset about your cousin's actions and didn't think it had bothered you very much. He didn't feel he could come to you."

"He didn't think it bothered me?" Kate was astounded.

"That's what he said."

"I guess Sean's never done anything he's ashamed of or he would know why I never brought it up."

"Kaitlin." Rigg's voice was tenderness itself. "You have *nothing* to be ashamed of."

"I must have encouraged him." Tears filled her eyes and Rigg felt something akin to violence for this faceless cousin who haunted the woman he loved.

"Katie, that's simply not true. You're a beautiful woman but that gives no man the right to touch you against your will."

Kate continued to fight her tears even as a single question haunted her.

"How long have you known?"

"Since the first night Sean stayed with me," he admitted quietly.

Humiliation washed over her anew to think that Rigg had known all along about Percy. And then another question came to mind and Rigg watched a look of horror cover Kate's face.

"Who have you told?"

"No one." Rigg uttered the words softly, almost to himself, and Kate shook her head as though to clear it.

"I didn't mean that. I'm sorry."

"Let's go to the house. You and Sean need to talk and I think I would like to be there if no one has any objections."

❑ ❑ ❑

Kate wondered how she got through the meal Sean fixed. The food looked wonderful but everything tasted like sawdust in her mouth. Sean noticed how quiet his sister and Rigg were and wondered, as they all worked on the dishes, if they'd quarreled.

Sean didn't know what to do with Kaitlin anymore. Didn't she know Rigg was in love with her? Didn't she see what a nice guy he was? He told himself that when he found the right girl, he was just going to tell her outright that they had to get married, then and there. None of this unsureness for him; none of this tiptoeing around in order not to scare her away.

Sean had worked himself into a tumult of emotions when Rigg spoke and brought him abruptly back to earth.

"Kate and I were talking before we left the store, Sean, and I think she needs to share with you what we talked about."

It was an awkward beginning but Rigg felt all of this should have been said long ago. Awkward or not, it was time to get their feelings out in the open.

"I got a letter from Scott today, Sean."

"Is Father all right?" Sean came completely out of his chair and Kate was quick to reassure him.

"Yes, I'm sorry I scared you." Kate waited until Sean was reseated and then went on. "The letter wasn't about Father and Scott didn't say anything upsetting, but he did ask me why we weren't in San Francisco.

"It made me start thinking and—" Kate couldn't go on so Rigg spoke up.

"When I came down and found Katie so upset I asked her about the letter. I then told her that I knew why you had left your aunt's. She told me she thinks the whole thing is her fault."

"Oh Katie, no! It's *my* fault." A look of near desperation crossed Sean's face and tears came to his eyes. The agony he felt on that day began to crowd in on him all over again.

"Sean, that's not true," Kate told him urgently. "I've never blamed you. And I didn't know until Rigg said something that you were that upset by what happened." Kate's voice faded on these last words. Brother and sister stared at each other. After a time Sean moved next to Kaitlin who sat on the sofa. Kate put her head against Sean's arm and sobbed. Through her tears she shared every awful thing she'd been feeling. From feeling badly about leaving Aunt Maureen to wishing she had no figure at all to be attracted to.

Rigg entered into the conversation when he felt a need and even though both Donovans were completely spent in the process, an hour later all was out in the open.

There was no longer any guilt between them or even anger toward their selfish cousin. The three of them would probably have talked all night if Kate hadn't noticed the time.

"We've got to get Marc."

"I can go get her," Rigg offered. Sean thanked him and said he would stay home, but Kate said she was in need of some air and went with him in the wagon. Rigg knew that she'd had a painful evening but there was one thing he needed to know. As the wagon moved toward his folks the setting sun bathed them in an orange glow. He couldn't think of a better time or place to ask her.

fifty

"I want to thank you Rigg, for giving Sean and me the push we needed to start talking. I don't know if we ever would have and, well, just thanks."

"You're welcome. I'm sorry it was so hard for you. I'll be praying that God continues to heal the hurt for you Katie, and if you ever want to talk, just find me.

"I need to ask you something Kate." Rigg went on. "Would you rather I didn't question you tonight?"

"No, I don't mind."

"It's a couple of things actually. Do I remind you of your cousin Percy?"

"*No!*" Kate said so vehemently that Rigg couldn't hold his laughter, some of which was relief.

"Why did you ask that?" Kate inquired.

"Because I'm hoping we'll grow closer than we are now and if I remind you of Percy then I'm going to repulse you. I don't want to do that."

There, Rigg thought, *it's out in the open. You'll certainly know in the next few seconds if the door is still open with this woman or not.*

"You don't repulse me." The words were said so softly that Rigg almost missed them. But hear them he did and they gave him courage to ask his next question. He did so without looking at Kaitlin.

"I've also been wondering if I upset you when I kissed

you? I didn't ask your permission to do such a thing and I want to apologize if I need to."

"And it almost happened a second time." Kate's softly spoken words caused Rigg to finally look at her. She didn't return his gaze, giving Rigg a wonderful view of her profile. Rigg also didn't bother to correct her about how many times he'd *almost* kissed her, times when she'd been completely unaware of his intentions. Like when she brought the account books over for his inspection and he thought he would drown in the fresh smell of her hair. Or when they shared little moments, like doing the dishes together or how her face would flush with laughter over something he'd teased her about. But for right now it was best to leave those times unmentioned.

"I'm not upset with you about the kiss but I don't think I want you to do it again unless you give me a chance to tell you no." The words were said sweetly and without rebuke. Rigg felt as though a great burden had been lifted from his heart.

"I can appreciate that and I'll certainly honor your wishes."

My wishes, Kate thought, and almost laughed.

How many times had she wished Rigg would kiss her again or hold her in his arms? For a time she doubted that Rigg cared for her in a romantic way, but now she understood that he was taking his cue from her.

Maybe she *was* too stuffy for her own good because she just didn't know how to subtly let a man know she was interested in him. Once again Kate wished Mother or Father were here to talk with.

She thought of confiding in Aunt Maureen but didn't see how that was possible either. There was May—they had grown closer each weekend they stayed there. *But how did a woman ask the mother of the man she was interested in, how to show him—*

Kate couldn't even finish that thought. She realized that even if she had someone to ask, she wouldn't know the questions.

Marcail was picked up without fuss and Rigg was as sweet as ever when he delivered them home. Marcail had to fall asleep with the lantern burning because Kate was writing to Father.

Dear Father,

I wish you were here more than I can say. I've always been able to tell you how I feel and I won't hesitate now. I think I'm in love.

I say think, because I have no idea what it feels like to be in love. I was never one of those girls who spent much time daydreaming about the type of man I'd marry. I mean, I thought of it certainly, but just in passing. And then, wham, right out of the blue, I'm looking at Rigg in a whole new light.

At one time he made me furious every time we were together. But now I'm disappointed when he leaves and ecstatic when I know I'll see him again. He's so tender with me; and not just me but Sean and Marc too.

Now you're probably wondering how he feels about me and I can't honestly say that I know. He told me tonight that he hopes we'll become closer. Well, he can't mean physically because we work in the same office every day, sit together in church and I spend all my weekends at his folks', so I assume he means closer emotionally.

Was that the kind of thing you said to Mother, when you fell in love with her? I'm so confused. What if he does tell me he loves me before you return? I don't even know where you want to live when you come back, and what would I say to him?

Kate continued on in a frenzy of thoughts and nearly unintelligible print. She went on to tell her father that she believed Rigg to be a man of God and that her heart did funny things when he was near, even though sometimes she wanted to strangle him.

Kate ended the letter with news on Joey and pleas for prayer. She also asked her father to write back immediately and to come home soon, wherever home was.

When she finally went to bed, she fell asleep swiftly—but not before she asked God to speed her letter across the sea and thanked Him for sending her to Santa Rosa and to a man named Marshall Riggs.

fifty-one

The middle weeks of summer sped by and Kate waited anxiously for news from her father. Aunt Maureen had been in touch several times and reported that Uncle Mitch was back out to sea. Once again she was lonely. Kate had long ago replied to Scott's letter, carefully giving him no hope of a future relationship with her.

Mr. Parker and Joey came to supper at the Taylors' nearly every week and Joey also continued his visits with Kate from time to time. Kaitlin was to learn new meaning for the word patience, as no opportunity afforded itself to talk with the little boy about his need to trust in Christ for salvation.

Mr. Parker blossomed slowly under the tender ministrations of this family and they soon found that no one had ever made a move to help this man. In bits and pieces it came out that he was an orphan, abandoned when he was five. He lived with a number of different families until he was ten and the father of one household beat him until he couldn't stand up. The next day he took every dime of money he could find on the place and left. He'd been on his own ever since.

Parker never outright admitted it, but the Taylors were able to gather that he hadn't been married to Joey's mother. He also didn't know if she was dead or alive. They hadn't laid eyes on each other since Joey was nine months old.

But of all the things that Parker shared, Joey's words to Kaitlin one night were the most revealing.

"One morning," the little boy said, "the marshall came and took my Pa. Said he'd hurt a woman. But he didn't do that, Miss Donovan. I know because he'd been drinking and Pa can't hardly stand when he's been drinking, let alone go off in the woods and hurt somebody.

"He didn't leave home all day, I told them that. But they wouldn't listen and when he was in jail I was the most scared I'd ever been in my life. I hated staying by myself. Even if Pa's passed-out drunk, I want him there. When they kept him a second night I snuck into town and slept outside his jail window."

Kate had no words for the sober confession from this child. She put her arms around him and held him close. Joey clung to her and Kaitlin begged God with a renewed burden to use her in the life of the boy.

While Kate's relationship with Joey became stronger, the closeness she'd always shared with Sean began to wane. It was heartbreaking for her but she knew the steps from boyhood to manhood were awkward and confusing. Some things you couldn't share with your sister.

Kate and Marcail were as close as ever, but Kate found herself dealing with an unexpected well of emotions over Marcail's closeness to May. Kate's heart asked God if nine was young enough to forget your real mother. It seemed that every week Marcail was with May she became more her daughter and less Theresa Donovan's. What would Father say?

It wasn't that Kate didn't love May—quite the opposite—she thought the world of her. But she was also having to realize that a 20-year-old's need for a mother were quite different from a 9-year-old's.

And very recently, as with most things in Kaitlin's world, she had talked to Rigg about it. They had grown closer just as Rigg had hoped and there weren't many things they hadn't discussed. Sometimes in calm logic, other times at the tops of their voices.

The subject of Marcail was the most recent to come on the table and Rigg would never know how close Kate came to throwing her arms around him for his sensitivity.

It was Wednesday night. Rigg, Kate, Sean and Marcail were all walking home from mid-week service; Rigg's wagon was undergoing repairs at the livery. When they'd arrived at the church Marcail had gone immediately to May and wrapped her arms around the older woman's waist. To watch them you'd think they hadn't seen each other for days.

On the way home Rigg seemed almost pensive as he walked at Kate's side, Sean and Marcail far in front of them, kicking a can as they went.

"You're quiet," Kate commented.

"Just thinking."

"About?" Rigg was usually very open, giving Kate the freedom to ask without feeling an intruder.

"I was thinking about Marc and my mother and feeling rather thankful that your father can't see how little she seems to miss your mother."

Kate stopped Rigg with a hand on his arm. "Oh Rigg," she whispered, "I've agonized over this. Please don't get me wrong. I adore May. But I can't believe Marc has forgotten Mother. I tell myself that Mother isn't here and May is but it doesn't make it any easier and I don't dare say anything to Marc."

"Kaitlin, I wish you'd have come to me. I just noticed it this evening."

"I've been seeing it for a few weeks. And just this week when Sean and I both had to work, I told Marc to write to Father because May always has ink and paper handy. But when I picked her up she said she'd been too busy cleaning house with your mom.

"I'm trying to remember how young she is but—"

Kate shrugged helplessly and Rigg reached for her hand. They walked that way for a time and Kate reveled in the comfort she found in the simple act of having her hand swallowed up in Rigg's. They were both disappointed when Sean and Marcail stood still and waited for them to catch up, causing them to let go of each other's hands.

Once at the house Sean didn't wait around but headed straight for Rigg's. Marcail went in to ready for bed and Rigg lingered outside, as always, reluctant to leave Kaitlin.

"You haven't heard from your father lately, have you?"

"No. I'm expecting a letter soon though. I always pray when I send mine that God will speed it to him but I'm afraid service to the island usually takes a while. Why do you ask?"

"I guess I was just wondering if you'd ever mentioned me to your father and if you did, what he had to say?"

"I've written about you, yes," Kate replied carefully, remembering how in her last letter she'd told Father that she thought she loved this man. "But like I said, I'm waiting to hear from him now."

"Has your father ever mentioned where he wants to live once he returns?" The question was a study in casualness but Kate wasn't fooled.

"As a matter of fact, I brought that subject up in my last letter. Like I said I'm—"

"Waiting to hear," Rigg finished for her, his eyes on hers, serious and intent. "I hope you understand Kaitlin, I can't just let you walk away."

Kate understood very well but could find nothing to say in response. She watched Rigg step close and let him take her hand once again. They stood for a moment, enjoying one another without words. Finally Rigg gave her hand a small squeeze and spoke.

"Good night, Kate-love. I'll see you in the morning."

Kate was sure she could still feel his hand holding hers long after he'd disappeared into the dark.

fifty-two

"Did we really agree to do this?" Kaitlin asked Marcail as they readied for church the next Sunday.

"Yes, we agreed," Marcail informed her. "Katie, what are you so upset about? You've sung in church a million times."

"This is different."

"Why is it different?"

Because Rigg will be there, Kate thought, but didn't bother to voice that sentiment to her sister. Kate was certain she was going to go in front of that church and make a total fool of herself. Why, she'd never be able to face Rigg again!

Kate knew the minute she saw Sean that he was just as nervous as she. They exchanged an agonized glance and did little more than play with their breakfast.

It would have helped to be called to the front immediately after the service began, but there were announcements to be made and then the congregation sang a few songs. When the time finally came, Bill was not satisfied by just allowing Pastor Keller to call them forward. He went into the pulpit and introduced them as though they were a traveling band.

"I know all of you have had the privilege of meeting Kaitlin, Sean and Marcail Donovan, and probably most of you know that they grew up as missionary children in Hawaii. But I don't think many of you know that all three of them are fluent in Hawaiian. And this morning they've agreed to sing for us in that beautiful language."

On those words Kate, with her heart pounding and wishing they'd had some sort of accompaniment, led the way to the front. None of the Donovans realized how beautiful they sounded a cappella.

The song they shared was the same one they had sung for the Taylors many weeks ago and since it was short, they sang it through twice. Both Kate and Sean were nearly giddy with relief that it was over, when Pastor Keller jumped from his seat and asked them for more.

For a moment the two older Donovans stood frozen, their minds blank and then Marcail saved the day by suggesting another hymn. This happened two more times making a total of four songs and at one point, Kate remembered they were singing to the Lord. As she committed the lyrics to God along with her voice, all self-consciousness disappeared.

When they moved from the front back to their seats, Kate sat down next to Rigg. She didn't look at him but could feel his eyes on her. When he reached over and gave her hand a squeeze her whole being melted with relief. Kate smiled at Rigg with her heart in her eyes.

Pastor Keller began his sermon just after that. Kaitlin had been too uncomfortable up front to look beyond the second row or she would have seen Joey Parker sitting in the last church pew.

She did catch sight of him as they exited, disappearing around the corner of the church toward home. She nearly ran to intercept him and he stopped reluctantly. He looked at her with shy embarrassment.

"Hi Joey. Did you hear me sing?"

"Yeah. It was nice." He smiled at her and as always, Kate's heart turned over.

"I could teach you a song in Hawaiian sometime. Would you like that?"

"Yeah." Joey's face came alive with the idea but when Kate asked him if he wanted to come for lunch he stepped away from her, declining as he went.

Kaitlin watched him walk away, her heart heavy. He was so young to be fighting God but Kate was convinced this was exactly what he was doing. Pastor Keller had challenged everyone in the room that morning to settle their eternity before leaving. Kate was certain that if Joey had trusted in the Lord that morning, he'd have told her.

"You're quiet," Rigg commented as they drove toward his folks.

"I was thinking of Joey. I know God is speaking to that boy but he's fighting Him and making himself miserable in the process."

Rigg agreed with her and then told her he liked the songs she sang.

"Were we really all right?" Kate's hand went to Rigg's arm and he was suddenly conscious of his brothers in the back.

"You were great. Your voices harmonize beautifully. I almost hope for Sean's sake that his voice never changes. He's a great tenor."

"Poor Sean," Kate commented. "He thinks he sounds like a girl. He hates it."

"There's nothing feminine about the way Sean sings," Jeff commented from the back. "He has nothing to worry about."

"Unless it's the number of teenage girls who nearly fall out of their seats when he passes by," Gil commented almost absently, but Kaitlin's head whipped around in surprise. She never thought about girls finding her brother attractive. Sean was cute, or at least she'd always thought so, and now she was seeing for the first time that she wasn't alone in that belief.

"I can see Gil surprised you." Rigg was watching her and Kate felt her face heat up.

"It's hard to see your own brother in, well, that way," she admitted.

"We know what you mean, Katie," Jeff called forward. "We don't see how you can stand to spend so much time with Rigg."

"She must feel sorry for him because he's so homely," Gilbert added in a stage whisper.

"You can both be replaced you know," Rigg informed them. A giggle escaped Kaitlin but when Rigg turned to look at her she gave him the most innocent look she could muster.

"Are you going to tell me I can be replaced too?"

"No. I don't like to tell lies."

"Now would you listen to this!" Jeff said with disgust. "What do we have to do to get a little appreciation around here?"

"For one thing, it would help if you smelled better."

Everyone laughed at Jeff's expense but he took it well. They were still chuckling when they got home and found Burt Kemp waiting for Miss Donovan.

"I know I shouldn't be doing business on Sunday but I missed you at church. And truth is, I just heard that they need a schoolteacher over on the west-side of town and I didn't want them to steal you away from us."

All of these words had been directed at Kate as he'd helped her from the wagon. She now stood staring at Burt in confusion.

"Mr. Kemp, you'll have to forgive me, but I'm not sure what you're talking about."

"Why teaching in the fall of course." He smiled at Kate as though he'd just offered her a lifetime contract. That such a thing never occurred to Kate was clear by the look on her face.

"Is there some reason you don't want to come back and teach at our school?" Some of Burt's enthusiasm drained away and he rushed on to sell Kaitlin on the idea.

"Oh, I know there was that whole mess with your salary, but Greg is sorry about that and you would be hired full-time at full pay. And if you don't like the dates we've picked for school to begin and end, we could certainly discuss that."

Rigg could see that Burt was prepared to go on all day. May and Bill were now on the scene and Rigg was thankful when his father interrupted.

"It looks like Kate needs to think on this, Burt. I don't think you need to worry about her going across town though."

Kate agreed with a smile, even as her mind raced. What if Father came back in the fall and wanted to move away? What if Rigg pressed his suit?

"Thanks Mr. Kemp, for checking with me but I'll need to pray about this and talk with Sean and Marcail."

"Oh certainly, Miss Donovan. I'm sorry if I was out of line in any way."

"Not at all. And I consider it a great compliment that you want me back." Kate was using her gift for making people feel at ease, something for which everyone was thankful.

Burt took his leave then and Kate went inside with May to fix lunch. The older woman noticed her house-guest's solemn look and commented on it.

"I know Burt didn't mean to upset you."

"I'm sure you're right May. But the truth is, I'm not sure what my father would want or if Rigg wants me to continue on the books through the fall."

"Or if he possibly had another job in mind for you, one a little more personal?" May said the words softly and Kate felt her lungs empty of air. She stared at her hostess for an instant and then busied her hands with potatoes. She tried to ignore the words she'd just heard, knowing as she did, that it was a mistake.

"How would you feel about that, May?" Kate asked

the question quickly before she could talk herself out of it.

"Oh, I'd probably rant and rave at him," May came close to Kate and smiled into her eyes, "and ask him why he took so long."

Kaitlin's jaw dropped in a most unfeminine way and May laughed. In the next instant the two women were hugging each other and laughing hard.

"Can I get one of those hugs?" Bill asked from the doorway and Kate watched in surprise, as May moved so that the table separated her and her husband. Bill's brows rose, telling her he'd accept her challenge if he had to.

"No hugging in front of the children," May stated as primly as she could and Bill laughed. She allowed him to close the distance then and Kate watched unashamedly as they embraced. When she did go back to working on lunch, she did so thanking God for the special family He'd sent her way.

fifty-three

Kaitlin and Marcail lay on their stomachs in the hay-mow looking out the loft door to the yard below. Lunch was over and the girls were feeling lazy. They heard movement behind them and a moment later Sean flopped down on Kaitlin's open side.

"Did Burt Kemp really ask you to teach again?" Sean wasted no time in asking the question that had been on his mind through lunch.

"Full salary."

"He did?" Marcail asked, wondering where she had been all the time this was going on.

"What will you do?" Sean wanted to know.

"You can't teach here in Santa Rosa, Katie. Father will probably want us to live with Aunt Maureen."

This was something she'd already thought of but hadn't bothered to mention to her sister.

"It would be easier to leave the mercantile than it would the school if Father came back," Sean stated logically. "But if you plan to make Santa Rosa your permanent home then you need to be discussing with Rigg where you should work."

Two in one day, Kate thought.

She wondered if Rigg had been telling people something that he should have discussed with her first.

You know better, Kaitlin, she immediately said to herself. *The way he feels about you is written on his face, for all the world to see.*

"I want us to be together," Marcail said after a moment.

Sean and Kaitlin would have been surprised if Marcail *hadn't* understood the gist of their conversation, so they made no pretense in front of her as they continued to talk.

"Marc," Sean began, "do you understand what's happening between Katie and Rigg?"

"They love each other."

"Right. And that's how it should be. We don't know when Father is coming back but we do know that until then, we'll be together. If Kate marries Rigg, and Father is still gone, then we'll still be here in Santa Rosa. She's not going to ship us off to San Francisco by ourselves. Isn't that right, Katie?"

"Right." Kate was relieved that that was all she had to say; it was all she *could* say.

"And you never know, Marc," Sean went on. "Maybe Father will like Santa Rosa enough to want to stay."

Marcail looked very satisfied and Kate put her face against Sean's shoulder to cover her tears. She couldn't stand the thought that Marcail would be hurt by her relationship with Rigg. The thought of being separated from her siblings, even if it meant a lifetime with Rigg, was more than she could deal with at the moment.

'Are you all right Katie?" Marcail asked softly.

'Yes."

'Katie, where would we live if you married Rigg?"

Kate's tears came harder and Sean kept still as she wet his shirt sleeve.

"You know," he said finally, "maybe we're jumping the gun here. He hasn't asked her—or has he, Kate?"

"No." Kate sniffed and then complained, "I don't know what's the matter with me these days. All I do is cry."

"That's okay," Sean said. "Rigg calls it a late reaction. As least that's what he said when I told him I hadn't cried much about Mother. He said sometimes we don't need to cry and then we find ourselves crying nonstop."

Sean was so sweet with Kate that she only felt worse and suddenly very tired. A few minutes later Rigg climbed up to join them and Sean eased away from his sister. Her head fell against her outstretched arm and for the first time Sean saw she was asleep.

Sean stood and looked down at her and then at Rigg. Whispering, he asked Marcail if she wanted to come, but she shook her head no. Rigg and Marcail watched him leave and then Rigg motioned for Marcail to join him where he sat against the barn wall.

"Was Katie crying?" Rigg immediately asked, still speaking in hushed tones.

"Yes she was. It almost made me cry too."

"That would have been okay," Rigg assured her.

"I don't like to cry, it makes my head hurt and sometimes I throw up." Her admission was so honest, her face so creased by her frown that Rigg couldn't help smiling. He adored this little girl.

"Tears aren't ever fun but they're sometimes very needed. Were Katie's needed?"

"I think so. Rigg, are you going to marry Katie?"

Rigg's eyes went to Kaitlin's sleeping form. He couldn't see her face but knew she was out cold. "I don't think it would be right to talk to anyone about that before I've talked with Katie. Do you know what I mean?"

"Yes." They fell silent again and then Marcail had another question. "Does the man always ask?"

"The girl to marry him, you mean?"

"Right. Can the girl ask the boy?"

"I guess so. It's tradition for the man to ask and from everything I've heard, most people like it that way."

"Do you?"

Rigg could see Kate stirring so he answered Marcail's question very softly. "I think when two people love each other, it doesn't matter who asks, just as long as they can be together." Marcail seemed content with that answer. She had more questions but Kate was stirring. They watched as she came slowly to a sitting position. Kaitlin blinked at Rigg and Marcail as if she were dreaming them.

"Hi Katie. How did you sleep?"

Kate didn't answer her sister; things were still too fuzzy. She continued to frown at them until Marcail giggled.

"Would you like to get down?" Rigg asked. "I can help you on the ladder." But again Kate didn't answer. She pulled her knees up and wrapped her skirt around herself. Once she had curled herself into a ball, she stared out the door at the trees.

"I dreamed that Father was back," Kate said softly. "He'd grown a beard and we didn't recognize him at first. I think I miss him more than ever." Marcail moved over to Kate and she drew her close.

Rigg's eyes met Kaitlin's over the top of Marcail's head and his look told Kate he was very aware of her pain. Quietly Kate began to talk, not reminiscing as they'd done on the front porch earlier, but about her fears. At first she held back, not wanting to upset Marcail, but Marcail shared a few of her own fears, surprising Kate with the intensity of her feelings.

Rigg listened attentively and spoke with tenderness, telling the girls how normal their fears were and how much he believed God was going to take care of their every need.

They talked until the heat of the loft drove them down the ladder. Once outside the barn they walked toward the house, seeking the cool interior and something to drink. They were almost at the back door when Joey Parker came shooting into the yard.

"My Pa's been hurt!" he cried in panic. "There's blood everywhere and he won't wake up."

The entire family heard his screams and within seconds everyone was gathered in the yard, trying to understand his hysterical chatter. When they could see that he was not going to calm down, Bill, Rigg, and Jeff jumped in the wagon, grabbed Joey, and headed for the Parker house. Kaitlin wanted to go along to comfort Joey, but Bill stepped in and forbade her.

"I have no idea what we'll find and I'm not about to take you into that situation."

Kate stood with the rest of the family until the dust had settled on the road, covering Parker and the loved ones in the wagon with their prayers.

fifty-four

The odor inside the Parker house was overpowering. It was also dark and therefore took a moment for the men's eyes to adjust and find Joey's father.

There was indeed blood everywhere but he was breathing. He had evidently passed out from drink and hit his head. Commenting that head wounds were typically gushers, Bill told Joey to try and calm Frank down. He was barking in a near frenzy over being shut outside. No one believed he would attack, but the noise he made was very annoying.

"Let's get Parker outside," Bill commented. "I need air and I think he must too."

Joey was sent to fetch water and using an old shirt, they attempted to clean Parker's head. Coming around some when the gash at his temple was touched, he tried to shove the ministering hands away from him.

"Should I go for the Doc?" Jeff wanted to know.

"I want your mother to see him first. She's always good with head wounds. If she thinks we need to go for the doctor, then we will."

They learned quickly that the easiest method for moving Parker was simply to let Rigg lift him in his arms. No small task, the muscles corded in Rigg's neck as he strained under the load. They were, however, on their way in no time with Joey and a half-conscious Parker in the back.

May examined Parker while he was still in the wagon and decided she could patch the cut herself.

"But first, I think he should have a bath. Are you up to it?" May asked her sons and husband and they agreed without hesitation. As it was, Parker awoke as soon as the water touched his skin and Bill stayed in the bathing room to assist him.

Joey would not believe that his father was going to be all right, so Rigg took him in for a brief visit. He then tried to get him to eat.

"This bread was made yesterday Joey, it's real fresh." Rigg put together a chicken sandwich for both of them while Kate poured lemonade. May cut apples into slices. All the adults watched the little boy's eyes move repeatedly in the direction of the room his father was in.

"What are you afraid of Joey?" May asked softly, thinking it was time someone addressed the fear usually masking this child's face.

"I'm afraid my Pa will die," he admitted. His face was so vulnerable that Kaitlin wondered if she might need to leave the room. "And I'll be left all alone."

"May I tell you a story Joey?" May waited for him to nod before she began. "When I was just a young woman I married a man and we had a baby—a son. I was the happiest woman on earth. But then, when my son was only two years old, my husband died.

"I didn't think I could go on. I loved him so much and he was a wonderful father to our son. I don't know when I've ever felt so alone . . . but then a wonderful thing happened. I remembered a Bible verse that said God would never leave me nor forsake me. I remembered that my husband was with the Lord and that the Lord still loved Rigg and me.

"But Joey, I want you to listen to me very carefully. I wouldn't have known that about the Lord if I hadn't made a decision to trust Him for my salvation when I was young. When I was about your age, I understood that I needed a Savior. Without my believing that Jesus Christ died on the cross for my sins, I would go to hell. I didn't want to go to hell, Joey, I wanted to live forever with God.

"I was sick with grief right after my husband died but God reminded me of His love and that changed everything inside of me. I was no longer afraid or believed I'd been deserted. I knew that God loved me and died for me and that meant there was nothing more to fear. Not being alone, not dying, nothing.

"Joey, do you have that peace, that special quiet inside of you because you know God is your Savior? Have you faced God and confessed your need for a Savior?"

There were tears puddling in Joey's eyes as he shook his head no. She went on to ask him if he wanted to pray right at the table. He then voiced his second fear.

"But what if Pa never believes in Jesus?"

"Oh, honey, I can't promise you that he will. But I do know that you are not responsible for your father. When you stand before God, He's not going to say to you, 'Joey, why didn't you save your father?' Only God can take care of that and right now the best thing you can do for your father is to trust God yourself.

"God died for your father too, and he might see the change in you and want that change for himself. But even if that doesn't happen—"

"I'd still be God's child," Joey broke in and May nodded, her own eyes beginning to fill.

The people in the room watched in awe as Joey looked up at the ceiling with his eyes wide open. His voice was clear and without hesitation as he spoke to God.

"I know You're up there. I've known it for a long time. I'm ready now to be Yours, if You still want me. I'm ready for You to take away my sins and live in my heart."

The look on Joey's face was indescribable. The peace of God had descended upon this small child and there was almost a visible difference. He didn't say anything for a few minutes and all in attendance found themselves afraid to breathe. Rigg, May, and Kate were in the kitchen with him. Just out of sight in the living room, sat Sean, Marcail, Jeff, Nate and Gil.

"Can I tell Marcail?" Joey finally asked. "And Sean too?"

"That's a wonderful idea Joey," May said. "They're in the living room; go right in. Then maybe you'll want to go in and tell your father what's happened." Joey nodded and left the kitchen.

Upon Joey's departure, Kate surrendered to the battle with her tears. She and May embraced for a long time and when they broke apart, Rigg hugged his mother.

"Thanks for stepping in Mom."

May's smile was still watery but her face was radiant as she made her way to the back stairway. As soon as she left, Kate and Rigg began to pray for the man to whom Bill was ministering. They both had a premonition that there would be a long road ahead for all of them when it came to Parker and his attempts to bury the past and present in drink.

fifty-five

Parker was sitting at the table eating when Rigg and Kaitlin left the farm. Joey was beside him and, as Kate thought back, she wondered if she would ever forget the poignant scene of Joey telling his father he'd trusted in Christ.

Parker had stared at his son for a long time before nodding and going back to his plate. Parker, with his forehead bandaged and wearing clean clothes, looked like a new man. Kate found herself praying that he would soon understand that he needed to be clean on the inside, too.

Sean did not have to work the next day but May did. So, thinking Sean might like the change of pace, May asked Sean to stay at the farm the next day so he and Nate could care for Marcail.

Rigg thoroughly enjoyed having Kate to himself for a few minutes and told her so.

"I like it too," she admitted softly.

"How are you feeling about Burt Kemp's offer?"

Kaitlin immediately remembered Sean's words about discussing that subject with Rigg if she was going to make Santa Rosa her *permanent* home. The thought made her blush, turning her face a fiery red, so red that Rigg noticed in the gathering dusk.

"You're blushing." He stated the obvious as he lifted her down from the wagon. He dipped his head to look her in the eye since she wouldn't raise her gaze to his. "What did I say?"

Kaitlin didn't answer him.

"Let me see." Rigg spoke quietly and continued to watch her. "My last words were about Burt's offer—oh! There she goes again."

Kate hated her lack of self-control as her face began to heat all over again. She wished it had been darker when they arrived back at the house.

"Please don't tease me Rigg." The words were spoken softly and Rigg took both her hands in his own as they faced each other.

"I'm sorry. You don't have to tell me."

Kate was silent for a moment. She could feel Rigg's eyes on her but kept her face averted. Finally, "May I ask you a question?"

"Sure."

"What would you do in my place?"

"I can't tell you what to do Katie."

"No, I guess you can't but you must have some feelings about it. I'm just asking you to share those with me."

"All right. Answer some questions for me. What do you *want* to do, teach or work at the store?"

"I love teaching but I think I might like working in your office just a little more, but then I feel guilty because I know they need a teacher. I also have guilt because you hired me and I can't just walk out on that job. And if Father returns I'll probably have to quit, no matter what position I take."

"But you need work now. And don't feel guilty on my behalf. Do what you feel the Lord would have you do. I'll be praying that you'll know His will and follow it."

"Thanks Rigg."

They stood for a moment longer and then Rigg bent and placed a soft kiss on Kaitlin's forehead. Her heart nearly burst at his tenderness. But she wasn't prepared for his next words.

"Kaitlin, I'm in love with you." The words, spoken in Rigg's soft, deep voice, were humble and sincere.

"Oh, Rigg." Kate breathed, wanting to tell him of her love also but being so unsure of her future, she held back. "If only I knew—"

"Shhh." Rigg's voice was gentle as he stopped her. "You don't need to say anything. But I wanted you to know how I felt and I also want you to be secure in my love, not intimidated by it."

Once again Rigg kissed her brow and then placed his arms around her. Kate held tightly to him, thinking that nothing had ever felt so wonderful.

We need to be together, she told the Lord as Rigg pulled away from her and climbed into the wagon. *He loves me and I love him. I've prayed so long to know Your will. Show us Lord, show us Your path for our lives. Give us Your blessing heavenly Father, to build a marriage in You.*

As though he could read Kate's mind, Rigg prayed as he drove home. He too longed to be with her and felt it was God's will. He also knew what a weighty thing it was for Kate not to hear from her father. Rigg sternly told himself that he needed to bide his time in pursuing her. In the light of his belief that it was God's will they be together, he needed to wait for God's timing.

❏ ❏ ❏

"I'm completely caught up on the past books, Rigg. Would you like me to start on this month?" It was Friday afternoon, and Kate and Rigg were in the office.

The week had sped by. Burt Kemp had checked with Kaitlin one more time but again she had put him off. It was as though her life hung in the balance until she heard from her father.

Rigg told Kate she could go home for the day and plan to start the next journal on Saturday. As she'd done every day that week, she headed to the post office. Today was different; today there was a letter from Father.

Kate noticed that, for the first time, it was addressed to her alone. She clutched it to her chest and hurried home. Kate prayed as she sat alone at her small kitchen table and asked God for help in dealing with the contents of the letter.

My darling Kate,

I write to you today with a bittersweet feeling in my heart. Bitter, because I'm so far from you at this wonderful time when you've fallen in love, and sweet, because I know—I remember so well how you are feeling.

Katie, I can't urge you strongly enough to follow God and your heart. If this young man desires you for a wife and you know that to be God's will, *do not hesitate*.

My words may surprise you, but your mother and I talked about the possibility of you meeting someone on our furlough and not returning to Hawaii with us. We both wondered how we would ever survive the separation but a child is not meant to live with her parents forever. Your desire to want a husband and a home of your own is completely normal. We would never have stood in your way.

Now, I'll admit to you that I always assumed I would know the young man, but you've introduced him in your letters, as have Sean and Marcail. And I will make this request: If he does want to marry you, that he write and ask me. I don't expect you to hold your plans until I reply. In fact, Marshall can tell me the date in his letter, but I would like this small courtesy if he's sincere about marrying my precious Katie.

If things have not progressed this far in your relationship, let me know. But I think now is a good time to warn you that I'll not be coming in the fall, as I'd hoped. It will be some time after Christmas.

Kate had to stop reading at this point. Her eyes had flooded with tears until she couldn't see the print.

She had been ready to deal with Father telling her not to get involved, something he hadn't done. But she wasn't ready to deal with his continued absence, even though he had warned them that it might be fall or later until he returned. Kate had not really believed him. She had not *wanted* to believe him. She needed him here.

There was no more doubt in Kaitlin's mind as to whether or not Rigg was going to ask her to marry him; it was just a matter of time. But this was August! How could she ever tell him they had to wait until after Christmas to be married? And then there was still no guarantee that Father would be home. The letter said *sometime* after Christmas.

It also said "do not hesitate." Kate pulled herself together and finished reading.

It hurts me to write this to you, but my reasons are joyful. There is tremendous revival going on here and the need for spiritual leadership is greater than ever.

When we left Hawaii I felt it would be good for the mission to be without me, and then in San Francisco I was not certain I could return as a ministering pastor. There are no words to describe my loneliness for you, but God is using me and I feel I must stay on.

Maureen has been in touch, she hopes we'll all be in San Francisco for the holidays. She will be keenly disappointed when I write her. Maybe you can see her? If not for Christmas, then possibly Thanksgiving. But do as you think best.

Having to communicate like this, with miles sep-
arating us, is difficult at best. I am praying for you as
you knew I would be, and trusting God to guide
your heart.

Give my love to Sean and Marcail.

Love,
Father

Kaitlin read the letter over a second time, knowing
when she was finished, what her next course of action
would be. This was what she'd been praying for. The
uncertainty was gone; she now knew what direction to
take.

With the letter tucked safely into the pocket of her
skirt, Kaitlin went to find her brother.

fifty-six

Kate found Sean on the loading dock at the back of the mercantile, preparing to leave for the night.

"Sean." Kate's voice was urgent. "I need to talk with you."

"What's the matter?"

"I want you to help me talk with Rigg."

Sean eyed her with a curious look. "You don't have any problem talking with Rigg. What's up?"

"This." Kate thrust the letter at him and waited as he read. She watched the emotions play across his face as he came to the part about their father's delayed return.

"I'm sorry, Sean. I know you're disappointed and I know my timing is bad but I need a favor. I want to tell Rigg that I love him but I know I won't be able to get it all out in English and I want you to translate."

They had begun walking toward Rigg's house and Sean turned his head to look at his sister as though she were crazy.

"Kaitlin, are you serious?" He sounded so incredulous that she felt ashamed.

"It's all right Sean. That was a terrible thing for me to ask you. Just forget it, okay?"

Sean didn't say anything to that. He knew she was embarrassed about having to ask him in the first place and then he had made it worse by ridiculing her. They walked on to Rigg's and Kaitlin asked Sean if she could wait for Rigg. Her question made him feel terrible and he nearly stuttered as he told her to make herself comfortable in the living room. Rigg looked very pleased to see her when he came in an hour later.

"I stopped by your place; we must have missed each other," he said with a smile.

There was no sign of Sean and Rigg noticed for the first time that Kate was looking rather agitated.

"I need to talk with you, Rigg."

"All right." Rigg answered, thinking that Kate had made up her mind about teaching in the fall. He sat next to her on the couch. When Kate sprang up away from him and stood in the middle of the room, wringing her hands, a frown covered his face and he doubted his own thoughts.

"I just haven't known how to approach you about this or really when to approach you. I mean I've prayed and—"

Rigg listened and watched without interrupting as Kate went from tears to anger and back to tears again, speaking all the time in Hawaiian. Near the end Rigg caught on that she was talking about them. But by now an intense look of regret had come over Kaitlin's face and Rigg felt his heart sink.

"I'm not able to say it," Kate finally said, and Rigg felt that she was apologizing, not for her foreign words, but for something far more personal.

"Maybe if you give me a little time."

"Sure." Rigg wondered what he had just agreed to and watched, his heart feeling as if it were caught in a vise, as Kate moved toward the door.

"Katie," Rigg called softly as she started to leave.

But Kate only looked at him with tears once again filling her eyes. "I'm sorry." With those words she was gone, leaving Rigg in painful confusion.

Sean, who had been listening from the kitchen, came into the living room and cleared his throat uncomfortably.

"I'm sorry Rigg."

The older man stared at him, misunderstanding his apology.

"She was talking about us, wasn't she? Kate was explaining how she feels about me?"

"Yes and I'm sorry. I had no business being here but after she asked me to help and I told her I wouldn't, I got to thinking about how much she cares for you and how—"

"Sean," Rigg cut in, "did you hear what she said?"

"Yes."

"I want you to come in and tell me everything."

Rigg was more baffled than ever. He thought Kate was telling him that she couldn't love him and now Sean had blurted out how much she cared. Sean was obviously ill at ease and Rigg reassured him.

"Just tell me what you can. First of all, what did Kate ask you to help with?"

"Kate told me that she needed someone to talk with, you know, about you and her, so she wrote to Father. She's been waiting to hear how Father felt about her getting involved with someone. And today a letter came."

"And that's what she said to me?"

"Some of what she said." Sean was looking uncomfortable again.

"You still haven't told me why she wanted your help."

"She wanted me to translate for her. You know how frustrated she gets and she knew she'd never be able to get it all out in English."

"Get all what out?" Rigg was feeling a little frustrated himself.

"That she loves you. But she's never flirted before and she probably *is* too stuffy for her own good because she just didn't know how to tell you or show you how she feels." Sean felt out of breath, but he guessed Rigg understood because he was grinning like a fool.

The bigger man came toward Sean and pulled him out of his chair and into his arms. He gave Sean a mighty hug, thanked him and headed for the front door.

❑ ❑ ❑

Kaitlin sat bent over the kitchen table. She was on her third piece of paper. She had cried all the way home over making a complete fool of herself and then, with a determined glint in her eye, she sat down to write a letter to Rigg to tell him how she felt.

The door opened without a knock and Kate looked up to see Rigg leaning against the jamb. His hands were stuffed into his pants pockets and his totally nonchalant stance belied the rush of emotions inside him. Kate felt herself blushing as he simply stood and looked at her.

"Do you know how many years I've prayed for you?"

Kate shook her head, unsure of how she was supposed to reply.

"I don't think there is ever a time Kaitlin, that I walk by those chairs in my store, you know the ones where the men sit while their wives are shopping, without wishing my wife was shopping somewhere in my store.

"And the times I've ordered dresses and undergarments, wishing as I did, that my wife could be with me when I unpacked them, so she could have first pick. Or when the boxes of children's shoes come in, wanting to have children of my own to put those little black shoes on."

Rigg pushed away from the door then and came to the table. He placed his hands on the top and leaned down, his nose almost touching Kate's.

"Do you understand what I'm trying to say Kaitlin?"

"Yes." Kate felt out of breath and she couldn't take her eyes from the man across from her.

"Then tell me, Katie, will you be that wife? Will you marry me?"

Kate couldn't speak. Her heart thundered with joy and wonderment that he had come to her. She finally managed to nod, searching Rigg's face as she did, to see if he understood.

"I have one more question for you, Kate-love. And it's the last time I'll ask. Hereafter, I'll take my welcome for granted. May I kiss you?"

"Oh, yes." Kaitlin had no trouble with those words at all. Rigg kept his hands on the table and leaned until their lips met. The kiss was brief and gentle. Kate was unsure as to whether or not she'd pleased Rigg and voiced her thoughts as soon as she could speak.

"I've never done this before."

"I haven't either." Rigg's voice was equally as soft as Kaitlin's had been and once again their lips met. No longer satisfied to remain so far from the woman he loved, Rigg moved around the table to take her into his arms.

When Kate could think once again, she found that Rigg had taken her chair and pulled her into his lap.

"I can't sit in your lap!" Kate was appalled and moved away from him. "We're not married."

"But we will be, very soon, Miss Prim and Proper." Rigg followed her right out of the chair and silenced her protestations with another kiss as they stood in the center of the room.

"You did say that your father was coming in the fall, right?" Rigg did nothing to conceal his enthusiasm— Kaitlin was finally going to be his wife!

Kate pulled the letter from her pocket and handed it to Rigg. As he read, she watched his face as she had with Sean. It occurred to her in the silence that she didn't know why Rigg had come after her and proposed. She was about to ask him when he sat at the table and took yet another fresh sheet of paper. He was a study in concentration as he began to write. A few minutes later he handed the paper to Kaitlin.

Dear Mr. Donovan,

It would give me great pleasure to be speaking with you in person but your delay doesn't make that possible. I would like your permission to wed Kaitlin. I just now asked her. She said yes, and showed me your letter. Thank you for the blessing to proceed in your absence. We have not discussed a date but my hope is that it will be this fall.

I have prayed long for a wife such as Katie and I thank you sincerely for the wonderful person that she is. I know the love that she bears for you will cause her grief at the time of our wedding but if you are agreeable, I would like you to marry us again at the time you return.

My prayers are with you and I look forward to the time we can speak face to face.

Sincerely,
Marshall Riggs

Kate read the letter and smiled through her tears. "Thanks Rigg. He'll be so pleased."

"It's my pleasure. I meant every word." He hugged Kate for a moment before taking her hand. Heading out the door, Rigg had one cryptic comment.

"That's one down, and two to go."

fifty-seven

Just as he'd hoped, Rigg found Sean at the house. He was eating supper and, with a mouthful of chicken, he stared at his sister and his employer. Sean noticed a marked difference about both.

Rigg's eyes, although always kind, held a certain tenderness that Sean had never seen before. And Kaitlin. She looked as if she needed a piece of string to keep her on the ground.

"I have a question to ask you Sean," Rigg stated quietly. "I just wrote to your father and asked if I could marry Katie. Now I want to ask you and then Marc. Do you mind if I marry Kaitlin?"

Sean wiped his mouth and hands on a napkin and then looked up at the two with an expression that was older than he was.

"I just have one thing to say to you Rigg," Sean paused and smiled slightly. "It's about time."

Kate laughed and moved to hug her brother. The two shared a long embrace before Rigg came to claim him. He held Sean by the upper arms and looked him in the eye.

"I love you Sean," Rigg told him honestly. "And I want to thank you for what you did to bring Kate and me together. I know you're disappointed about your father and I'm praying that he'll come home soon.

"But I want you to understand that you still have a home. I think Marcail will probably want to be downstairs here or have you upstairs with her. Whatever you both want. If you'd like to be upstairs, go up and pick out a room. Or better yet, do that later and come to my folks with us now, so I can ask Marcail."

Sean's eyes were shining with happiness and when Rigg finally hugged him, he held on tight. Being offered a home and a choice on a bedroom might have seemed a small thing to someone else but to a boy whose life had been so unsettled of late, it was a lifeline in a stormy sea.

As it was they all went upstairs together, a first for Kate and Sean. There were three bedrooms and Sean, surprisingly enough, chose the smallest. It had a large bed, dresser and a standing full length mirror.

"It's cozy," he told them. "And I like the view."

Sean planned to move his gear in the morning so they headed back to Kaitlin's so she could get a sweater and then on to the farm. Rigg was careful to hide his disappointment once they arrived and found both Jeff and Gil gone. A friend of Jeff's, who'd been away from the area had returned so he was at her house for supper. Gil, May informed Rigg, was coming back anytime. He'd just had some errands to run.

Rigg knew that his parents were suspicious with the way he and Kate asked Marcail to go for a walk but they stayed quiet even though they were more than a little curious.

"How was your day, Marcail?" Kate asked as Rigg sat quietly and watched them. The three had climbed into the loft in the barn.

"It was okay. I wrote a letter to Loni and one to Father. I think you need to read the one to Father though, Katie, because I told him I want him to come home. I don't want to send it if you think it will hurt his feelings."

"I can read it for you, Marc, but I got a letter today and Father said he wouldn't be coming until sometime after Christmas."

"But Katie, Father said he was coming in the fall." The little girl's face showed her disappointment and Kate didn't know what to say. Too much more of this and Marcail would begin to doubt her father's honesty. As Kate searched for the right words to reassure her, Rigg stepped in and saved the moment.

"I've only known you for a few months, Marcail. But even though it's only been since March, I really like being with you and talking with you. I can only imagine how much your father likes to be with you because he's known you your entire life.

"You can believe, honey, that if he can't be here, it's not because he doesn't want to be."

Marcail nodded and both adults could see she was relieved.

"You know Katie," Marcail stated a moment later in a logical tone, "you should marry Rigg, he's very nice." Marcail's hand flew to her mouth as she stared in horror at her sister.

"I'm sorry Katie, I'm so sorry."

Rigg rolled from his sitting position to lay in the straw, until he was nearly nose to nose with Marcail.

"I'm glad you brought that up Marc," Rigg told her. "Because today I wrote to your Father and asked if I could marry Kaitlin. Now I want to know if it's all right with you?"

"What did Katie say?" Marcail asked cautiously, not wanting to make another mistake.

"She said yes."

"Did you ask Sean?"

"He said yes."

Kate had been doing fine up to that point, letting Rigg handle everything. But Marcail's next words were her undoing.

"I knew this would happen Katie, I just knew. Rigg looks at you just like Father looked at Mother."

Kate reached for her sister then and held her tight. She couldn't stop the tears that fell and Rigg gathered them both in his arms as Kate sobbed. Finally he pressed his handkerchief into her hand and she made an attempt at containing herself.

"I told you she does this a lot," Marcail informed Rigg seriously.

Rigg thanked his young, future sister-in-law for the reminder giving her a conspiratorial wink.

"We were at my house when I asked Sean, and I told him he would be living with us, as will you. He decided to take another bedroom upstairs so you can have his old room on the first floor or pick one of the other ones upstairs.

"Sean's new room has a bed and so does one of the other bedrooms. If you want the room that doesn't, then we'll just move furniture around."

"Thanks, Rigg." Marcail smiled at him. "Katie, are you going to teach school or work with Rigg?"

"Oh!" Kate said in surprise.

"We haven't talked about that yet," Rigg informed the little girl. "But we'll let you know what we decide. How about we go down now and tell everyone else?"

"How come you asked Sean first?" Marcail suddenly asked, frowning at her sister as though she'd been betrayed.

Rigg scooped Marcail up and planted a kiss on her cheek, effectively wiping the scowl from her face. He also stole a kiss from Kaitlin as they were climbing down the ladder. Before Kate was even back on the ground, Marcail was running for the house and shouting at the top of her voice that Rigg and Kate were going to be married.

fifty-eight

Gil had returned while the three were in the barn and he was as excited as everyone else to hear the news. May was ecstatic and couldn't stop hugging Rigg and Kate. She brought out her good dishes for the cake she'd just baked and coffee.

"What date have you picked?" This question came from a beaming Bill and Rigg told him they hadn't talked about it. May had more questions and everyone did a lot of laughing over how many times Rigg was forced to answer, "We haven't talked about it."

Gil asked how the whole thing had come about, and Kaitlin learned for the first time how Sean had been in the kitchen and emerged to translate what she'd said. She thanked him from across the room with a grateful look.

As the evening grew long, Kate began to wilt. She wondered if it was normal to tell people so soon. Everyone had very logical questions for them and they had no answers. Kate hoped they would leave a little early so they could talk. She hadn't even had a chance to tell Rigg that she loved him.

Feeling teary all over again, Kate mentally scolded herself. *He'll change his mind Kate, if you don't pull yourself together.* Kate never took into account that she was tired for several good reasons. It was the end of the week, the emotional upheaval of hearing her father was being delayed again and going to Rigg to tell him how she felt only to make a mess of the whole thing.

She told herself that Rigg's proposal and her acceptance just might have a bearing on her physical and emotional state as well. And if all that wasn't enough, she had completely forgotten to eat supper!

Bill noticed that Kate hadn't touched her cake or coffee and his voice came softly to her from his place next to her on the couch.

"Katie, are you all right?"

"I don't think I am, but I don't know why." She felt tears at the back of her eyes, but she was too tired to let them fall.

Rigg had heard his father's question and Kate's answer. He was feeling rather drained himself and, even though he knew his family would be disappointed, he said it was time to go.

Sean had to work in the morning but said he wanted to stay at the farm with Nate. Marcail wanted to stay, too, and Rigg was quietly thankful to get his intended alone.

"We didn't eat supper," Rigg commented when they were almost to the house.

"No, I guess we didn't."

Kate was silent as Rigg stopped the wagon and helped her down. She wondered why she wasn't out of her head with excitement. They were leaning against the side of the wagon and Rigg had his arm around Kate. She let her head fall against him.

"I don't know what's wrong with me."

"We're both tired. There are a million things to talk about, but I think they'll wait until morning."

"I think so, too." Kate moved from his embrace and stopped just out of reach. "You're probably too tired to kiss me, so I'll see you in the morning. Good night Rigg."

Kate's hand was on the doorknob when Rigg's hand covered her own, stopping her retreat into the house.

She tipped her head back to look at him and he could see she was smiling.

"I said I was tired, Kate-love, not dead."

Kaitlin laughed and said softly, "I love you Marshall Riggs."

"And I love you Kaitlin Donovan." He smiled and kissed her in such a way that Kate didn't doubt his words at all.

❑ ❑ ❑

Kate woke up feeling rested and refreshed. She turned to some of her favorite Bible verses in the book of Lamentations. Chapter 3:22-26 said, "It is of the Lord's mercies that we are not consumed, because his compassions fail not. They are new every morning: great is thy faithfulness. The Lord is my portion, saith my soul; therefore will I hope in him. The Lord is good unto them that wait for him, to the soul that seeketh him. It is good that a man should both hope and quietly wait for the salvation of the Lord."

Kate prayed after she read these verses, taking time to thank God for His saving love and say that she had accepted that gift.

Spending such a long time praying for her loved ones, Kate was late for work. She hurried along the boardwalk rehearsing her apology only to find Rigg waiting out front for her.

"Good morning."

"I'm late," Kate stated, her planned apology melting away the minute she set eyes on Rigg. August was hot so Rigg was in simple dark slacks and a crisp white shirt, already rolled at the wrists with no vest or coat.

"Did I forget to tell you last night *not* to eat breakfast?"

"Yes, you did forget to tell me."

"So you've eaten?"

"Yes."

"I'm sorry. Maybe you'd like a cup of coffee while I eat?" Rigg took Kate's arm and led her up the street. She naturally wanted to know where they were going.

"To the hotel. I've told my clerks that I'll be out for a while. You and I need to discuss a few things and since there's nothing pressing today, I think this is a good time."

Saturday mornings were busy in the hotel dining room but Rigg found a secluded table for two and led Kaitlin to it. He'd been carrying something under his arm and as soon as they were seated he pulled it out: It was a calendar.

"I think the first thing we need to do is pick a wedding date."

"I already have. I checked my calendar this morning, just before I left the house."

"Great," Rigg grinned. "What's the date?"

"December second. It's a Saturday."

"October seventh is a Saturday, too," Rigg stated, having also checked the calendar. Kaitlin blinked at him.

"October? I don't think that's enough time."

"For what?" Rigg asked in all honesty and Kate looked a little frustrated. "You *are* marrying me, aren't you Katie? I mean, you don't need more time to decide, do you?"

"I am definitely marrying you, but doesn't it take a while to plan a wedding?" Kate had never participated in one before but when they had been in San Francisco, Aunt Maureen had helped with one and the way she carried on you would have thought the Queen was coming. She was also hesitant to tell Rigg that she needed time to save for what was sure to be a major expense.

Rigg watched Kate's face and spoke honestly. "Katie, I wish we were already married, so October sounds good to me. But if you want to wait until December, I'll go along with your plans."

A harried young woman appeared at their table and splashed some coffee into their cups. Rigg told her what he wanted before she moved off in the direction of the kitchen.

Kate studied her coffee cup a moment. She didn't really know what she wanted, except that she wanted it to be special. Other than that, and thinking a white dress might be nice, she didn't have any other desires. But she knew from weddings she'd attended in Hawaii that there was always plenty of food. Sean didn't have a decent suit and Marcail would certainly want a new dress; although the one May had made her was very pretty.

"Tell me what you're thinking."

"I'm thinking that it's different in Hawaii. I don't know as many people here as I did there. In Hawaii, dozens of people would have come forward to offer their help, their food, their homes, or whatever was needed.

"Along with the fact that I have almost no trousseau and I've never done this before—"

"Money!" Rigg broke in, suddenly understanding. "You're worried about the money."

Kaitlin wouldn't answer him.

"I don't know if talking here was such a good idea," Rigg said after they'd been interrupted by the arrival of food. Kate was looking so uncertain that Rigg wanted to hold her.

"How would you feel if we found my mom as soon as I'm done eating, and talked some of this over with her?"

Kate nodded and tried to drink her coffee.

❑ ❑ ❑

May was at home with Marcail. Rigg sat in the living room with Kate at his side, his hand engulfing hers. When May had given Marcail a job in the kitchen, she joined them. Rigg's explanation was brief and May listened silently until he was through.

"Tell me, Katie, when do you *want* to be married?"

"I wish we already were."

"So, your wanting a December date is not because you're unsure about marrying Rigg?"

"No, I'm not at all unsure about that. But this is August nineteenth, and I can't imagine having everything ready for a wedding by the seventh of October."

May spent the next hour reassuring Kate about her wedding. Kate learned that the church had a special group of ladies, of whom May was one, to handle wedding arrangements. May also told her daughter-in-law-to-be, that she would love to make her a wedding gown. Kate was feeling like the sun had broken through on a cloudy day. She was actually going to be married seven weeks from today.

"Are you ever a hard guy to track down!" Jeff stood at the entrance to the room and spoke to Rigg, "I understand congratulations are in order." Rigg stood up and Kate watched the two men embrace.

"I can't think what you've done to deserve her," Jeff commented as he leaned to kiss Kate's cheek.

"You've got some nerve, insulting me and then kissing my woman," Rigg laughed.

Kaitlin and May fled on that note, both thinking that the two of them were hopeless. They joined Marcail in the kitchen and filled her in on the news.

Kate and Rigg did end up going to the mercantile just after lunch, but Kate was in a fog. She couldn't have told anyone what she'd done that day if her life depended on it.

fifty-nine

Kate found it delightful to be greeted with a morning kiss. It was Sunday. She had stayed with the Taylors and when Rigg had come to take her to church, he'd kissed her as he helped her into the wagon.

They talked as they rode, and Kaitlin brought up a subject they'd completely forgotten to discuss the day before.

"Burt Kemp is going to want an answer from me today and, in all fairness Rigg, I need to give him one. Do you mind if I teach again this year?"

"I have only one problem with your teaching and that is the chance that you'll be pregnant before the year is out." Kate thought her face would flame it was so hot.

"I wonder how many years we'll be married before you stop blushing in front of me," Rigg remarked softly.

"You took me by surprise," Kate explained without looking at him. She took a deep breath and continued.

"You've got a valid point, though. Mother taught when she was carrying Sean and Marcail. In fact Marc's delivery was so easy that Mother's labor began about an hour before school was to let out, but she didn't tell anyone. And then she sent for Father after she dismissed. We were only home about two hours before Marcail was born.

"There is, of course, no guarantee that things will be the same for me but I don't think the possibility of my having a child should keep me from teaching."

They were not yet within sight of the church and Rigg pulled the team to a stop in the middle of the deserted road. He put his arms around Kate and she looked up into his face, so near her own.

"We've never talked about children. You do want some, don't you Katie?" His words, said sweetly, almost hesitantly, made Kaitlin wonder if he was feeling a little insecure about something.

"I wouldn't mind if we waited a little while, but I would like some—no less than five, to be exact." That statement earned her a beaming smile and another kiss.

As Rigg drove the remaining distance to church, Kaitlin told him of her conversation with Joey. "You should have seen his face, Rigg, it was heartbreaking.

"'Miss Donovan,' he said, 'you are going to teach school this year, aren't you?' He nearly burst into tears when I said I hadn't decided."

"Maybe he'll be there this morning," Rigg commented, "and you can tell him the good news."

Rigg and Kate's wedding plans spread like wildfire and many members of the congregation offered felicitations, before and after the service.

Kate had been correct about Burt Kemp. He tracked them down within seconds of the benediction and then nearly hugged Kaitlin for saying yes. Kate and Rigg both felt comfortable with the decision and Burt made an appointment with Kate later that week to go over anything she might need.

When they finally made it to the wagon they found Jeff waiting for them. For the first time Kate could remember, he wasn't alone.

"Kaitlin," he said by way of greeting, "I want you to meet Sylvia Weber. Sylvia, this is Rigg's fiancée, Kaitlin Donovan."

"It's nice to meet you Sylvia," Kate greeted the other woman and tried to keep the awe out of her voice. Sylvia was beautiful, strikingly so. Her dress was a deep rose velvet which accented every curve of her perfect figure. The feather on her matching hat was so high it brushed Jeff's forehead when Sylvia stepped close to him.

"Congratulations." Sylvia's voice was smooth and cultured. "I'm sure you and Rigg will be very happy." Kate couldn't help but respond to the genuine sincerity in her eyes and the four of them talked for awhile.

It seemed that Sylvia and Jeff had finished school the same year. Sylvia's family, all except her married sister, had then moved east shortly afterward. Sylvia was here staying with her sister for an indefinite period of time.

"Are you coming to the house for lunch?" Rigg asked.

"No, Sandra and Carl are expecting us," Jeff supplied.

"Sandra is my sister," Sylvia told Kate. "And her husband is Carl, Carl Boggs."

The couples went their separate ways a moment later and Kate turned in her seat to watch Jeff and Sylvia climb into a snappy little buggy pulled by a dapple gray mare.

"She's beautiful."

"That she is. I've always liked dapple grays."

Kate's head whipped around to see if he was teasing her but saw in an instant that he was dead serious.

"I meant Sylvia."

"Oh."

"Rigg, are you really trying to tell me you didn't notice that mass of blonde hair and those huge blue eyes?" Kaitlin's voice told him she wouldn't believe him no matter what he said.

"Sylvia is very pretty," Rigg said, his voice full of logic. "But my tastes run to Irish girls, black hair, eyes as soft and brown as pansies and stubborn chins."

Another wagon was coming toward them or Kate would have thrown her arms around Rigg. He had meant every word.

"I love you Rigg." Kate was feeling so emotional that the words were not in English.

"Are you going to translate that for me?"

Kate shook her head. "Just trust that I meant it." Those words weren't in English either, but Rigg could tell by the look in her eyes and the sound of her voice that he was loved.

❏ ❏ ❏

"Now if you will come into the living room," May said with barely contained excitement, "your father and I have something to tell you."

Rigg and Kate exchanged a glance and seated themselves on the sofa.

"We've been discussing a wedding gift for you. I think we've just the right thing. We want to fix up Rigg's house—the cost will be on us! We'll paint, wallpaper and make new curtains. We also want to replace any of the rugs that are worn, such as the one in the living room.

"I figured we would need to do most of it after the wedding but we'll start in the bedroom and see how far we can get. What do you think?"

Rigg leaned forward on the sofa to see Kaitlin's face. She looked worried.

"Katie?" When Rigg spoke her name she looked at him.

"Rigg, have I said something to make you think your home isn't suitable?"

"Oh no, Katie," having heard the question, Bill broke in. "We know you would live there without a single complaint but things are showing their age and it's nice to start out with a few new things."

"Is it all right with you?" Kate asked Rigg. "I mean, it's your house and if you'd rather things were left alone—"

"It's *our* house and I like the idea. I probably won't be much help in the color selection but whatever you and Mom come up with will be fine."

"Well, it's all settled," May beamed. "Come in the kitchen Kate and I'll show you some fabric I picked up yesterday."

Rigg looked at his father after the women left. Gil was sprawled in a chair with the newspaper but Rigg knew he was the soul of discretion.

"How long did it take for Mom to start thinking of your things as hers? And money . . . how long did it take for Mom to get comfortable enough to say she needed some money?"

Bill looked at his son with compassion. "It'll come, Rigg, just give her time. Tradition states that the bride's family pays for everything and Kate has been somewhat worried, since the day she arrived, that she was a burden to us. Keep reassuring her that you're going to take care of her.

"And unless I totally miss my guess about everything I've heard about Aunt Maureen, I think Kate will have a wedding the likes of which she's never dreamed."

sixty

Rigg had mailed his letter to Patrick Donovan in Hawaii first thing Saturday morning. On Monday, Kate sat down and wrote to her father, as well as to her aunt. Aunt Maureen was in Santa Rosa a week later, on the first of four such trips she would make before the wedding.

Maureen Kent was a welcome surprise to the Taylors. She genuinely desired to help yet did not take over. And she wanted to pay for everything!

After two days, Kate stopped arguing with her because Aunt Maureen's response was always the same: "This is the way your father would want it."

On Aunt Maureen's third trip to Santa Rosa, three weeks before the wedding, she brought her niece a sizable box of nighties and feminine apparel. Maureen watched as Kate took the clothing from the box and exclaimed in delight over each one.

"Thank you Aunt Maureen," Kate breathed when the box was empty. "They're all so lovely and I've never had anything like these before."

"The pleasure is all mine, Katie," the older woman assured her warmly. "Katie," Maureen spoke again and something in her voice immediately snagged Kate's attention.

"I can't help but think that you must miss your mother *more* at a time like this. Am I right?"

"Yes," Kate replied softly.

"I know you and Theresa were very close and I'm assuming she has talked to you about the intimate side of marriage."

"When I was fifteen."

"I'm glad to hear that, honey, but your mother isn't here now and I want you to come to me if anything is bothering you. But I want to tell you something, Kate, that not many women practice. After you're married, the best person you can talk to is your husband.

"Rigg adores you; I can see that every time he looks at you. If anything is bothering you be sure you go to him. He might suggest you see May or contact me and that's fine, but I'm in my second happy marriage and I've found that men want their wives to enjoy every aspect of married life. And they'll go to any length to see that we're happy and cared for. I'm quite certain Rigg is no different."

The words were spoken so tenderly that Kaitlin felt for the first time that she'd missed something precious and dear by not being able to be closer to this woman.

Kate thanked her aunt with a hug and they talked for a while longer.

"Kaitlin," Aunt Maureen spoke almost hesitantly. "Have you ever forgiven my son?"

"Oh, Aunt Maureen," Kaitlin said with deep feeling, sensing that her aunt had agonized over this issue. "I can't tell you that it didn't bother me, but I'm all right. Sean and I have talked about it and so have Rigg and I. Percy has been forgiven and blame is not being cast on anyone, including myself, as I once did."

"You don't know how happy that makes me, Katie," her aunt spoke tearfully. The women embraced again and, because it was Saturday, Kaitlin had to excuse herself soon after to work on her school lessons.

School had gotten off to a good start for everyone but Sean. Kate had worried when they'd arrived in Santa Rosa that Sean would want to quit school and work full time. Kaitlin's suspicions had been correct, but it happened in the fall.

Rigg promised him as many hours as he could handle, but Kate could see he was still unhappy. He did his schoolwork, but with no extra effort. Two other boys who sat near him were able to distract Sean with barely a word or glance, and Kate was just sick each time she had to reprimand him in front of the class. She finally told him one day after school that he should write to Father.

"You're angry because he hasn't come and I think I understand. What I don't understand is why you're taking it out on the rest of us. If you've got some anger to vent toward Father, then do so. But when you're in my school, you'll show proper respect to me and the other students."

Sean had slumped low in his seat and looked at the empty desks around him. It took Kate a moment to realize he wasn't going to say anything. Her sigh was almost one of defeat.

"Just think about it, please, Sean." The surly 14-year-old finally nodded, acknowledging this time that he'd at least heard her.

The problem with Sean was not the only ripple on the surface for Kaitlin. She had cried for a solid hour after she and Rigg met with Pastor Keller to discuss the ceremony.

"My father should be here, Rigg. I feel like I'm betraying him. He should be here to marry us."

Rigg had been tender with his distraught fiancée but also adamant that they were making the right move. He reminded her that her father had encouraged them to go ahead with their plans.

"Katie, we don't know when he's coming, you said so yourself. If I thought it would be soon after Christmas, I'd say let's wait. But it could be months and I don't think I'm being selfish in wanting us to start our life together now.

"Like I said, we could set a date sometime in January and let your father know. But that only pressures him to come here even if the time is all wrong. I believe he was sincere when he said don't hesitate and follow your heart."

Kate was comforted by Rigg's words and admitted to him that she hadn't really wanted to delay the wedding. She also told him he was going to have to be patient when she missed her father so much that all she could do was cry.

The ever present handkerchief appeared from Rigg's pocket and he informed Kate that she could cry on him anytime she wanted.

May had the wedding dress done in record time and Kate couldn't believe how beautiful it was, especially considering it was made of cotton.

"You'll thank me Katie," May had told her when they'd decided on a pattern and fabric. "We always have Indian summer in October and your wedding day is sure to be a scorcher."

Kate stared in awe at her reflection in the mirror. The dress was snow white with a high neck and three quarter sleeves, the cuffs of which were trimmed with valenciennes lace. The skirt fell straight to the knees and then flared to the floor with a deep flounce.

Kate fingered the intricate embroidery on the bodice and wondered in amazement how May had accomplished such a feat in so short a time.

"Oh May," Kaitlin whispered.

"Don't hug me, Katie," May said with a smile, "you'll wrinkle."

"But where did you get this lace and how could you have embroidered this so quickly?"

May was grinning at her with an impish light in her eyes, when someone knocked on the door.

"Come in, unless you're Rigg and then you'd better not open that door!" May called in a loud voice.

Jeff's head appeared through the crack and the rest of him emerged when he spotted Kate. He whistled appreciatively at the sight of her.

"It's not too late to change your mind and marry me," Jeff teased as he plopped in a chair.

"What would Sylvia say?" Kate asked, her brows raised in censor.

"Did you need something Jeffrey?" his mother wanted to know. She was somewhat immune to his charm.

Jeff hemmed and hawed a bit and Kate had the distinct feeling that he didn't want her to know what he'd come to say. She excused herself without giving anymore thought to Jeff's actions and headed to "her" bedroom at the Taylors'.

After the wedding dress was hung on the wardrobe door and Kate was once again dressed in her calico skirt and simple blouse, she stood and stared at the dress. *Can you see my dress, Mother? Has God let you peek down and see how happy I am and what a wonderful husband Rigg will be? Can you feel how much I miss you Mother, or would that make you sad?* Kate was not even aware of the tears that streaked her cheeks.

There wasn't a day that passed when she didn't think of her mother and had to face the fact all over again that she really was gone. Today was no different. The fact that Aunt Maureen was coming and had been so valuable in the past weeks was a balm to Kaitlin's pained heart.

Kate's mood lifted when she remembered that Aunt Maureen was scheduled to arrive on October second. When that happened, Kate had only five days to wait until she became Mrs. Marshall Riggs.

sixty-one

Santa Rosa was blanketed in fog the morning of the wedding. The CLOSED sign that Rigg had hung on the doors of the mercantile the night before, was still in place long after the store should have been open.

Uncle Leo had surprised everyone by showing up on Thursday evening with his wife Ruth. It was his first visit since he'd moved to Texas. He announced that he'd come to run the store while Rigg was on his honeymoon.

This news came as more of a relief to Jeff than Rigg, since Jeff had agreed to take care of things while the bride and groom were in San Francisco. But even though Leo Riggs was on the scene, Rigg opted to keep the store closed on Saturday. That way everyone could enjoy the wedding.

Rigg had not banked on being so nervous that he couldn't eat. Jeff had stayed the night at the house with Rigg and Sean and was able to observe his older brother in as close to a state of panic as he'd ever seen.

"Why don't you eat some breakfast Rigg?" Jeff suggested.

"I'll get something on my shirt."

"You're not wearing a shirt," Jeff pointed out, but Rigg only stared right through him.

The wedding was set for one o'clock and, when Rigg disappeared to get dressed, he spent so much time in his bedroom that Jeff finally pounded on the door to tell him it was twelve-thirty.

Rigg hurried out, struggling into his coat and asked Jeff how he looked—something he'd never done before.

"You look good. In fact, Kate is so in love she'll even forgive you for not shaving."

Rigg's hand flew to the heavy stubble on his jaw before he began tearing his jacket off with enough force to rip the seams.

"You don't have time Rigg," Jeff pleaded, but found himself ignored. Sean told Jeff he should have stayed quiet.

While this scene of bedlam was being played out at Rigg's residence, a most serene bride was being helped from the wagon at the back of the church.

"Thank you, Gilbert." Kate adjusted her skirts. "Do you suppose they're here yet?"

"I don't think so. Let's get inside out of the heat."

May had insisted that Kate go in Gilbert's wagon and that they use the back door of the building in an effort to avoid most of the dust.

Tables had been set up under the huge trees that lined the churchyard. Arriving guests delivered every type of food, from hot dishes to fruit salads, to be shared at the reception following.

At three minutes to one, Gil joined Kaitlin in the small room in which she was waiting and told her that all the guests had been seated.

"Are they here, Gil?"

"No," Gil answered and watched Kate in amazement. She didn't seem to be the least bit upset that her intended was nearly late for his own wedding.

"What do you suppose happened? You don't think Jeff is up to something, do you?"

"No, I don't," Gil said with conviction and then muttered, "he might do something after the fact but not before."

"Should I be getting worried?" Kate asked but just then Bill came in with good news.

"Here's Sean. We're all set."

Brother and sister were left alone to wait for the music that was to be their cue to come down the center aisle of the church.

"You're beautiful, Kate."

"You look quite handsome yourself." Sean grinned over the compliment and straightened the neckline of his shirt.

"What happened to you guys?"

"We were all ready to go and then Jeff reminded Rigg that he hadn't shaved."

Kate giggled. "Did Rigg really forget to shave?"

"You can laugh, Katie, but I swear the man nearly panicked!" Kate was still chuckling when the music sounded and they moved into position at the back of the church. Kaitlin caught sight of Rigg and then lost him again when the congregation stood.

At the front of the church Sean handed Kate over to the waiting groom. She felt Rigg's hand tremble within her own.

"Second thoughts?" she teased in a soft whisper.

"Absolutely not," he assured her, his eyes dark with emotion.

The ceremony was perfect, not overly long but with everything they'd wanted. Kate thought her heart would burst when she was finally able to turn and look out over the sea of friendly faces as Mrs. Marshall Riggs. They came down the aisle, her hand in his, their smiles nearly stretching off their faces.

The reception was a delightful affair of laughter, best wishes, good food and precious fellowship.

Rigg no longer looked ready to flee and Kate teased him about being late.

"The best things come to those who wait," Rigg teased her back and stole a pickle off her plate.

At different times throughout the afternoon, people had pressed in on the newlyweds and they'd been separated. They thought nothing of this, secure in the knowledge that eventually they'd be alone.

Kate was talking with Joey when Jeff approached and announced that he needed her inside the church. Kate figured he was taking her to Rigg who was going to tell her it was time to leave. She unsuspectingly accompanied her brother-in-law.

"Now Katie," Jeff began to speak the moment they were indoors, "you just need to stay quiet and go along with my little plan. I promise Rigg won't be the least bit upset with *you*."

"Jeffrey," Kate said, "what are you up to?"

"Oh, it's just an old custom called, 'stealing the bride.'"

"No!" Kate spoke adamantly and turned to leave but Jeff grasped her hand and began to hurry her toward the front of the church. He was making jokes as they went, and Kate became weak with laughter. She also didn't believe he would really go through with this.

Kate tried to reason with Jeff but he was talking as fast as he could and she couldn't do anything to make him release her hand. Jeff stopped at the front of the church and opened a small door.

"In you go."

"Not on your life," she refused. Kate glanced into a small room, little more than a cubicle really, and gasped in surprise. Jeff had set a chair and small table in place on which sat a cup filled with something and a plate full of food.

"How long have you been planning this?"

"Since I found out Rigg was in love with you and if you don't get in there right now, you're going to ruin all my work."

Kate looked at him indulgently. "Jeff," she said with the patience of Job. "There is nothing to keep me in there, just as soon as you walk away, I'll let myself out."

"That's a risk I'll have to take," Jeff told her sagely.

Kate shook her head, but being the good sport she was, she walked in and sat down. Jeff grinned, winked at her and shut the door.

"I hope you'll forgive me Kate!" Jeff said softly as he flipped the small lock shut—a lock that Kaitlin hadn't noticed. "Now that I think about it," Jeff said, still speaking out loud, "I hope Rigg forgives me."

❑ ❑ ❑

"Where in the world is Katie?" May asked her newly married son.

"I don't know. I haven't seen her for about fifteen minutes. But she was talking with Joey just before I saw Jeff come and claim her."

"Well, if you see her, please ask her to find me. I want her to meet the Crawfords." May sailed off at that point to check on the food.

Rigg was stopped by a few more people but he answered them a bit distractedly. Where was his wife? Rigg checked with his father, Sean, Marcail, and then Nate. He'd decided to run Jeff and Gil down and question them when he spotted them in deep conversation at the edge of the reception. The closer he got to them, the more convinced he was that Kaitlin had not disappeared on her own.

"All right, where is she?"

"Who?" Jeff's face was angelic.

"You know who!" Rigg said with a smile.

"You're not having trouble keeping track of your wife already are you Rigg?" Jeff was appalled. "Now, let me see, why it's only four-thirty! Married just these few hours and already apart. That's not good, Rigg my boy, not good at all."

Rigg was trying very hard not to laugh. Gil, on the other hand, had succumbed until tears came to his eyes.

Jeff opened his mouth to start again when suddenly the shoe was on the other foot.

"Hello Rigg. Hello Jeff and Gilbert." Kate's voice was saccharine sweet. "I'm sorry I was gone so long, but a certain gentleman detained me. He insisted that I sit down in *private*, and have a bite to eat."

Jeff's eyes were sparkling with laughter and he gave Kate a mock bow. "You, madam," he stated with great finesse, "are a worthy opponent."

"Thank you."

"Just what did he do with you?" Rigg finally asked.

"I'll tell you later, after we're on our way. Hopefully by the time we return, you won't want to strangle him." Gil began to laugh again and Jeff joined him. Rigg broke into their glee.

"Speaking of being on our way—" the bridegroom let the sentence hang.

"I'll get my things." Kate said good-bye to her brother-in-laws, her eyes telling Jeff he was forgiven.

"How did you get out of there?" Jeff whispered when he hugged her.

"Joey followed us and witnessed the whole thing." Kate's smile was so audacious that Jeff roared.

They took some time to say their good-byes to the family and remaining friends. Their plans for a honeymoon trip began in town with supper at the hotel and then back to their own home for the night. They would board the mid-morning stage the next day and start in the direction of San Francisco.

When they arrived in the city they'd stay at Aunt Maureen's for a few days before taking the stage home again. A substitute teacher had come for the following week and Rigg left without a qualm, knowing Uncle Leo was in charge.

The days in San Francisco were idyllic as they toured the city by day and spent most of their evenings in the privacy of their lavish bedroom, having supper and falling even deeper in love with every minute they spent together.

"We start home tomorrow," Rigg said almost sadly; it was their last night at Aunt Maureen's.

"I'm looking forward to getting back."

"You are?"

"Mmm hmm. My class will call me *Mrs. Riggs*. Doesn't that sound wonderful?"

"Indeed it does. But I know something that sounds even better."

"What's that?"

"I love you Kaitlin, and praise God for our marriage."

Kate gaped at him. He'd said the words in perfect Hawaiian. "How did—"

"Sean's been working with me ever since I proposed."

"Say it again."

Rigg obliged. Kate, laughing in delight, threw her arms around her husband.

"The language isn't important you know," Rigg said as he kissed her softly. "No matter how I say it Katie, I'm head over heels in love with you."

epilogue

"Stay dry!" Jeff called to Sylvia as she dashed from the shipping office to her carriage in the pouring rain. "And I'll see you tonight."

It was December twenty-third and Sylvia Weber was hosting an informal Christmas party at her sister's house She'd invited nearly all the young people from church

Bill, who was watching from his office doorway, struggled with his feelings. He had no right to ask Jeff to change his plans but Rigg, Kaitlin, Sean and Marcail were coming to trim the tree and stay the night. This would be the first tree party where one of the boys would not be with them. It was also their first Christmas with Kate, Sean and Marcail.

"Dad," Jeff turned when Sylvia's carriage was out of sight, "What were you saying?"

"Come in and sit down." The two men made themselves comfortable around the desk and then Bill looked his son in the eye.

"I was saying that your mother has been praying about her work here at the shipping office for many months. She doesn't want to quit outright but she's ready for a break.

"And now that Katie is expecting, she told me she'd like to take a little time for herself before she becomes a grandmother."

"Well, we can certainly fill in, Dad, for as long as we're needed. In fact, she doesn't ever need to come back. We'll get by."

"That's what I've told her and that was going to be our plan until yesterday when Jake Bradford was in." Bill watched his son closely and continued.

"Bobbie is coming back to town. She's going to be married and wants to come home for a while before she makes that step. Jake tells me she's been working at the shipping office in Jenner for over three years. She's not going to be here permanently but it sounds like it will be enough time for your mom and me to make a decision on her working with us.

"I haven't discussed this with anyone but your mother. If you say the word, I'll drop the whole idea and no one need know we were considering Bobbie. We would all be working in this office together and if that's going to be too uncomfortable for you, I'll understand, and we'll figure out something else."

Jeff was thoughtful. It certainly wasn't the first time he'd thought of Roberta Bradford. In fact, he wished she'd come home years ago. But never did he picture himself working with her six days a week. And how would *she* feel about it?

A few minutes of silence elapsed and then Jeff spoke with quiet conviction. "I hope we've all done a good deal of growing up in the last five years. I can't say as I ever imagined myself working side by side with Bobbie, but I would like to see her. I don't really have a problem with her working here, but she might."

"That's true. But if it doesn't bother you, then I'll ask Jake for her address."

"I think that's fine. She's obviously an answer to prayer, and I mean it when I say it will be good to see her again."

❑ ❑ ❑

Kaitlin sat down in the living room to reread her father's letter. It was a letter of joy. There was tremendous revival going on in the islands and, understandably, that was almost all her father could talk about.

He explained that his return would be delayed for an indefinite period of time and although Kate was disappointed, she was also accepting of the fact that he needed to stay in Hawaii. She shifted on the sofa to a more comfortable position and kept reading.

"Did the baby move?"

"Oh Rigg," Kate laughed. "Your mother tells me I won't feel that for a long time."

"I guess not," Rigg admitted softly and Kate smiled at him before going back to her father's letter which, unfortunately, told them he would be delayed again.

"Did the baby move, Kate?" Marcail had heard the question from the kitchen and Kaitlin's reading was interrupted once again.

"No," Rigg answered. "And if we don't leave her alone, we're going to drive Kate out of the house."

Rigg's statement wasn't too far from the truth. Rigg had been thrilled with the news that they were expecting and whenever he and Kate were in the same room, he could be found measuring his wife's waist with the span of his fingertips.

Marcail had been a different sort of problem. For a solid week after hearing the news, she had stared at Kaitlin's stomach. The question Kate had been awaiting came a week later. Kate remembered so clearly when her mother had explained the mysteries of conception and birth to her.

But Marcail had more questions at nine than Kate had had at 14. After an hour-and-a-half of intense conversation, there wasn't much that Marcail didn't know. Kate had recounted their conversation to Rigg and he'd been very practical about the whole thing; telling her that rcail had obviously been ready and that explaining facts to her was the best possible move.

Sean's reaction had been much briefer.

"Good grief, Kate! Already?"

Kate had blushed to the roots of her hair but that only used Sean to grin mischievously at his sister and ther-in-law. Rigg remembered very clearly what it s like to be 14 and gave his young brother-in-law a rn look.

Now it was December twenty-third and the four of m were putting on wraps to leave for the Taylors'.

"I won't have any trouble being thankful this year."

"About what?" Kate responded to her husband's cryp-remark.

"Mom has us share every year what we're thankful "

"And what will you say?" Kate asked and slipped her is around her husband's large frame.

"Well, that we've had plenty of rain for the crops, of rse."

"Of course," Kate agreed, and smiled into his eyes.

"Ah, Kate-love," Rigg sighed, "you're awfully nice to e around."

"And I'll stay around too, just as long as you keep ing me that." Kaitlin sealed her words with a kiss.

"The rain has stopped what's holding them up?" n called to Marcail from the porch.

"The usual, Sean," Marcail stated in calm logic. "Just usual."

Current Books by Lori Wick

A Place Called Home Series
A Place Called Home
A Song for Silas
The Long Road Home
A Gathering of Memories

The Californians
Whatever Tomorrow Brings
As Time Goes By
Sean Donovan
Donovan's Daughter

Kensington Chronicles
The Hawk and the Jewel
Wings of the Morning
Who Brings Forth the Wind
The Knight and the Dove

Rocky Mountain Memories
Where the Wild Rose Blooms
Whispers of Moonlight
To Know Her by Name
Promise Me Tomorrow

The Yellow Rose Trilogy
Every Little Thing About You
A Texas Sky
City Girl

English Garden Series
The Proposal
The Rescue
The Visitor
The Pursuit

The Tucker Mills Trilogy
Moonlight on the Millpond
Just Above a Whisper
Leave a Candle Burning

Contemporary Fiction
Sophie's Heart
Pretense
The Princess
Bamboo & Lace
Every Storm
White Chocolate Moments